The Red Leaves

of Autumn

Dana Cornwell Bodney

ISBN: 152324206X
ISBN 13: 9781523242061

1

The shrimp boat moved lazily along Johnson Creek toward the dock at Harbor Island, South Carolina. It was Monday and the boat traffic was light; a blessed change from the weekend cluster of amateur captains clogging up the docks. Duncan jumped from the boat to the landing and lit a cigarette. The rumble of the refrigerated transfer truck behind him was music to his ears.

The move to Harbor Island a few years ago had been a most profitable one, and essential, according to Mr. Paulos. The competition was getting heavy these days and they needed an intermediate location between Miami and the northern hubs to ensure their contacts remained loyal. Transporting was a breeze thus far, and the operation as a whole seemed to be benefiting greatly from the new set up. Moreover, Duncan was benefiting. He had been in the fast lane for twenty years and it was killing him. He still smoked, sniffed and enjoyed his share of women, but the glitz and glamour of it all was gone. Yes, the Lowcountry lifestyle seemed to suit him just fine.

Duncan lit another cigarette from the butt of his last while he watched the new employee. After several lame attempts, the kid finally secured *The Rennie* to the dock. Duncan glanced up at the Captain and shook his head at the boy. The dock shook as the heavy teen-ager jumped off of the boat onto the sturdy two-by-fours.

Several weeks ago Duncan had been instructed to hire Phillip Dubose as a favor to one of the bigwigs in the trucking division of their network. It seemed harmless enough at first, but now it was becoming a real headache. The kid was clumsy and dense and Duncan worried that he might happen upon something that he shouldn't, just out of sheer stupidity.

Supposedly the kid was sampling the profession, so to speak, and his rich little Mommy was going to buy him a boat of his own if he liked what he learned. Since it was only temporary Duncan could live with it. He was accustomed to no outsiders in the business. But after all, he was in the Lowcountry now and things were more relaxed. The boss seemed to treat things on this end differently than D.C. or Chicago.

Duncan thought of his own rules of the trade he had developed over the years: follow instructions; watch your own back first; keep your mouth shut; the strong usually survive. Somehow those thoughts did not ease his frustrations at the moment.

He knew one thing for sure though. The kid was a loser. He was really starting to get on Duncan's nerves.

2

Stella began to wonder what was keeping her lunch date. She'd sat on the terrace at Gatsby's Café overlooking the beautiful Beaufort, South Carolina, waterfront for half an hour and Walker was late. The leaves on the trees glistened brilliantly in the sunlight just waiting to be swept away by the salty sea breeze. The Spanish oak trees edging the boardwalk along the water were old and large. Their limbs cascaded over the terrace and its moss dangled and teased her as though it might drop at any minute. Tourists were taking pictures of passing sailboats or lazily strolling along the cobblestone paths that led to the broad boardwalk. A mother and two young children sat on the grass and enjoyed an ice cream cone. Shoppers took a break from roaming in and out of the unique boutiques along main street to relax on park benches. No doubt, Beaufort was an alluring town and once its charm captured you there was no turning back.

It really had all begun this time of year, and now, finally, they were beginning another phase of their lives together. Since their first trip to Fripp Island, a short boat ride away from

Beaufort, they'd dreamed of living here. Neither had fathomed the thought that so early in their lives they would be experiencing the beginning of this distant hope.

Immediately after law school Walker had launched a law practice and worked long hours. Together they had made smart financial investments and now the hope of retiring at a very young age was a reality that had begun a month ago.

Walker had spent at least half of that time at the golf course on Fripp Island or the clubs on the neighboring islands, or so Stella thought. Yesterday he had complained that his short game was suffering a little and, knowing Walker as she did, odds were that he had stopped to buy a new putter at the golf shop on Lady's Island on his way to their lunch date.

Stella was lost in the sound of the gulls overhead and the sight of white caps in the water, but kept an eye on the antique French doors that led from the inside of the established restaurant onto the sprawling terrace. The lunch crowd was building and the terrace was filling up quickly. The weekend was upon them once again and the small town of Beaufort would be packed by nightfall. She was watching for her tardy husband as well as the waitress who had poured her water earlier. Her throat grew increasingly dry as she saw the other customers being served drinks. A gentleman at the table beside her had ordered a trendy foreign beer in a long neck bottle; small pieces of ice were still frozen to the label. As Stella watched the ice melt and run down the pretty bottle onto the white starched tablecloth, a voice from behind her asked, "Would you like to order now?"

"Yes, I would, thank you. I would like a beer like that gentleman is having please," she said and subtly nodded her head at the man to her right. "Why don't you just go ahead and bring two and a couple of frosty mugs along with them. My husband will be along soon."

She watched red and golden leaves float to the ground and became lost in memories and thoughts of family traditions. Ironically, the season that marked the end of summer was the time of year when Stella Stevenson began anew. Perhaps it was her October birthday or because they had married in late September or it could be the autumn birth of their only son. Maybe it was a feeling simply brought about by the bare limbs and exposed open space which, only weeks before, had been hidden from view; a sort of "wipe the slate clean" theory.

As the red leaves rustled past on the edge of the lawn between the terrace and the water, she lifted the small crystal saltshaker from the table and sprinkled a small amount into her beer. This was a bad habit that she had learned from Walker on their very first date. That too, had occurred in the fall.

She took a second sip from the longneck bottle and poured the rest into the chilled mug. Stella reached for the saltshaker again and as she did she recalled a near dilapidated wooden shack with a sign near the top, which read The Tiger Den.

It was a day just like today, but instead of the Beaufort waterfront to set the mood, there was a blaring jukebox, neon lights glaring through the blackness of a shack with no windows and a single ray of daylight creeping under the door leading to a rickety old deck. The sound of loafers scuffing across a dirty floor in time to the tunes from the jukebox rang in her ears.

The high-pitched dinging of the pinball machine sounded often as it coaxed more quarters from the college students' pockets. The smell of hot dogs, pizza, popcorn, stale beer and cigarette smoke welcomed each patron as they entered the bar. It was paradise.

There had been days, and a few too many nights, that Stella had spent ten to twelve hours straight at The Den. Some of those days had included time spent with an old boyfriend who would buy nothing except the beer that was on special for the day. She smiled at the memory.

She looked down at the pretty beer bottle in front of her now as a gust of wind blew small leaves around her chair. Jagged slivers of ice fell from the sides of the mug and into the beer as Stella continued to sip it and remember that day once more.

The infamous Tiger Den in Clemson, South Carolina, was located only two stoplights from her dorm room on the university campus. Walker had phoned her around noon on a Saturday. She was still asleep in her short twin bed propped up on cinder blocks to make space available under the bed for things like dirty laundry. When it appeared that her roommate, Cathy, who never slept in, was not budging to answer the call, she slowly walked five steps to the telephone as her head pounded with each ring. The parties around the fraternity quad had been wild last night. She had no idea what time she and Cathy arrived home.

She lifted the receiver. "Hello," she said in the loudest voice she could muster, which was still only a whisper.

"Hello, may I please speak with Stella."

"This is she."

"This is Walker Stevenson."

Stella froze with the exception of her pounding heart. Beads of sweat broke out on her forehead. Yes, it could be the hangover, but it wasn't. *He* was on the telephone. She couldn't believe it. He was actually calling her. Walker Stevenson was on the telephone right now. The whole day following their brief meeting last week she had thought of him and what a great name he had, not to mention body, face, hair and even personality.

"Are you still there?"

"Ooh, yes," she said, embarrassed that she hadn't spoken sooner.

"We met Wednesday at The Tiger Den. You were wearing a lobster hat made of red felt. Did you win a prize at the Hat Party?"

"No, I didn't. I didn't even make it home with the hat. Someone dropped it in a pail of party punch at the KA house."

"Did I wake you?" he asked apologetically.

"Oh, no, no," Stella said shaking her head rapidly as if it would hide her lie.

"Good. How about coming out to the Tiger Den and joining me? The game will be coming on TV in about half an hour."

"The game?"

"The Clemson football game." Walker was not surprised that Stella hadn't caught on. The game was an away game and of much less concern than the home games played at Death Valley when the entire campus became a sea of tailgaters in a united quest for a party.

"How about I pick you up in twenty minutes?"

Stella glanced toward the mirror above her desk and quickly said, "No, that's O.K. I'll find my own way out. Give me about an hour."

"You'll miss the kick off."

"But the beer will be colder by then."

After two goodbyes, the conversation ended. Stella screamed her roommate's name twice and jumped on top of Cathy, who was still huddled beneath the covers.

"It was him. It was him," she shouted. "I can't believe he called. What am I going to wear?"

Stella hurried to the only window in the room and rolled the bamboo shade up to the ceiling in one swift motion. The sun flooded the room and a cool breeze squeezed its way under the windowsill.

"This is sweater weather, yes, definitely sweater weather."

Another bolt of excitement through her veins and she screamed for joy and twirled round and round in the middle of the floor.

The noise combined with the bright sunshine brought Cathy to an almost upright position. "What are you screaming about?" Cathy asked quite annoyed.

Stella ceased her pirouettes and looked at Cathy.

"Oooh, you look awful," Stella said. "I don't look good, but you look...well, you look like you are in terrible pain. Here let's both take a headache powder."

Stella grabbed a small can of orange juice from their short refrigerator and they medicated themselves.

"I was hoping you could go with me to The Tiger Den, but you don't look like you'd be much fun. You need to stay in the bed. I'll get Leila to go."

"Thank you Doctor Stella. Why are you going there?"

"You must have been comatose. Walker Stevenson just called and wants me to join him at The Tiger Den."

"Who is Walker Stevenson?"

"Remember the guy I met before the Hat Party. The real handsome," Stella trailed off. "It's no use. You're not functioning well. We'll talk later." Stella grabbed her shower pail and started for the door.

"Wait a minute," Cathy said. "Didn't we go to the same party last night?"

"Yes."

"Well, why is it that I feel so badly and you're getting ready to go out again?"

"You probably let your tolerance decrease during the summer, or it could be all the dancing you did at the KA house."

"Dancing?" Cathy looked puzzled.

"That's right," Stella said, walking into the main hallway of the Chi Omega dorm. "Cathy Russ, our devoted sorority President, was dancing on the speakers in the Kappa Alpha lounge last night." Stella was screaming by now and knew that anyone with ears on the second floor of the Chi-0 dorm had heard her announcement. She heard a crash behind her and saw Cathy's Tax Accounting textbook lying in a heap in the middle of the hall.

"Just a little friendly harassment, roomie."

Cathy's rebuttal came in the form of a slamming door that rocked all of Smith Hall, the Chi Omega domain.

Stella knew from the reflection in the mirror that she had some work to do in order to look her best for her date with Walker. She had forgotten to wash her makeup off again last night, but no pimples had surfaced because of it. The chill of the cold ceramic tiles on her bare feet sent her to the shower without dwelling on the image in the mirror.

Forty-five minutes later she arrived at The Tiger Den with Leila Roddla, a sorority sister who lived down the hall. Leila had a huge Lincoln that had been handed down to her from her father several years before. It was a great party car. As they got out the noise from the fans cheering inside filled the parking lot. Clemson must have scored. Although Stella's heart was racing, she appeared cool and calm. Even though no one could see them from the bar with no windows, she didn't want to appear nervous.

Without notice, her anxiety won over her calm and she turned abruptly to her sorority sister with questions. "Oh, Leila, how do I look? What do I say? Do I have zoo breath?" she asked all at once, and then breathed heavily into Leila's face.

Leila staggered back a few paces and reached into her pocket, "Here have a breath mint. You look great. Why are you nervous? I've never seen you like this."

"Leila, I really think this is the man I'm going to marry."

"You don't even know him."

"I realize that," Stella said defensively, "but I just feel electric at the thought of seeing him. I know I'm going to marry him. This day will change my life."

"What you are feeling is hormones. But if this is what you want then I wish you the best. Go through the door," Leila said as she pointed to the wooden slab before them, "and sit down on the stool beside him and ask for a lite beer. If he buys you one without recommending the beer that is on sale, then you can feel free to pursue the marriage idea."

This idea brought a smile to Stella's gorgeous face which is just what she needed to be wearing as she entered The Tiger Den on the very day that she believed would change her life.

The old door squeaked loudly, like the front door of a haunted mansion, and all eyes inside turned to see who was entering, or at least tried. The bright sunlight was piercing to the eye after any length of time in the dark establishment, and for a few of the patrons, they'd been here a while. Walker stood from his stool at the bar and walked toward Stella. His urgency to greet her was well disguised as politeness. But the truth was he didn't want to give any of the other guys in the room a chance to even think that the beautiful blonde was up for grabs. "Yes!"

he thought to himself, as the sight of her legs sent chills down his back. Stella had worn shorts. He remembered those legs from the other night. He ushered the two girls over to the bar where he and his friends had a good view of the TV.

After everyone was introduced, the beer orders were placed and Walker not only bought Stella the beer of her choice but he bought Leila one as well; Leila, in turn, gave Stella her sign of approval.

It had not taken very long at all, fifteen minutes at the most, before Leila and Walker's friends could see the obvious and began talking among themselves.

Stella overheard Leila say, "I've never seen her like this. I've known her for four years and I've never seen her like this before. She's usually not one for such P.D.A."

"Neither is Walker," a friend confirmed, "but I think they might just do it right here."

"Oh, don't be ridiculous. They haven't even kissed yet," Leila scorned.

The Tigers intercepted a pass and ran sixty yards for a touchdown and Walker and Stella were no longer the topic of discussion or scrutiny. Their eyes were locked and the only look away was the occasional glance to soak in the remainder of the others body.

Walker was pleased with Stella's choice of attire. She wore a pink polo shirt with the collar turned up under a navy cotton pullover sweater. Her shorts were white and only a tanned, shapely pair of legs were between them and her white tennis shoes. He had had an uncontrollable urge to touch athem the moment she sat down, but he had waited at least two minutes before he placed his left hand on her knee. She had not seemed to mind. Now, thirty minutes after her arrival they sat facing each other, still on their bar stools, with their knees intertwined as the distance between them grew less and less.

The opposing team scored a touchdown and crowd gathered closer around the television at one end of the bar. Walker took Stella's hand and quietly slipped out the door to the back deck. No one noticed their exit since all other eyes were focused on the television.

The deck clung to the shack at the mercy of dozens of exposed rusty nails. It was shaded by a wall of the fastest growing weed in the south: kudzu. Large tree limbs grabbed at the rails of the neglected deck and spilled the colorful leaves onto the floor. There were no words spoken, only the sound of the crisp leaves scratching along the rough planks beneath their feet. The autumn breeze blew in what seemed like every direction.

Stella's blonde hair blew recklessly about her face as she and Walker continued their marathon trance. He untied the white ribbon in her hair and watched as the blonde locks flooded her shoulders. Walker cupped his strong hands on either side of her face and they kissed.

The kiss, or series of kisses, lasted a very long time. Walker reached down to the pile of leaves that had congregated around their feet and picked up a red one with yellow tips. He handed it to Stella and said, "This is the beginning of something big."

They both laughed out loud and kissed again. Stella twirled the red leaf around between her fingers and looked up at Walker who held her tightly around the waist.

"What is your middle name?" she asked.

"Ely."

"I like that. We can call our first son by that name," she said.

"I'll take that as a yes, you will marry me."

She nodded in the affirmative and Walker lifted her perfectly shaped body high into the air and buried his face in her chest as he hugged her with complete joy. He gently slid Stella back down to the ground kissing every inch of her body as it passed his lips.

The tinkling noise of the china and flatware being set around a table nearby brought Stella's thoughts into the present. She gave an enormous sigh and took a sip of her icy beer to cool down. Whenever she remembered that portion of the afternoon that they fell in love she always became incredibly amorous, though she'd had a different word for it then. Sure, it was absolutely ridiculous that Walker had proposed marriage after only a very short while, but each of them had had other relationships before and could distinguish between being in love and being in heat. Theirs had been a heated love affair. She smiled unconsciously as she thought of last night and was assured that it had been, and was still, a very heated marriage. Walker could still make chill bumps cover her entire body with the single touch of a finger to the back of her neck.

The sun slid slowly across the sky and her once-sunny seat was now in the shade of an ancient oak draped so thoroughly with Spanish moss, it looked as if it were placed there delicately long ago by its creator. Stella sat in the wrought iron patio chair absorbed in thought. They were going to be so happy as year-round residents of Fripp Island. She envisioned all the things they had been putting off due to the long hours spent on the quest for a successful career. The waiting was over and another beginning was upon them.

The terrace was full and the bar inside was filled with people who chose to wait their turn for a prime table outside. Stella was unaware of any activity around her except the motion of the trees blowing in the wind and the swift passing of boats on the waterway until suddenly her body broke out in a spray of chill bumps. She knew without looking that her lunch date had arrived.

She turned her head to meet his eyes and her lips ran into his. One hand lay gently on the back of her neck and the other presented her a single red leaf.

"Sorry to keep you waiting."

"A red leaf. You know it's been a few years since you've given me a red leaf. I still have the very first one you gave me right after you proposed."

"That was some day wasn't it? Where is that leaf? We should have it framed."

"It's in one of the college yearbooks on the bookshelf in the den. I just unpacked it last week."

The Stevensons had finally unpacked the last box of the possessions they had accumulated over the span of their marriage. Now it was time for the real relaxation to begin and Fripp was the place to do it. There was an abundance of activities to fill their day if they ever tired of sitting on the beach. From golf, tennis, croquet and biking to fishing, boating, crabbing and shopping. The pleasures were endless, but it was apparent which of Fripp Island's amenities the Stevenson's enjoyed most of all: the ocean and beautiful beach.

The ocean at Fripp was the epitome of what one envisions as they think of the charm and brilliance of constantly moving surf. As the tide rolls in past the sandbars, the roar of the water increases to a full crescendo and then, gradually, the waters slide back toward the horizon. Then the only sounds are the sea gull's laughter and the occasional lapping of the water on the sandy beach.

The Stevensons were not alone in their opinion of Fripp Island's perfections. Two summers ago a stretch of the Island's beach, and the private home directly behind it, had been turned into a Hollywood set for the film *The Prince of Tides.*

It was most exciting to see their beach on the big screen, especially since the homes they used were only eight houses down from their own. Walker and Stella had joined the ranks of a prestigious group of people who were year-round residents. To be a part of that group had been a dream they shared since they had purchased a lot years ago. Their home was fabulous. Wide porches rambled along three sides of the house and all were equipped with rockers and wicker lounges positioned to view the ocean and the golf course.

A three-car garage encompassed half of the ground floor, and a one-bedroom apartment and storage room filled the rest. The living room was on the second level and was ridiculously huge with high, white ceilings and antique exposed beams. Watercolor and oil paintings lined the walls; memories of their journey together thus far. The kitchen was past the dining area through a pair of swinging doors with circular windows in each. The windows had been Walker's idea, as well as the rest of the kitchen design. He had insisted on a large Sub-Zero refrigerator and all stainless-steel appliances. Stella could not argue because she was sure he would be spending more time in there than she. Walker loved to cook and he even cleaned up, so Stella had agreed to leave the kitchen up to him.

The master suite and two other bedrooms were also on the second floor. Their bathroom was large and roomy; a dressing area was attached with a big bay window and window seat along one wall.

On the third floor were two more bedrooms and a large open room they referred to as the library. From ceiling to floor were bookshelves with a sliding ladder attached. Books of all types filled the white shelves along with family snapshots and special things that the children had made over the years. Everything in the room was white except for the black baby grand piano, which sat next to the massive arched window that looked out over the ocean. The view was tremendous.

From the bar in one corner of the room, the living room below could be seen through the bannister of the balcony. When Stella or one of the children played the piano the sound would ring out through the house and Walker loved to listen. The library was his favorite room even before the kitchen. This library did not house one law book and for that Walker was most proud. Even during the busiest part of his career he had never brought his work to Fripp. He felt like if he had to bring it, he didn't need to be here at all. When he passed through the guard gate at the end of the bridge that connects Fripp to Hunting Island, Walker Stevenson was a stress-free man, at least until the telephone rang. Those days were over and all he was going to do now was play golf, enjoy the weather and his wife. Not necessarily in that order.

He was definitely enjoying his wife now most of all as they held hands across the narrow table and discussed their morning. Stella suggested they leave now and go back to Fripp. She wanted to jump his bones. He had agreed, but the sudden smell of the fresh croissants, shrimp salad and cabernet put their libido on hold.

A male guitarist with long hair and a beard walked onto the terrace carrying his instrument and a stool. Without introduction he began to sing.

The music was a lovely addition to the near-perfect atmosphere. Walker drank the beer Stella had ordered for him and then ordered a bottle of William Hill Cabernet Sauvignon, 1989. The musician played favorites by the great James Taylor mixed with a little bit of Buffet.

The waitress served their food and Stella dug into the shrimp salad croissant as Walker took a big bit of the smoked salmon that lay before him. They were enjoying the food, music and each other when a shrill voice from the other side of the terrace shouted, "Why, it's the Stevensons."

Stella and Walker looked at each other in a frightened sort of way. Every head on the entire terrace turned in the direction of the voice.

"Heaven help us," Stella said so only Walker could hear.

Walker shook his head. "She's everywhere. There's no escaping the wrath of Marguerite Dubose. Let's just be nice and maybe she'll move along quickly."

"Nice? Why should I be nice when all she does is shake her store-bought tits in your face."

Walker smiled and sshhed Stella at the same time. He stood and extended a hand to the short, big-breasted woman who approached him. Stella heard the clip-clop, clip-clop of her sleazy shoes as they moved along the brick floor toward them. Stella loathed the shoes Marguerite always wore: too-high heels and single narrow strap over the toe. Where did she shop anyway?

Marguerite bypassed Walker's hand completely and stood on the tips of her red painted toenails to hug his neck. Her jumpsuit was unbuttoned to the waist and revealed an elastic tube top, which pushed her implants together and upward. Earrings so large that they had a life of their own dangled below the bottle-black teased hair and required Marguerite to speak even more loudly than usual to be heard over the noise.

From a distance, Marguerite was really not as bad as Stella perceived her to be. Some might even like that type of woman, but Stella could not tolerate it and the sight of her genuinely turned her stomach. Marguerite was a shallow, self-centered, sex-crazed, friendless fake. Most of the islanders steered clear of the woman with the loud voice trapped in the squatty body, but there were others like the bozo who stood behind her now clad in the sissy navy double breasted blazer who had not quite wised up to her methods.

Stella smiled politely and said as little as possible while Marguerite rambled on about herself and her son, "Little Phillip", as she referred to him. Finally, she said, "Have your guy call my guy. Let's do that lunch thing."

Following another series of loud clip-clops Marguerite was seated a safe distance from the Stevenson's at last. Bozo had followed close at her heals and sniffed her the whole way back to the other side of the terrace like a disgusting poodle.

"I bet she found him at the shelter for the homeless, dressed him up, and promised to buy him a case of cheap wine if he would escort her to lunch and service the account."

"Unkindness does not become you, my dear. Why do you even let her bother you?" Walker asked. "There are people in this world who are just basically full of it and Marguerite Dubose is one of them."

"I disagree with you, Lovie." Stella used the term signifying she didn't see eye to eye with him, but that the issue wasn't worth arguing over. "I think she's hiding something."

"Well we know it isn't her bosoms." Walker laughed at his own wit.

"You are so clever." Stella raised her glass in a sarcastic toast to her spouse.

"I think underneath all of that makeup there is an extremely unhappy person. If it weren't for 'Little Phillip,' who by the way was tipping in at 265 according to Ely who saw him in August, I doubt if the woman would have any joy in her life. Now don't get me wrong. I'm not sure if she is the perfect mother, but she does worship the ground that boy walks on. Who is and where is his father anyway? I wonder what the poor kid will do after he graduates from Beaufort Academy this spring. They say Marguerite's loaded and loaded and loaded. Maybe he'll just spend her money. I don't think it's good when a mother depends on her child for her own complete happiness. But what do I care, all she wants from me is my husband."

The cabernet had kicked in and Stella was talking a mile a minute. Walker could take no more.

"Are you quite finished?" he said with a broad grin.

"What?" Stella starred at Walker.

"Remember why we are here Stella. Forget about Marguerite and let's celebrate us." Walker lifted the lone leaf that lay beside Stella's glass. He twirled it around by the stem. "Remember? I think you wanted to jump my bones or something like that."

Stella apologized for getting off track and promised that Marguerite Dubose would never cause them to lose one precious moment of togetherness again. Not ever.

3

Stella pulled into traffic on Bay Street, the main thoroughfare in Beaufort, and circled the block. Traffic was at a standstill and ahead she could see the drawbridge was up and two sailboats were making their way along Harbor River toward Port Royal Sound. Walker's car was not in sight. Obviously he had made it across the bridge before the little man on top, who controlled the fate of all Beaufort motorists, decided it was time to let some sailors have the right of way. Slowly the bridge opened and she watched as a gorgeous sailboat floated through. Stella imagined that it was going south for the winter. They may be a little premature in their voyage, she thought as she pressed the buttons in the middle console of her car and lowered all four windows. Fresh air rushed through the open spaces. It was a great day. Not a cloud in the sky and the marsh was picturesque with shades of blue and green. The thermometer was rising. Perhaps they were having a bit of an Indian Summer. Perfect beach weather; a true gift from above.

The breeze and sounds from the bay relaxed her. Stella was still mildly perturbed by Marguerite. What a piece of work. Well, as her mother always said, "If you can't find anything nice to say about someone, a good Southern woman always says, 'Bless her heart'". Somehow that just did not seem to fit with Marguerite. She was a nuisance.

Stella waited patiently as the boats passed and vowed to put Marguerite out of her mind and enjoy this spectacular weather and the rest of her day. She thought of their little Boston Whaler docked back at the Fripp Island Marina. They had had a splendid time in the waterway this summer during the annual Beaufort Water Festival.

"The River," as the Intracoastal Waterway was commonly referred to in these parts, had been packed from bank to bank with floating vessels during the festival. You could walk from Beaufort to Lady's Island, directly across the bay and first in a series of islands between Beaufort and Fripp, simply by stepping from boat to boat.

The Beaufort Water Festival had been scheduled later in the month of July than usual this year due to the tides. It was a necessity, of course, that high tide was during daylight hours in order to accommodate all of the activities to be held on The River. Thus, the specific dates of the festival changed from year to year. The action always began on Monday and ended on Sunday with the much-publicized Blessing of the Fleet.

Boats of all types and sizes, each decorated uniquely, and most humorously, took their positions in the extensive caravan and sailed by the grandstand at the Waterfront Park. Each was blessed and judged by the one and only Commodore of the Water Festival. The Stevenson's had never won, or even placed, but for years they had participated. It was a tremendous amount of fun. For most people, that is.

As with most organized functions, especially those on as large a scale as the Water Festival, there is a lot of work involved. Stella had heard that the planning for the upcoming festival usually began the day after the last one ended. To be a chosen member of the Beaufort Water Festival Planning Committee was an honor and a position in the community, which held lots of clout. Although it also carried the burden of hours and hours of long work, it was opportunity that was rarely turned down. People worked for years and years on the committee striving and competing for the most honorable position of Commodore.

Once you achieved the famed title of Commodore, the struggle was over. You could sit back and relax with the other members of The Admiral's Fleet, which was made up only of men who had once served as Commodore. This elite group usually viewed the party of all parties from the grand ballroom atop the National Bank Building on the waterfront.

More Fripp Island residents had participated in the festival this past year than usual because The Fripp Island Company's President had been the Commodore. It was sort of like a block party on the water. Yes, Marguerite had been there too.

She had not been her usual flirtatious self. There was a man with her. Stella remembered the man's face now as she watched the bridge lower. It was amazing to her that she could envision his face so vividly. It was a hard face. A slightly handsome one, but scary in an odd indescribable way. Their boats were too far apart to hear the exact words spoken, unless it was a shout hello, but Stella watched as the man jerked his hand from Marguerite's as she attempted to get him to wave to them.

As the boats passed at cocktail cruise speed Marguerite tipped the captain's hat she was wearing to them, beeped the horn and waved. Her boat was not decorated. It needed no added touches to be a hilarious sight. Her 20-foot Sea Ray was painted purple with pink glittery swirls on all sides. It should be against the law to paint a boat in such an undignified way. Although Marguerite sat with her bare legs draped over the man's lap, he did not appear to be just another one of her puppies. In that single passing, Stella had sensed the roles were reversed in this affair. The man had an aura that cut through the complete chaos of The River that day and reeked of power and obsession. His eyes devoured Stella's flesh to the bone as he managed a fake smile.

Stella had not been the only one affected by his gaze. There was a hush in the continual conversation in their boat immediately after they had passed the Dubose's and guest. Then someone had commented about the captain's hat Marguerite wore and laughter prevailed once more.

Traffic ahead began to move along and Stella listened to the high-pitched hum vibrating through her ears as her car passed over the metal portion of the bridge. The view from the top took her breath away. What a glorious place to live. There was a line of trucks with trailers at the boat ramp on Lady's Island waiting their turn to put their boat afloat and devour the water. This made her more than anxious to return to her own piece of paradise along the beach at Fripp Island.

The humming ceased as the wheels of her navy Mercedes rolled onto the paved road. Only twenty-one miles to go, and what a picturesque path to travel. Three islands lay between Stella and the private bridge, which accessed Fripp. Lady's Island, Harbor Island and Hunting Island, in that order. She soaked in the Lowcountry charm while the wind whipped wildly around her as her speed increased. Lou Rawls sang loudly from the radio and she sang with him off key and at the top of her lungs, "Lady love, your love is peaceful like the summer's breeze. I keep on needing you a little more and more, and I thank you my Lady Love." Talk about timing she thought.

Adrenaline was pumping through her veins. Music was one of her favorite things in the world. A sad song could make her cry in a heartbeat and a good vivacious song could pump her up but good. She noticed a speed limit sign whiz by on the right. She was already in Frogmore and better slow this mammoth sedan down.

Frogmore, South Carolina, was a terrific little town just oozing with character and atmosphere. At the one traffic light in Frogmore stands the original building that was the general store in Post-Civil War days. It now houses several different shops that are full of tourists spending money on anything from t-shirts to jewelry and interior home décor to pet supplies. Across from the slightly renovated general store is a great little restaurant called Froggies. Not a very original name, but has the meanest bloody mary in the Lowcountry and fresh delicious seafood entrees.

The citizens of Frogmore were their own biggest fans and felt like motorists should slow down and examine more closely the assets of their fair town. Once she had not complied with the thirty-five miles an hour rule and had the pleasure of meeting a Barney Fife type. She had pulled into the parking lot of a local restaurant called The Shrimp Shack, in answer to the embarrassing flashing blue lights, and ended up with a ticket and two fried shrimp burgers. The Shrimp Shack was now one of their favorite places.

The small island town was also famous for a Lowcountry stew. Stella decided that Frogmore Stew would be perfect for dinner. Since they already had the corn, smoked sausage and red potatoes at home, a couple of pounds of shrimp was all she needed. It could steep to perfection in all of the spices the recipe called for while they played on the beach. She flipped her blinker on and made a quick right turn.

Duncan heard the familiar sound of crushing oyster shells in the drive over that of the rumbling generator on the refrigerated truck. He turned to see who was approaching. Through the settling dust he could make out one tanned leg with a red high heel shoe extending from a Mercedes. He traced the leg up to the long blonde hair pulled back in a very sophisticated black bow. She wore a short houndstooth skirt and white blouse. The dark black sunglasses added to her intrigue. She closed the car door with her left hand and that's when Duncan gave up hope.

The colossal diamond ring nearly blinded him as the sun's rays connected with the stone. He turned back toward the creek. Never again. He had almost had his privates removed by a jealous husband in Chicago and his two-week recovery stay in the hospital convinced him that there were plenty of single fish in the sea. But there was no harm in looking. Perhaps this would calm his nerves and help him to appear more composed when the deputy did arrive. He lit a cigarette and walked up the plank toward the market where he leaned against the building and waited.

Stella had a bounce in her step and was humming a song when she exited the seafood shack through the screen door.

"Hello. Beautiful day isn't it?" She continued her bounce and hum.

"Hi," was all Duncan could say. He hadn't expected a beauty like her to even speak to him.

Maybe it was worth it. Her quiet engine began to purr and she backed out of the parking space. Duncan noticed the Fripp Island resident sticker on her windshield. The ring glistened again through the glass as he watched her drive away. She turned right toward Fripp Island just as a Sheriff's Patrol car entered the drive.

Duncan nodded to a worker loading the Gray, Inc. truck to close the rear doors of the trailer.

4

A trail of melting ice followed her all the way up the back steps of the porch. There was evidence on her red pumps as well. Stella sat the messy bag of shrimp on a bare wood table she had bought from a local Gullah woman for ten dollars. The asking price had been half of that, but her conscience had made her hand the trusting woman a ten. The table was well over a hundred years old. The heritage of the Lowcountry Gullah's had always fascinated Walker and Stella. She had surprised him with this "artifact" as a birthday gift one year. The once enslaved Africans who dwelt along the coast as far north as Cape Fear in North Carolina and all the way to Jacksonville, Florida, spoke in a Geechee dialect. They were artisans in basket weaving and quilting and the Stevensons frequented their annual festival.

She opened the back door and picked up the dripping bag and hurried through the laundry room into the kitchen. Walker was sitting at the kitchen breakfast room booth watching some golfers through the bay window.

"Let me guess. Frogmore Stew." He turned his attentions toward her.

"How'd you know?" She dropped the bag into the sink.

"I just did. The crab pot is full of boiling water and bay seasoning. Go put your suit on and let's hit the beach."

Stella smiled at the man who could read her mind. It did not surprise her. She could read his too. Or maybe neither read the other's mind at all and it was merely a process of thought in which two minds were so totally connected via the heart, that they actually had the same thought at the same time.

Stella was used to it now and didn't feel psychic any more, only fortunate.

"How many ears of corn do you usually put in the stew?" he asked.

"Six. Sometimes seven," she answered as she slipped the pumps off and surveyed the damage.

"We'll never eat all of that," Walker insisted.

"I'll do something with the leftovers. I just read an article last week about juicing up food the second time around. I'm going up to change." She patted Walker's behind as he leaned in the refrigerator to retrieve the sausage and other ingredients.

"How can you do something juicy with the leftovers when you don't ever come in the kitchen?" Walker mumbled to the contents of the fridge.

"Excuse me?" Stella said.

"I said I love you honey."

"Sure you did. I'll be right back and you can show me." She laughed and walked through the swinging doors.

The telephone rang. Walker shouted, "I'll get it," from the kitchen.

Stella passed the mahogany staircase with glossy white trim and turned toward the master suite. She put on her old faithful black bikini, slipped her feet in a pair of deck shoes with near rotten laces from the salty water, then grabbed a denim sarong and hooded jersey on the way out. She made it to the kitchen just in time to hear Walker say, "I'll be in touch."

"Who was that?"

"Ed. Come on let's go."

The side porch of their house connected with a private boardwalk to the beach. They each wore shades and carried reading material and one beach chair each. They had done this before. One of the greatest luxuries of having a home on the beach was not having to pack an overloaded beach bag. If you forgot something, no big deal. The house was only seconds away. It was like being in your backyard.

Walker explained to Stella why Ed had called. A case that Walker had been involved with before he retired was scheduled to be heard before the Georgia Court of Appeals in a few days. It sounded to Stella like Walker's longtime friend and recent ex-partner needed some moral support.

Walker invited Stella to accompany him to Atlanta and suggested they call the McFee's, close friends from Clarkesville, Georgia, and ask them to come along. Stella jumped at the chance and dug around in the beach bag to retrieve her cell phone.

Their friends had been what she missed most about leaving Clarkesville. Their friends and their small Episcopal Church where the friendships were deep and the fellow parishioners were a family dedicated to helping one another. "Let's not get melancholy now," she thought as she pressed the buttons of the phone.

By the time she was back in her chair beside Walker, Lois was on the line. Stella angled the heels of her shoes into the sand and created a sort of natural footrest. She gazed at the great Atlantic Ocean and held the telephone toward the breaking waves for Lois to hear the sweet melody.

"You're disgusting," Lois said loudly. "It's barely fifty degrees in these North Georgia mountains and I've been digging winter clothes out of trunks all day.

Stella milked the moment for all it was worth. She gave Lois a detailed description of the perfect day and added, "I really wish you were here." They ceased the joking conversation and moved on to planning the getaway to Atlanta. When all of the arrangements had been decided they moved on to the happenings in Clarkesville that Stella had missed.

Walker pointed to his watch and gave Stella the wrap it up sign. She knew her girlie chatter was interrupting his solitude. After asking about all of the children they said their goodbyes.

The pair sat quietly on the beach. Walker was reading *The Sporting News* and Stella was glancing through several magazines that had arrived in the mail that day. The tide was coming in with a rush today and the never ceasing beach breeze was picking up. Stella stood and put on the jersey she had brought down with her. It was a terrific day, but the breeze carried more of a touch of autumn than she had realized.

"Let's take a walk," she said.

"You go ahead. I think I'll call Ed back and assure him that I am definitely coming."

"O.K. don't talk to any strange women that pass by," Stella warned.

Walker looked to the north and then the south. There was no one in sight except a twosome shell hunting on the distant sandbar. "Looks like I won't have any trouble following those orders."

She put her hands in the front pockets of the pullover and walked north. She could see the Point Villas in the distance and decided to go check on the progress of the condominium renovations.

From the direction the oats were leaning her instincts told her that the tide was coming in. Stella had acquired a precise sense about the positions of the tide. Her sense of direction had always been keen. She looked at her watch and began to mentally plan the rest of the afternoon as her rapid gait carried her over the sand.

The shrimp salad she had ordered for lunch had been prepared with mayonnaise, and Walker's salmon was cradled in a delicious dill sauce, so their fat intake for the day was blown anyway. Why stop now? She would bring out the Brie cheese she had been hoarding since their last trip to the Fresh Market in Savannah and pop the cork on one of the bottles of champagne that Walker kept in that massive refrigerator of his, and create a surprise happy hour. It shouldn't be too hard to tap back into the romantic mood of their lunch date.

Stella climbed the rickety steps that led to The Point Condos. Obviously the stairs were in the last phase of the renovation plan. The upkeep of beach access stairs was an ongoing project. At high tide crashing waves could do some damage but there was also the wear and tear of salt air to consider. The Stevenson's had to deal with the same problem themselves, but it was worth every bit of it to wake up each day to the sound of the ocean; that was just part of the price of living beachside.

When she reached the landing at the top of the stairs there was still no visible signs of new construction. She walked down the path toward the tennis courts. The white lattice arbor with wisteria intertwined, welcomed the property owners to the courtyard of the condo complex. Stella admired the foliage and walked into the courtyard.

It was beautiful. Work had definitely been going on in here. New shutters and window boxes made the grey stucco building come alive. It made her think of her favorite childhood book, *The Secret Garden*, as the peaceful atmosphere engulfed her. After a few moments of solitude on the teak benches she exited through the other arbor at the opposite end of the courtyard.

The front of the condominiums faced the ninth green of the golf course. After examining the new landscaping between the complex and the parking area Stella noticed the tall arched windows they had installed in each unit. This was some facelift. Their home was a mere three-minute golf cart ride from this much-improved piece of real estate and she knew this was a plus for the value of their property. Not that they would ever sell, but it does feel great to see an investment continue to increase in value. Fifteen years ago they had paid one hundred and twenty thousand for their lot and now if you could get anyone to sell a beachfront lot it would cost about a half a million. Yes, Walker would be pleased about these improvements.

Stella's extensive snoop through the condos left her on the far north side of the property. There was no beach there, only the inlet on one side and a jetty directly in front. Thus the name The Point. She knew that she could get to the beach by a quick walk over the jetty. It was a rocky route but it was the fastest and she was eager to get back to Walker to share this new information about the condos.

Stella stepped onto the first wet boulder and began a slippery balancing act as she moved across the jetty. This wasn't so hard after all.

Gulls circled the tip of the jetty, which seemed very odd to her. The violent crashing of the waves there sent a spray of water high into the air every ten seconds. Stella continued in the direction of the beach, now only a few yards away. The gulls screeched louder and dipped down into the water in quick sharp dives.

Her heart sank at the thought of another dead loggerhead sea turtle. For some reason a few would get off course and end up smashed against the jetty.

She changed her direction and started toward the tip to investigate. The rocks became more and more slippery and she thought about turning back, but she wanted to be sure it was a turtle before she bothered the habitat authorities. She continued on as the spray soaked her face. An unusually large rock lay to her left and she braced herself against it as she peered yet farther to the tip.

She waved her arms and the gulls moved away and she went on. An odor swirled in the wind that Stella did not recognize immediately. Waves from all directions were breaking on the rocks and the water sprayed into her eyes. She was a few yards from the tip now and caught a glimpse of something yellow. Confusion and curiosity propelled her forward.

"What in the world," she said in wonderment.

Was that a huge starfish floating in the surf? No. No. It was a human hand.

All at once the vision was before her. She could feel the stinging vomit rising in her throat, and she gagged. Her knees shook uncontrollably and she fell to the rocks beneath her feet.

Her eyes grew wide and her mind was frozen. She stared at the body in a yellow shrimper's slicker that lay at the base of the jetty, only a foot below her. The ocean life had marred it beyond recognition. She reached down to move some seaweed blocking some letters on the slicker. Now she could read the name across the chest of the slicker written in black ink. She forced herself to look at the sickening sight once more before she burst in tears. All thoughts were lost from that moment until much later, as she said the name, Dubose to herself. There before her lay Little Phillip.

5

The pounding water on her neck and shoulders helped relax her tense, sleep deprived body. For the past several nights she couldn't fall asleep and was always awakened by the same picture in her mind: the grotesque face of Phillip Dubose. The nightmares were vivid. His swollen face had lesions and bruises and pieces missing. In the dream he had eyes that screamed to her to help him. That's where she always woke up.

She was no longer frightened, simply sad and exhausted. She turned off the shower, stepped onto the marble floor and reached for the fluffy terry robe with the distinctive Ritz Carlton emblem. After twirling her hair up in a towel, she walked through the bedroom and into the sitting room of the elegant suite Walker had reserved.

She reached into the refrigerator behind the honor bar and pulled out a Diet Coke, paused, and exchanged it for a regular Coca-Cola. She had eaten nothing for the first two days, and now she was eating only at Walker's insistence. She opened a small bag of cashews and thought how this should really please him. He had been her crutch since the whole horrible incident and it was time for her to regain her stability.

She pulled the drapery cord of the heavy striped curtains and looked far to the ground below. Dusk in Atlanta. Peachtree Street was packed with commuters, some with the lights of their car beaming through the twilight and others, who refused to admit that the days were getting shorter, becoming lost as the dimness progressed to darkness.

Stella leaned closely to the window and let her forehead rest on the glass. Its chill was a welcome contrast to the hot shower. It felt clean and crisp and numbed her forehead. Her eyes closed. She stayed there a while hoping it would numb her brain.

Stella's mind wandered as she continued to lean against the window. What an invigorating time of year. Walker and the children had always dreaded the end of Daylight Savings Time, but she had welcomed it because it meant family time was usually more frequent since the four of them weren't dispersed about, either on the golf course, basketball court, office, or any number of other places in Clarkesville.

This was the time for spontaneous trips down to Fripp on a nippy Friday afternoon for a long weekend of togetherness, with oyster roasts on the beach, old cotton sweaters and hooded sweat shirts, and slow cruising boat rides, not the time to find a body at the beach in front of your house.

She pulled the robe tighter around her neck and opened her eyes. Darkness had fallen over Atlanta. How quickly each day passes. How quickly day turns into night. How quickly a day sharing love and time with your mate can become a nightmare filled with death and grief and detectives.

They had been the worst. At least, that night. They had asked question after question, almost to the point of interrogation as though she had dredged the gory mess up from the depths of the sea herself. Walker had asked them to leave and they had. She wished Walker could ask the death and grief to leave too.

Stella knew this was something she had to tackle on her own. She exhaled a heavy breath onto the window and then drew a heart in the fogged glass. She left the window and stretched out on the soft sofa upholstered in a companion fabric to match the drapes. As she sank into the down pillows the vibrant yellow, green and burgundy flowers and vines lifted her spirits. "Finally," she thought.

She had not been depressed since post postpartum blues with Ely. She had simply not allowed herself that option. But she had also never found a dead and decomposing body either. Especially one of a young man whose mother she had just spoken so unkindly of that very same day.

Part of the problem was guilt and she knew it. There was really no harm done since no one had heard her remarks except Walker, but her conscience was heavy and that was not the norm for Stella.

She laughed to herself. Maybe she was feeling better. She had conquered the first stage of the healing process, denial, and hoped that the remaining phases would pass quickly as well. She would proudly announce the progress she had made the minute Walker returned. He had gone back across the street to Lenox Square to pick up her new dress from Neiman Marcus. The personal shopper had insisted on delivering the dress to the Ritz after a few minor alterations were made, but Walker wanted the exercise after the trip in the car.

The Atlanta getaway tradition had started when the children were young. Atlanta, a short one-hour trip from Clarkesville, had been their favorite spot for years. It had all begun one

Thanksgiving, or actually the day after, the biggest shopping day of the year. The McFees and the Stevensons were on a toy-shopping mission for the kids and decided to stay over-night at the Ritz and an exciting tradition began.

Mimosas in the lobby bar before the group split up signaled the kick off to the day, making for a more relaxed spirit when pulling out the wallet for Yuletide gifts.

Those of the same sex grouped together and did not meet again until late afternoon, unless they happened to bump into one another at the bar at Nick's or Houllahans. It was the pre-ferred way to shop. The crowds seemed smaller and the waiting for a salesclerk wasn't nearly as frustrating with a "toater" in your hand.

When the shopping was over the nightlife began. Dinner reservations at a hot new restaurant or an Atlanta classic—103 West, Pricci's, Bones and Chops, The Abbey, Raffello's, The Buckhead Diner—were made a month in advance to insure a table. Between the food, drinks and company, it was a favorite time of the year.

The foursome usually acquired a second wind that kicked in about midnight often resulting in a trip to Rupert's to dance. At that hour the three-story, late night entertainment spot in the heart of Buckhead was just beginning to hop. The live bands that played way into the morning were their main attractions and "meat market" reputation it's other. Even though the trendy dance club was new and cutting-edge, the group preferred Johnnies Hideaway by far. Red carpet, disco ball, tight group with ages ranging from 21 to 92. Dancing at Johnnie's was the greatest. From shagging to beach music to disco dancing to the sound of *Saturday Night Fever.* Generally, they closed the place down and couldn't believe it was three o'clock in the morning.

After the cab ride back to The Ritz, they ordered room service. They followed that old college hangover philosophy: eat something greasy; in fact, the more grease the better. Fat, juicy hamburgers were their first choice followed by omelets with bacon or sausage or both. One day of sinful eating habits shouldn't kill you.

As time passed the group began to venture to Atlanta more than once a year. Birthdays, anniversaries, PMS were all good reasons to get away for a good time.

She twirled the sash of the burly robe around her finger. What a dud she had been this afternoon with sweet Walker. He had given her carte blanche with his credit cards and she had been dismissive to the point of rudeness. He had picked out the short, red-beaded cocktail dress at Niemen's with the back that hung to her waist in a loose swag. She had insisted that her black pumps back at the Ritz would look fine with the dress, but Walker had sent the salesclerk to the shoe department anyway to find some size sevens more suitable. The clerk had returned and presented them to her and Stella had only nodded, throwing in a disinterested "They're fine" as a formality.

She was getting embarrassed. How insulting she had been to that nice girl and more over to Walker. What happened to the beginning of dream life? "Snap out of it," she almost said aloud as she stood from her reclining position on the sofa and snapped her fingers.

She strode to the bar, pulled out the Finlandia Vodka and some cold orange juice and made two cocktails. Walker should be returning any time now.

She walked toward the big window of the suite, cocktail in hand, and in a gruff, sexy melody she sang, "Put on your red dress, Mamma, because we're going out tonight."

6

The pool and fitness center in the hotel were well equipped. He had spent some of his morning there on the treadmill jogging his usual four miles a day. It wasn't the sandy beaches of Florida, but it was nice. The equipment was top of the line and a wide screen television centered along one wall helped to pass the monotony of running and going nowhere.

He had worked up an appetite and decided to go to the dining room for a bite. Brunch at The Ritz was more savory and filling than his usual bowl of Life cereal. Nathan Kenan Gray III sat in the dining room long after he had finished his meal and read the *Atlanta Journal-Constitution* and people watched.

The Stevensons' time of arrival was uncertain and he could use this time for a little practice. This entire trip to Atlanta seemed bizarre to him, but when Nathan, Jr. had phoned the panic in his voice revealed his desperation and the urgency of the matter, so he asked few questions and packed a bag.

Something else was on his mind as well this morning and he contemplated it while he continued to people watch. Why in the hell had his father chosen the shrimp industry as a diversification for Gray, Inc. anyway? They had to purchase a dozen refrigerated trailers, and trucks to haul them, when they had an entire fleet of regular trailers and trucks, all updated equipment, stationed in dozens of major cities throughout the country.

The whole idea is to utilize what you already have in a more efficient and slightly different way in order to boost the profits. Spending well over a million dollars to crank up a new division had never been on the drawing board. He would need to get up to Richmond soon to check over the books on this division. Maybe that's part of the problem. Maybe this shrimping folly of his father's was costing the multimillion-dollar family-owned business a bundle. Or maybe his father's concerns really were over the death of one of his employees. Doubtful, but one can only hope.

His father, Nathan Kenan Gray, Jr., was a hard, unfeeling man. He and his son had made outstanding progress in the past two years with their relationship, but he was still an indignant, humorless, untouchable loaner. His strong, towering physique was topped with jet-black hair and dark brown eyes.

One would never suspect these two were father and son. But it was true. The same blood; the same family name and heritage. The family had welcomed the blonde, blue-eyed baby with affection and surprise just as they had his mother years before. It had been several generations since the affluent Virginia family had a blood relative with blond hair and blue eyes.

He signed the tab *Kenan Gray*, and walked out of the dining room toward the lobby with the newspaper tucked under his arm. It would come in handy later when the surveillance began. He laughed at the thought of it all, yet he knew there was more to it than his father had divulged. He wondered again what was in this "seaman's capsule" he was on a mission to find.

7

The brass elevator doors closed as Lois leaned against one of the mahogany walls that surrounded her. She leaned forward to the control panel and pressed twenty-four and felt a subtle movement upward.

She could hardly believe what Walker had just told her and Mike. Poor Stella. She would go straight to the room and call her. From the picture Walker painted she was still very upset. And understandably so, since the detectives from Beaufort had informed them only this morning, that the case had turned into a murder investigation instead of suicide.

The elevator stopped on the twenty-fourth floor and Lois, tall, athletic and redheaded, stepped into the foyer. Lois was alone on the twenty-fourth floor except for a man at the end of the hall letting himself into his room. She moved swiftly down the spacious hallway toward the end, where she was confident she would find room 2401. Along each side of the hall were exquisite pieces of furniture, strategically placed to ensure the fastidious decorum. The man at the end of the hall was still standing in the same spot. He must be having a problem with the computerized key. That had happened to them before, but not at the Ritz.

Lois continued to move down the long corridor as the man with his back to her turned the bill of his Atlanta Braves baseball cap to the rear and peeked into the peephole. By now she was at the door of their room and the man was directly across from her. She noticed the number of the room he was trying to enter was 2402.

"It's no use; you can't see a thing through this side of the peep hole. I've tried it before. Having trouble with your key?" Lois asked.

The startled man turned his cap back around quickly and spoke very softly after a pause to catch his breath, "Yes, I left it inside. It seems my wife is in the shower and is unaware that I am locked out in the hall."

Lois inserted her key in the door and waited for the green dots to blink. She opened the door to 2401. "I didn't mean to startle you. Would you like to phone her from our room? There's a telephone in the bath you know, she could hear the ring."

"Yes, thank you. That would save me a trip to the lobby. I left my cell phone in the room."

Lois held the door open for the tall young gentleman with an extremely handsome face. He hurried past Lois thanking her for her kindness and stopped with his back to her beside the king-sized bed and lifted the receiver. Before he began to dial the number Lois said, "I'll be right back. I'm going to get some ice."

She knew the bellman was moments away with their luggage and he could get the ice, but decided to get it herself. Lois grabbed the ice bucket and was gone. When she returned, the young man was just hanging up the telephone. His thanks were overwhelming. He explained that she was on her way to let him in and he said goodbye, blushing, as he closed the door behind him.

8

Lois sat the ice bucket down and walked directly to the telephone. She realized that Walker had forgotten to tell them their room number. She pressed zero and the hotel operator quickly connected Lois with Stella's room. She was so anxious to speak with her long-time friend, but she hardly knew where to begin.

Stella answered on the second ring. There was more enthusiasm in her voice than Lois had expected.

"How are you doing?" Lois asked, twirling the telephone cord nervously.

"Better. I just mixed a couple of drinks. I thought Walker would be back by now, but since he's not, you better come over and drink it. We wouldn't want to be wasteful," she laughed.

"It's great to hear you laughing. I wasn't sure what state I would find you in. Walker said he really started to worry today when you didn't want to shop. We've never seen that side of you."

"No need for concern. I'm coming out of it. We'll do some power shopping tomorrow and ease his mind. So where did you see Walker?" Stella asked.

"We bumped into him in the lobby. Your dress is terrific. I can't believe you were actually going to wear plain black pumps with it." Their dialogue was on its usual course. Lois breathed easier now and stopped twirling the cord.

"He tells everything he knows now that he is not a tight-lipped barrister. I need to have a chat with him." Before Lois could respond Stella continued, "I don't know what I would have done without him these last few days. I haven't handled this well at all, Lois. I've been a basket case, and you know that's not me." She paused to allow Lois to agree with her.

"I know I've written you about how Walker and I really wanted our first few months living at Fripp to be perfect. The first one was and now this happens. I'm sorry. I'm just a little mad about it all now. It's been an emotional roller coaster, as the cliché goes. From shock, which the doctor said I was in for a while by the way, then fright, sadness and grief. And suddenly I find myself mad and resentful."

"That's really a blessing, Stella. Because when you're mad you can usually get the job done. You can put this all behind you, not all at once, but soon."

"Have you been taking a psychology course?"

"No, but I've raised two girls."

"Yes you have. Then I say you have your doctorate. Why are we talking on the telephone? Get over here and enjoy this cocktail," Stella demanded.

"I'll be right there. What is your room number?" Lois asked.

"2402."

9

The gavel banged three times and the Clerk of the Georgia Court of Appeals said, "All rise," as the white marble doors parted and three black-robed judges ceremoniously appeared. The Clerk informed the Judges of the calendar for the day, announcing that the case Walker had come to assist Ed with would be first.

Walker and Ed left Stella alone on the pew and walked toward the front. The two lawyers sat shoulder to shoulder on the right hand side of the intimidating courtroom ready to plead their case for yet another time.

The Judiciary Building housed both the Georgia Court of Appeals and the State Supreme Court and was in close proximity with the State Capitol. The grand old building was a sea of dark suits when they had arrived this morning. While Walker and Ed were meeting near the courtroom to discuss some specifics of the case, Stella strolled through the lobby admiring the marble floors and watching droves of people, attorneys she supposed, pour in from the street.

In the mass of dark hues, Stella felt as though she had just been plugged into a light socket with the fuchsia woolen blazer draped across her shoulders. The crisp autumn breeze told her not to consider removing it, but to just ignore the mostly male multitude that starred as they passed, and studied the woman in the hot pink coat. It never occurred to her that they were admiring her beauty.

She sipped coffee from a vending machine that was surprisingly good, and began to count the red neckties that passed. She counted seven in one glance. Nine times out of ten Walker wore a red necktie into the courtroom and in the unusual event that he didn't, it was probably because he had not anticipated being in the courtroom at all that day. Perhaps it signified power or intelligence, or maybe it was just good luck.

She glanced at her watch and moved toward the elevator. She waited in the crowd of same-suited professionals for the doors to open then inched her way inside. Eight, nine, ten, eleven red neckties stared her in the face. There were probably more but it was so packed there was no way to be sure. It was useless to think she could get close enough to the elevator control panel to press her desired floor. Surely one of these starched white shirts was going her way.

All but six of them did get off on her floor and many of them spoke to her handsome spouse who was waiting outside the courtroom for her. Walker had a reputation within the Georgia court system as an awesome litigator and numerous articles had been published in the *Fulton County Daily Report,* a legal newspaper, regarding his work with specific cases. They usually included a photo of him, so many casual colleagues recognized him and spoke as if they knew him personally. Walker always smiled and returned the hello in a kind way although he didn't have a clue about their identity. Relentless and mean as hell in the courtroom, but a nice guy otherwise.

As Stella approached Walker she was chuckling to herself over her idea that she should go into the red tie design business. He kissed her on the cheek and whispered in her ear, "It's nice to see you smiling." She slipped her hand into the crook of his arm and they entered the courtroom.

Now Stella watched as the green light in the middle of the room flashed on and instantaneously Ed began his opening remarks. She had been in this courtroom before to watch Walker and vaguely remembered how the lights worked. They resembled a traffic light laid on its side, enclosed in mahogany wood, of course, to match the rest of the room. Their semblance was very straightforward: green for begin, yellow for two-minute warning, and red for stop. No need to speak any further when the red light flashed because the Judges had stopped listening.

She did not know very much about the case at hand, but she was determined that she would be here with her husband today. Walker had encouraged her to sleep in and order room service, drink coffee with Lois, and relax. That plan sounded perfect to her but she felt she needed to repay Walker for all of his support in the past few days, and make something other than her problems the center of their lives for at least a morning anyway.

Stella gazed out the window to her right as Ed continued to speak. She could see a lovely little courtyard in the distance and watched as the trees dropped their leaves before her eyes. An undying philosophy rose once again in her mind. Autumn; a genesis. The birth of another year in its untainted purity. Her eyes filled gradually with tears, sort of like they always did when she was at a wedding, and then one solitary tear weighing two tons escaped over the edge of her eyelid and rolled down her cheek clearing all of the makeup in its path.

And then she felt better. Maybe she hadn't allowed herself enough tears. She didn't remember crying a lot, only dreaming those bad dreams. She reached into her small black purse for a tissue and the chain shoulder strap hit the edge of the seat with a bang. She glanced around and no one was looking at her. Good. Maybe they won't notice the flaw in her makeup either. She was sure it was there.

Let's see, what comes after denial? Tears maybe, and then recovery. Stella was a determined woman who lived life with zeal and always kept moving forward.

The yellow light flashed on as the green faded to nothingness. Two minutes she thought. The beginning of our new life will begin in two minutes. "I will," she spoke to herself without making a sound. "Put this behind me. It is over." Her jaw was locked down with conviction as her teeth grated together.

The red light blasted on. She had missed the entire forty-minute argument in her midst, but had won a grand battle with reasoning in her mind. The newness was upon her and the shocking episode in her life was now history, including the mysterious man in the Braves baseball cap that the Ritz security men had been unable to locate.

10

Nathan Gray gently replaced the receiver on the hook and leaned back in his leather desk chair. He knew it had been dangerously wrong to send Kenan to Atlanta, but he had done it regardless. How many more times would he make mistakes as far as the wellbeing of his son was concerned?

How could he change the past filled with years of neglect? He had ignored the small fair child all the years of his childhood and now he was trying to make amends for his selfish and juvenile behavior. So why in the hell had he chosen him to send to Atlanta? There were plenty of choices in the ranks.

If Anthony Paulos would get off his back, he would not be forced to make such hasty decisions. He would have to report to Paulos soon that the seaman's capsule had not been found yet. Paulos would put the pressure on Nathan in his usual way with a few quiet words. This was the first time in all their years of business together that Nathan wasn't quite sure of the procedure to follow to please the man in charge. Paulos wanted the capsule found, and refused to send any of his men to help.

It had been "Nathan's screw up," so Nathan could fix it. Nathan knew he had to concentrate his efforts on finding that capsule.

He had hoped that the search wouldn't stretch back to Fripp Island, but after talking with Kenan he accepted the fact that it must. The poor kid. Nathan knew Kenan was right during their telephone conversation when he said that he hadn't graduated from Princeton, undergraduate and MBA, to sneak around like a private eye.

Kenan had conveyed complete frustration to his father during their discussion. For the last two years he had worked closely with Nathan and now, in an obvious time of crisis, Kenan was clearly in the dark about the specifics and ramifications of this matter, yet instructed to do the dirty work. He was indignant, but agreed to proceed solely out of loyalty.

Nathan had sensed Kenan's nervousness through his rigid speech but had no advice to offer him. He was up to his ass in alligators and was having dinner with the biggest one tonight. Currently, there was not a drop of good news to report to Paulos, but even with the dread of the evening ever-present Nathan couldn't shake the thoughts of Kenan and what he must be feeling.

The entire father-son relationship felt more depressing as the day wore on. True, they were making much headway, but Nathan felt as though he had let Kenan down yet another time. Nathan knew he could never tell Kenan the whole truth, partially to protect his son, and more certainly because he was ashamed of his own ethics.

The ardent, controlled man, who filled the leather chair with his solid stature, whirled it around to view the grounds of their family estate below. He looked through the enormous window and unconsciously leaned both arms across his chest matching each strong finger of one hand to its mate on the other hand. He pumped them up and down against each other as he watched the yellow and red leaves detach themselves from the aged oak trees, which stood about the Gray Estate in profound silence.

From his second floor study of the Gray Estate in Richmond, Virginia, Nathan felt that perhaps this time of year was a bad influence on his emotional state. Nathan looked at the trees his father had planted throughout the grounds when the construction of the mansion had been complete. He had staggered them along the edge of the drive that curved up through the alee. His mind delved into the past and he remembered a time that made him even more depressed.

Nathan imagined that Priscilla and Kenan were once again meandering across the lawn during one of their many playful times spent together exploring the grounds. Kenan hiding behind each massive tree trunk and Priscilla pretending to be so surprised when she found her precious young son.

He could see them now. The two bosom buddies were adorned in jeans and sweatshirts, each carrying a rake in their hand. That particular day they had made their way to the knoll on the left side of the property never knowing that they were being watched. Nathan had brought his car to a halt just inside the black iron gates of the fence that bordered the estate. He watched the two frolicking about, raking the leaves into a pile then running and jumping into them, hand in hand. He felt so detached from them, but at the time didn't know why.

He had parked his car and walked toward the pair who were oblivious to the fact that anyone was approaching. They had raked another collection of the red and golden leaves into an oddly shaped mound and were chanting the familiar childhood phrase, "On your mark, get set, GO." Nathan watched them repeat the procedure, holding hands for dear life and throwing themselves into the leaves. The sound of their laughter still burned in Nathan's ears.

They looked up as his broad shouldered shadow swept down upon them. The laughter stopped abruptly and they rose to their feet brushing the crumbled leaves from their hair and clothes. They saw only the large intimidating silhouette of Nathan as the brilliant sun shone directly into their eyes.

His reaction to the situation was exactly as they had grown to expect: condescending verbal abuse. Nathan did not recognize fun when he saw it and they had learned to accept that disappointment as well. His first biting words proved their theory correct again.

"Priscilla we have a grounds keeper to rake the leaves. I would prefer if the neighbors didn't see you with a rake in your hand."

"It's a game. We're playing, and besides, the neighbors are not exactly right next door dear," Priscilla had answered in her cool, quiet voice that he longed to hear.

"I can hear them now, 'He just can't fill his father's shoes. They must have had to fire some of the help. I saw poor Priscilla working about the grounds the other day. The company's just going to hell in a handbag since the old man died.' It will be all over town," Nathan spat the words out.

She pulled Kenan to her as if to protect him, although she had never had a reason to fear Nathan physically.

With jealousy jumping from his words he continued.

"We're due at the Fauntleroy's in an hour and look at you." She had looked beautiful even then with the leaves all over her, but he had never told her so when she was his. "I suppose this was Kenan's idea, and by all means, drop every damn thing and make the boy happy."

His face turned red with embarrassment now as he thought of what a pompous ass he had been. He had thrown his hands up in disgust and stormed away, but the gentle tone of Priscilla's voice calling after him pounded through the nothingness, "She called again today."

This stopped him in his tracks but he did not turn around. His stillness, which filled no more than a couple of seconds, was the only acknowledgment he gave to Priscilla to let her know that he had even heard her words.

He had returned to this very same room and watched them continue their play, seemingly unaffected by his display of disapproval.

He wanted to be a part of their lives but didn't know how. His jealousy and possessiveness always made him say and do the wrong thing. Priscilla had created a family atmosphere at Gray Estate for their son, but he didn't feel a part. If he had only realized then that the word "family" meant sharing, perhaps it would have helped him. But sharing was not in his vocabulary then and only in a concerted effort now.

"Why did she stay with me all of those years?" he asked himself aloud as he continued to pump his fingers against each other across his chest.

Her words, "She called again today," rang in his ears once more. The breeze sent some leaves crashing into the arched window. They clung to the glass until the breeze ceased, then fell to the ground below.

The neighbor's opinions, which Nathan had imagined concerning his lack of success with Gray, Inc., were actually a reality. It was true that he lacked the charisma and sincerity that his father had possessed with clients. Sadly, his true character, one of a spoiled and selfish child, never failed to surface during a business meeting. He had lost some of the clients his father had held for years to their competitors because of these shortcomings. The business was on a course to financial ruin and there was no mistaking it was his fault.

That very night so many years ago, after he had snarled at the family he silently longed to be a part of, he met Anthony Paulos. They had been at a dinner party. Most of the guests were neighbors on Ampt Hill but a few new faces proved to be an interesting find for Nathan. He met Mr. Paulos near the bar on the veranda as they both asked the bartender for vodka on the rocks with cocktail onions at the exact same time. They both laughed loudly and simultaneously gave one another a gentleman's punch to the shoulder... and the bullshit began. Paulos' position at that time was not nearly as significant within the organization as it was now, but the man was so convincing. He had quietly told Nathan about a business venture that could net millions.

This proposal had gotten Nathan involved and in six short months Gray, Inc. was back on track, financially speaking. His father would roll in the grave if he knew what Nathan was doing to the company, their heritage and his son. On the other hand, life was a perfect dream for Nathan. The best part was that Nathan didn't have to kiss any ass to get the company far into the red. Forget those clients who left his company because he failed to entertain them frequently or say exactly what they wanted to hear. He had one major client now, or maybe the client had him, but profits soared. The stockholders smiled over their dividend checks and everyone was pleased with Gray, Inc. once again. Maybe for the first time, they were pleased with the old man's son.

Nathan watched now as the groundskeeper, Richard, slowly raked the leaves near the gate. His work was as painstaking as it had always been, but it seemed to take him longer than it used to. Nathan noticed the gray hair atop Richard's head and wondered when that had happened. The old man seemed to be raking and getting nowhere. He might have to consider replacing him. But Priscilla had hired Richard right after Kenan was born, so maybe he would keep him around in some token position.

Nathan remembered how his mother had worried about Priscilla strolling the baby down to the gate with all of the leaves on the drive. "She could slip on those dreadful leaves. We must hire someone to sweep the drive daily before you stroll the baby." It was a command and Priscilla had wasted no time in hiring Richard away from the Eight O'clock Superette. He had been her favorite grocery bagger and when she offered him the job he seemed honored. Surprisingly, he untied his apron, laid it on the checkout counter and followed her out of the store.

It was a definite increase in salary and his job duties entailed far more than raking leaves. He became Priscilla's personal page and friend. Kenan loved the black man who taught him to run and jump and play every sport that involved the use of a ball. He had done what Nathan should have done for the boy.

Nathan turned his chair back around. The sight of the old man made him sad, and all those damn leaves. The days would be getting shorter and late afternoon golf games would disappear until spring. There would be more hours spent in this cold, lonely mansion. Nathan could scarcely bear the thought of it.

Sure, he could get away and do what he did best when he became lonely and depressed, but that too would end and he would eventually have to return to this morgue. He really missed Kenan. Maybe, he thought, I should bring him home from Florida. He shook his head confirming Florida as the best place for Kenan's residence until this problem was solved.

"She called again today." Would it ever stop blasting through his head? Maybe it would have been better if Priscilla had moved out of their bedroom after she had received that first telephone call, but she hadn't. She continued to share his bed, never allowing him to touch her. To lie in that bed beside Priscilla Gray, with her long and lean body warming the sheets beside him and not touch one golden blonde hair on her head was torture for Nathan.

She knew about none of those flattering feelings of her unfaithful husband. The only impressions that were communicated to her were ones that made her feel inadequate. She felt Nathan had other, more exciting means by which to be satisfied and cared nothing about her. Priscilla was not an aggressive person and never once entertained the idea of making an advance toward Nathan in the bedroom, although she really did still love him even after she found out. At least for a little while anyway.

Their lack of communication sent the marriage into a vicious cycle that grew larger and larger until it was beyond help of any kind. Had he only asked for Priscilla's forgiveness after the first incident she would have bestowed it upon him. Instead, he had one illicit affair after another. He was certain that Priscilla knew of his constant adultery, but he was convinced she could not have cared less. All that interested her was Kenan. He wanted her to hurt, because he was hurting. He had possessed her completely until that child had been born. All of his attempts to get her attention failed. Priscilla never once raised her voice in a fury to express rage over Nathan's infidelities.

The years passed and Nathan continued to show no remorse and Priscilla continued to ignore the situation. Nathan was his usual possessive self, always questioning any outings she took and discouraging any close friends. She had been accustomed to those bad habits in the beginning and was unaffected by them still, as she seemed to be about everything except her cherished Kenan.

The wall between them grew thicker and thicker until Priscilla's love that remained for Nathan grew only into hate and deep resentment. Nathan didn't understand why she had never left him.

Though he was not consciously aware of it, he was staring at the large oil portrait of Priscilla and Kenan that hung on the wall before him. He began to study the portrait in which the tall confident boy stood behind his incredibly beautiful mother. His lean fingers curled around her shoulders as she sat with such dignity. Neither were smiling. He thought the portrait timeless.

Nathan's eyes widened as he stood and approached the large picture on the wall. It was if he were viewing it for the first time. Priscilla and Kenan were almost mirror images. Their beautiful blue eyes and golden blonde hair were exactly the same hue. The shape of their eyes, nose and face were identical.

Even though he knew now that his own jealousy had exiled him from his family he couldn't help but feel detached as he looked at the portrait. His own physical appearance—intense, dark and burly—was so drastically different from theirs. It still hurt to think of it.

Nathan ran his finger along the edge of Priscilla's shoulder and stopped when he came to Kenan's hand. It was then that the realization came to him. "It was for Kenan."

It had been for him all along. She had lived with a man she detested only for one reason: her son. Sure, lots of married couples stay together for the children, but this was different. Nathan had been a horrible father; Kenan would have never missed him. Priscilla would have had all the money she needed. It would have been most unusual if the judge hadn't awarded her the family estate after all of Nathan's indiscretions.

Nathan shivered at the thought that this woman knew him so well. She was smart and knew that Kenan was Nathan's only legitimate child and she intended to keep it that way. Had Priscilla ever divorced him, and that surely would have been the case because he could never give up the need to possess her, he would have remarried. His excessive sexual behavior would have allowed him no other marital status in life. Perhaps his choice would have been "the other woman" who called Priscilla from time to time, and if that were the case, Kenan would have ceased to be the sole heir to the Gray fortune. The past two years had been painful ones and Nathan's tunnel vision of self-centeredness had denied him the ability to reason through this matter earlier. And why now, he wondered when he was in such deep trouble? He didn't know.

Sentiment seemed to fill the large man's heart as he contemplated his love for Kenan. Would it ever match that of Priscilla's love for their son? Could it? She had loved Kenan so much she had never told him about his father's constant affairs. She had worked hard to give Kenan a happy and harmonious home life in the midst of a broken marriage.

Priscilla pretended to care for Nathan in public, as the silent attentive wife. All for Kenan. She had been Kenan's source of stability and love but more than anything she had protected him from the sadness Nathan created.

Nathan reached for the silk handkerchief in his breast pocket and used it to wipe his watering eyes. He looked at the handkerchief—it was embroidered with the Gray family crest—remembering that Priscilla had given him and Kenan each a set two Christmas' ago. It had been a good Christmas thanks to Priscilla and her insistence on family tradition.

Priscilla Gray had instilled some extraordinary characteristics and morals in their son. If she could live a life of pain and misery to protect her only son and ensure his benefit of the future, surely Nathan could play some part in the game as well.

More leaves were clinging to the window. He felt like he was sinking fast into a more depressed state. Maybe he should call Dr. Minor, his shrink, and arrange for a session this afternoon. He walked toward the large desk and picked up his cell phone. He pressed a speed dial entry and his spirits were lifting with each ring. Finally, the ringing ceased and a provocative voice said, "Good afternoon, The Mecca Escort Service. May I assist you in making today a day to remember?"

11

"Which do you like, the Gorham," Stella asked holding up the stem of crystal in her right hand, "or the King Edward?" she glanced toward the one in her left.

"Which will hold the most wine?" Lois asked.

"The Gorham."

"There's your answer."

"I love the way you shop," Stella said approvingly.

She instructed the clerk at Tiffany's to send a dozen of the wine glasses to her address on file. The two continued to browse the shelves and showcases of the exquisite jewelry store and discussed taking a cocktail break at the Pleasant Peasant on the upper level of Phipps Plaza. With a laugh, they both agreed it was the right thing to do.

The shopping adventure had begun around eleven when the Stevenson's returned to The Ritz after the court hearing. Lois and Mike had been waiting in the lobby having a bloody mary. Both ladies were anxious to explore the new department store at Phipps, the Parisian, and the men felt sure they could squeeze in nine holes of golf before they were to meet back at the Buckhead Diner for a late lunch.

The mall was not very crowded since it was a weekday and Stella's shopping stamina was at an all-time high. They loved the Parisian, but also made a trip through Saks Fifth Avenue simply out of years of devotion. They passed by their favorite children's store, Chocolate Soup, and confirmed that children really do grow up too fast just like everyone said they would. A trip to Lord and Taylor proved to be most successful in finding Ely some birthday gifts. She almost had them ship the gifts directly to him at Clemson, but decided against it at the last minute. She would do it herself after Walker had a chance to see them.

Lois suggested they sit at the bar instead of waiting for a table since it would be quicker. "We've still got a little bit of shopping time left. Can't waste a minute."

Kenan was glad they made that choice. He welcomed the break in the hard core shopping routine. He could browse in the bookstore across from the restaurant and watch them as they sat at the bar near the front.

The crowd was thin today, making following them far from easy. He almost went into a coma when Mrs. Stevenson had emerged from The Ritz with the redhead whose telephone he had pretended to use yesterday. He knew the Stevensons' had dinner plans with another couple because he had overheard a conversation as such, but since he dismissed the plan to follow them at that time in order to search their room, he was not privy to the identity of their guests. His second attempt at entering room 2402 was a success, but no capsule was found.

Kenan thought how fortunate he was that his income didn't depend on his ability as a sleuth as he was certain he would be penniless. He continued to observe the ladies now drinking what appeared to be screwdrivers. Kenan was almost one hundred percent certain that this fascination his father had with the Stevensons was completely in vain. He believed that there was not even a remote possibility that Mrs. Stevenson could be the person harboring the infamous seaman's capsule that his father was stroking out to find.

Even the words "seaman's capsule" sounded far too dramatic to Kenan's ears and seemed to only exaggerate the seriousness of the situation. Nathan had described the object in great detail as though it were an exquisite masterpiece of art. It was a cylinder approximately seven inches long and one and a half inches in diameter. The cylinder screwed apart in the center and usually housed a small knife the shrimpers used. A nylon cord was attached to the top portion of the capsule and allowed it to hang around their neck for easy access. Nathan went on to say that the slickers the shrimpers wore were very thick and heavy and how impossible it was to get in and out of them.

Kenan thought how his father sounded like he had been in the shrimping business all of his life rather than for only the past two years. When Kenan asked what had been in the capsule to demand this intense search he was given no answer. His father only pleaded with him again to just get the search over with and return to Florida as quickly as possible.

Kenan set the Gucci shopping bag on the floor beside his feet and picked up a book. He had felt conspicuous walking around the vast mall empty handed so he had ducked into the Gucci store and purchased a subtle signature necktie and a pair of black socks. He continued to watch the ladies and pretended to be deeply interested in the prenatal care book he held in his hand. After a moment he realized the nature of the book he held and moved a row back to the men's health section.

Kenan shook his head and his eyes did an incredulous roll at the absurdity of this situation. After a day of observing the Stevensons, there had been no activity whatsoever that was out of the ordinary. The only thing peculiar was Kenan's actions.

"This is ridiculous," he said out loud.

Sneaking around The Ritz, of all places, ease dropping on conversations, and now reading prenatal care books. The six foot three inch, very intelligent, single heir to a three-generation fortune was, in his view of the situation, losing credibility fast.

Kenan concluded that this method of snooping would never result in the probable means to an end that he was so anxiously awaiting. From conversations he had overheard, the Stevensons were leaving Atlanta this afternoon and heading back home to a place called Fripp Island, South Carolina, wherever the hell that was. He was hopeful that by the time they all arrived he would have devised a plan that did not involve these sneaky methods.

Mr. and Mrs. Stevenson were a perfectly normal couple and were probably very likable as well. There should be no reason why he couldn't procure passage to their home with only one little white lie. He could be a county employee checking for radon, or maybe a visitor on the beach with a sudden abnormal heart palpitation. Anything was better than this.

Kenan peeked over the pages of the book he was holding to check on his prey and saw that Mrs. Stevenson had turned and was now facing the bar directly. Her blonde hair fell perfectly beneath the gold clip that gathered the thick strands at the base of her neck. Less than twenty-four hours ago Kenan's heart had skipped a beat when the long awaited Mrs. Stevenson crossed the lobby of The Ritz. It had not been difficult to distinguish her from the other attractive women who passed by. With the brief description Nathan offered, coupled with bellmen, concierge's and registration employee's greetings of, "Hello, Mrs. Stevenson!" and, "Good to see you again Mrs. Stevenson," he would have had to be deaf, dumb and blind not to know that the woman who passed by him sending shock waves through his entire body wasn't Mrs. Stevenson.

He had breathed heavily to restore some sense of calm to his dismantled emotions. The lady who walked confidently past him was a lady named Mrs. Stevenson. True, she was tall and blonde, impeccably dressed and incredibly attractive, but her name was Stella Stevenson and not Priscilla Gray.

He had gripped the newspaper tightly in one hand and dug his nails into the leather sofa with the other. A ghostly sensation crept over him and he began to wonder if his mother had a sister she had never told him about. His mother had never told him very much about her family other than her parents had been killed when she was a young child. She had been raised by an aunt in West Virginia and had met Nathan at the University of Virginia.

Kenan composed himself by dwelling on the single distinguishing characteristic that made this woman completely different from his mother. Stella Stevenson possessed the art of conversation. As she passed through the lobby it was as though she spoke to everyone, be it with a simple nod of the head or a spoken word. Her kind smile was heartfelt and sincere. Her trait of sophistication filtered through an undisguised fun loving spirit and a never-met-a-stranger personality.

He dismissed the idea that the two women could be related and chalked it up to the adage that everyone had a double.

Kenan wished for his mother that same outward motivation, but he understood the cause of her broken spirit. Nathan, clear and simple. Two years of therapy had yielded some promising results for his father, but the many years before could not be changed.

Kenan imagined that Priscilla Gray had not always been viewed as the wealthy, silent, recluse of Ampt Hill Road in Richmond. Nathan was a paranoid and powerful husband and his jealousy and possessiveness had unfortunately molded Priscilla into a person with characteristics that she had disliked. Kenan was unaware that she felt as though her life was such a lie she could hardly bare to show her face in public. She would and she had, but only when Nathan had demanded it of her.

If he had only demanded that she attended the event with him on that dreadful night, rather than some still unidentified hooker, perhaps things would be different now. It was after seeing Mrs. Stevenson yesterday that this thought came to him and Kenan realized his emotions were growing tender. He forced himself to stop thinking of his mother. He knew he must face the immediate task of following the Stevenson's.

When Kenan finally loosened his grip on the leather sofa and came back in tune with his surroundings it was too late. The couple was nowhere in sight. Luckily one of the bellman was blessed with a voice that carried and Kenan was able to hear him say to another employee, "This is the Stevensons' luggage. Take it on up please. They've already gone shopping across the street."

After riding the elevator to the twenty fourth floor and exchanging small talk with the bellman, he had casually watched while the luggage was deposited in her room. He then took the elevator back down to his floor and experimented with the lock on his own door until he determined the tools he would need to get into 2402.

The yellow pages, contained in two separate books, each five inches thick, listed an electronics/computer store only a few blocks away. He returned directly to the Stevensons' room. A knot formed in his stomach as he recalled the redhead appearing out of nowhere and offering to let him use her telephone. He had returned to his room and ordered some dinner. He needed to regroup.

And now here he was in a bookstore far from the answers he was searching for, somehow understanding more clearly the dynamics of his family. He moved down the aisle away from the window. The books before him all had titles pertaining to mental health. Kenan chose a book with a blue cover to browse through which dealt with the subject of grieving. The table of contents listed steps of which he was well acquainted.

The profound words of the attorney two years ago surfaced in Kenan's mind again, "I do hereby give, devise and bequeath all of my estate, both real and personal and mixed, to my only child, Nathan Kenan Gray, III." Kenan had shown no reaction. He was still in a state of depression and disbelief. Nathan, however, reacted to the reading of his deceased wife's will by flying into a selfish, childish rage. "This is a slap in the face to me," he had screamed, "after all the years I kept her. All those years of ignoring her secret accounts and then she doesn't even leave them to me."

No one in the plush attorney's office was aware how diligently Priscilla had worked to accumulate the twenty million dollars she successfully concealed in a West Virginia bank. She bought elegant dresses and jewelry that Nathan urged her to charge to his account so that others in their social circle would be aware of his continued prosperity. She wore them once, and then returned them after she was sure Nathan had paid the bill, and received cash in return.

She had been very good at the game. Her shopping excursions took her to boutiques as far as the D.C. area. No one ever questioned the gorgeous quiet woman whose husband could afford to buy her anything.

Compared to Nathan's mega millions, Priscilla's twenty million was a scant amount. Although she had lived most of her adult life in complete torment of the man just to insure the security of her son's future she was not completely certain that the original plan alone would yield all of its supposed profits. It would not be out of character for Nathan's hatred to cloud his decision making ability concerning the future of the Gray fortune. At least this account could help Kenan start a business of his own and he wouldn't have to rely on Nathan in the slightest.

Nathan was shocked that Priscilla had deceived him. As the rage persisted it was obvious that it was not due to the financial consequences of her Last Will and Testament, but to the undisputed message his wife was sending him from the grave. Did his beloved Priscilla hate him that much that she didn't want him to possess anything that had been hers during their life together? His tantrum continued until he grabbed his chest and fell to the floor.

A stroke was the original diagnosis, but eventually psychiatric treatment was suggested as well. Thanks to a brilliant Dr. Minor in Richmond, life improved for Nathan, physically and emotionally. A life for a father and a son was evolving.

Kenan believed he understood the reason for his mother's complete dismissal of Nathan in her will. He was so possessive of her and only in death could she sever the rein he had held over her for so many years. By leaving him none of her worldly possessions possibly Nathan Gray might understand that he had left his wife with only a hollow, depleted emotion that Priscilla had once known as love.

Maybe she had hated him, and had every right to. Maybe he should hate Nathan, as well, Kenan thought. He was a pitiful excuse for a father except where the checkbook was concerned. But Kenan had long since resented the money Nathan shoved around in efforts to buy love, loyalty, trust and a hundred other things you earn by being a decent human being.

Kenan had seen it work with some people and for those people he held no respect at all. Nathan's antics had never worked with him or his mother. Perhaps that was the cause of the distance in their relationship, or one of the reasons. He knew his mother could have never anticipated the devastation her husband would experience after her death. Her objective would have never been to damage someone so totally, not even Nathan, if it was true that she did indeed despise him. If she hated him that much why didn't she leave him a long time ago? He wondered occasionally if there weren't parts of the puzzle missing. But only occasionally did he think of it during the past two years because it hurt so much to dwell on the horrible past.

Kenan often looked on the bright side at the possibility that Priscilla had known all along how Nathan would react, and it had been an effort by her to disparage Nathan Gray and to force him to feel an emotion other than jealousy and possessiveness. Perhaps she had the foresight to see that his ultimate breakdown could help to cultivate a relationship with his only son. Priscilla's image seemed to shine brighter in Kenan's eyes when he viewed that day from this point of view. He had dearly loved his mother and had her on a pedestal of honor where he knew she belonged.

He felt like she was right beside him at times, encouraging him or praising him for his accomplishments while running the business in Nathan's absence. Nathan had recuperated well from the stroke and was dismissed from his medical doctor's care after a couple of months, but the psychological therapy continued even now.

The meetings with Dr. Minor had decreased to only twice a month. In the beginning, however, they meet three times a week and on occasion, Kenan had been asked to sit in on certain sessions. Dr. Minor had helped his father to admit to Kenan that he was full of guilt for having manipulated Priscilla for most of her life. Nathan also admitted that he had resented their child from the cradle and even though Kenan was not surprised by this statement of truth, the words ate at his heart.

That same evening at dinner in the enormous dining room of the mansion, the two men had sat across from each other occupying two of the eighteen chairs around the oblong antique table. The silence in the room was overpowering as Nathan broke down and cried in front of his son for the first time in his life. He kept apologizing for treating Priscilla the way he had and repeated over and over that he really had loved her.

Kenan embraced him and thought how awkward it felt to hold the broad chested man. He did not remember a time when he had been so physically close to his father. He called Dr. Minor the next day and told him of the previous evening. The doctor seemed pleased and hoped that this occurrence would help Nathan to let down his defenses and open up more during their sessions. Kenan sensed that the doctor knew Nathan was harboring other feelings of guilt inside. He felt the same way about his father, but had no idea how deep and devious the truth really was.

Life on Ampt Hill improved after that autumn night. It was a progressive kinship between two men who were grieving the death of a woman who had held them together for so long. Day by day they attempted to heal their wounds, and sometimes the heartbreak of the other.

Kenan closed the blue book and squeezed it back onto the crowded shelf. The ladies were standing. They each held a white Styrofoam cup in their hand.

He picked up his Gucci bag and walked toward the door. The salesclerk behind the counter gave him an annoying glance. He realized he had been in the same spot of the book-store for nearly thirty minutes and was leaving without making a purchase. The older woman's crooked lips turned upward into a smile as Kenan grabbed the first paperback book in reach and threw a ten-dollar bill on the counter as he raced out of the door.

12

The cab came to abrupt halt in the valet section of the parking lot wrapping around the aluminum and neon building.

"I'll catch this one," Lois said as she reached into her purse.

"Thanks," Stella said, "I can see the boys from here. They're at our favorite booth."

The two women entered through the double doors of the restaurant and were greeted by a pretty hostess who so kindly offered to keep their packages for them while they enjoyed their lunch. Another hostess showed them to the circular booth next to the window where Walker and Mike were already dipping onion rings with scattered jalapenos into a tangy barbeque sauce.

"What? No packages?" Walker asked in disbelief. "I thought you were feeling better, Stella."

"Don't worry Walker, she's feeling great, and so are the salesclerks at Tiffany's, Sak's and the Parisian."

A waiter approached the foursome and asked for cocktail orders. According to the silver badge on the lapel of his white waiter's jacket he was waiter number 53. Walker declined since he faced the five-hour drive back to Fripp Island, but the other three decided on a bottle of cabernet.

Even at three thirty in the afternoon, the Buckhead Diner was packed. Glossy wooden booths bordered the windows and either side of an imaginary line in the center of the restaurant, were full. All but a few of the tables that filled the remaining areas of the popular dining spot were occupied as well.

The waiter returned with the wine and asked if they were ready to order. Stella spoke up anxiously and said, "Why don't you bring some potato chips with blue cheese dressing and the quesadillas for an appetizer, then I'd like a Caesar salad with a double order of soft shell crab on top with a side of dill sauce." She paused long enough to take a breath. "You know your cole slaw is the best. Bring me a small order of that, too. Oh, and don't forget the bread. I love the bread."

She closed the menu in her hand, sat back in the booth and breathed deeply with a satisfying exhale. Mike, Lois and Walker were all staring at her in disbelief.

"Were you ordering for all of us?" Walker asked.

"I'll share the appetizers, but nothing else. And I'll probably have dessert too."

Walker reached and gave her shoulder a massaging rub. "I love to see you eat. I couldn't be happier."

The remaining orders were easy for number 53 to remember, but Stella's would put his memory to a test.

Lois unzipped her purse and pulled out her phone. "Oh no, not that again," Mike moaned.

"Didn't you get enough incriminating evidence last night?" Walker asked.

"I did get some good shots of you three drinking the B-52s at Otto's piano bar last night. And the one of Mike in the middle of Peachtree Street trying to hail a cab should turn out pretty well too."

"I think the best one will be of Walker and the Jamaican cab driver singing that song about, 'If you want to be happy for the rest of your life, you've got to make a pretty woman your wife,'" Mike sang as he poured the wine.

They passed Lois' phone around and took a few candid shots. "Say cheese," Lois said. The flash blinded them both. "Darn, I hope the window behind you two didn't cast a glare on the photo. If it turns out well, I'll send it to you. Oh, I need to send you Ely's birthday gift, too."

"Have you told Ely about the murder?" Mike asked.

Stella and Walker looked at one another and Stella answered, "No."

They had discussed informing both children of the tragedy the day after the funeral, but Stella was still shaken and they were afraid the children would sense it in her voice. There was no need to upset them when there was really nothing they could do any way.

"I'd like to call them both tonight or tomorrow," Stella said looking at Walker.

He nodded just as number 53 sat the appetizers down in the middle of the table. The conversation quieted as they ate, ravenous, savoring each bite.

"This," Stella said, holding up a quesadilla slice, "may be what I miss most about living so far away from Atlanta."

"You can say that now, but wait until the soft shell crab arrives," Lois said reaching for a bread stick.

"Ooohh, you're right, they're to die for. This is so much fun. I could never choose between eating and shopping. They are two of my favorite things to do."

"That's right, honey," Walker said as he topped her glass off with more wine. "Get your tummy real full and you should sleep most of the trip home. Then you won't complain about listening to the talk radio shows I enjoy so much."

"That's a great idea." She woofed down some chips covered in warm blue cheese. "I especially want to sleep if that lunatic, David, what's his name? Paulie? Is that it? David Paulie? Any way, if he's on I just can't take it."

"Now honey, he's had some interesting ideas. His theory about the traffic on the perimeter highway around Atlanta causing problems with the magnetic field, does make you stop and think, now doesn't it?"

"I heard that one," Mike interrupted. "His solution was to change the directions of the traffic flow. He is really a scream."

"I can't believe two intelligent men like you, would even waste time tuning into his show," Lois said.

"It's entertainment. You warm up to his ways after a while," Walker said as Mike nodded his head in agreement.

Stella made no further comment, she just kept eating. The sun beaming through the restaurant window felt warm on her back and she thought how Walker was probably right, she would catch up on her sleep on the way back to Fripp.

Number 53 cleared the table when it was apparent that the foursome could eat no more and asked if anyone cared for dessert. There were no takers, not even Stella. The dreaded moment of saying goodbye was upon them and the women handled it gracefully with talk of when they would be able to do this again soon.

The valets were much too efficient in bringing the cars around and before Stella knew it Walker was ushering her into the car. She waved goodbye to Lois through the window and snuggled down into the passenger seat of the navy Mercedes. She detested goodbyes, especially when it was to a friend she so trusted and loved. She closed her eyes as the temperature in the car rose from the heat of the sun, and emptied her mind of any thoughts.

Traffic on Piedmont Road was busy as usual and Walker had to wait several minutes before finding a break in the madness to make a left hand turn. Stella was already in the arms of Morpheus and certainly didn't notice the casket gray Audi that pulled into traffic behind them.

13

The young brunette kissed him as she slipped from the sheets of the king sized bed with her garter belt and stockings still intact.

"This won't take long," Nathan insisted as he lifted the receiver to his ear. "This room has a great view of the city," Nathan motioned toward the window. He watched the girl move across the room and grew more annoyed with his secretary for interrupting him.

She reached the window and opened the drapes. The sunlight poured in and Nathan was left to marvel at the tantalizing silhouette her body created as he tried to concentrate on the conversation with his secretary.

"Yes, Barbara, I know I have a meeting with Mr. Paulos tonight. I only gave you this number to call in cases of real emergencies."

"Mr. Paulos was adamant that your dinner engagement be moved up to six o'clock tonight. He seemed very anxious about it," Barbara said in her drill sergeant tone.

Barbara Crowe had been Nathan's secretary since the first day he had joined his father at Gray, Inc. She was not intimidated in the least by any of Nathan's remarks. She did her job well and was richly rewarded. She also had the ability to keep Nathan's personal life as confidential as possible. This was not the first time she had called him at the Poinsett Hotel, a landmark and exquisite old hotel in downtown Richmond. There were never any questions asked or personal judgments made, only business matters discussed.

"All right, I'll be there." Nathan hung up the telephone. He watched the girl at the window as her long brown hair brushed from side to side over her bare shoulders as she moved her head. He always asked for brunettes or redheads, never blondes. They reminded him of Priscilla.

"Sorry we had to stop in the middle of things," Nathan said, "but I think we can probably resume our activities now without any further interruptions."

The girl who now held her arms over her head and against the sunny, warm window did not respond. Nathan watched more closely now as she moved her body in an extremely sensual motion pressing her breasts and pelvis against the glass.

He rose from the bed and walked to the window and stood behind her. She did not shudder or slow her movement as he reached to massage her large breasts. As he bent his head to kiss her shoulders, that is when he saw her audience.

Calmly, Nathan pulled the drapes closed and watched the lustful smiles of the yuppie businessmen in the building next door disappear. He turned the brunette toward him and with the warmth of her body against his, said, "I paid for you, they didn't."

14

The Audi motored along the interstate, slightly exceeding the speed limit. Kenan had finally gotten used to driving the unassuming Audi rental car he had chosen at the airport.

Following the Stevenson's on the interstate without being noticed was easily done, but he knew it would become more difficult when they reached the two lane highways. He had found a road map of Georgia and South Carolina among the various forms included in the car rental agreement and thought that the last couple of hours of the trip would be spent on back highways, starting and stopping in small towns.

He wasn't sure at all how he was going to handle that leg of the trip, but he had a couple of hours to come up with a solution.

The leaves along the interstate were flaming with color and Kenan thought how nice it would be to be behind the wheel of his road hugging Porsche, driving through the curving elegance of a mountain road. He and Julia, the only girl he had ever dated long enough to refer to as his "girlfriend," used to take long drives in the mountains when they were at Princeton.

Kenan wondered about the girl he had dated for nearly two years. He was not even sure which state she lived in now. The break-up had been a clean one. She had wanted a commitment from him and although Kenan had cared for her deeply, he knew he didn't feel enough emotion to warrant the life-long commitment of marriage. He wasn't sure what the feelings were that he was missing, but he knew there had to be more to love than his feelings for Julia. If that was all there was to being totally in love, then he had obviously set his expectations too high.

Kenan had watched some of his fraternity brothers at Princeton who vowed to remain bachelors for life, melt like butter in the palm of their chosen one's hand. He was sure there was something out there he had not yet discovered if a woman could bring these guys and their active sex lives to a screeching halt, and then on to surrendering forever to one single woman.

Kenan dated and did so frequently, but never the same woman twice in a row. He was afraid of the commitment problem reoccurring. It just wasn't worth the hassle, and then in Richmond at least, there was always the fear that a girl would be interested in him for the money alone. His handsomeness made him all the more intriguing for the fortune seekers and Kenan had learned through experience to beware.

His social life in Florida was more relaxed. The name Gray didn't turn any heads at all in Pompano Beach. The small coastal community a short drive from West Palm Beach was an elegant area and the residents there respected one another's privacy. Golf course options were excellent in that area and great weather all year long. Kenan had definitely taken advantage of the warm days to play as often as possible.

He was leasing a four thousand square foot, oceanfront condo and had greatly enjoyed the six months he spent in Florida. A diversification decision he had suggested during the time he was acting President of Gray Inc. due to Nathan's breakdown after Priscilla's death, had targeted this area of Florida as being beneficial to the new division.

The new division was set up as Gray Mechanical and many of the initial marketing strategies were being handled by Kenan in Pompano Beach. The work entailed a large amount of entertaining, thus justifying the lease payments on the gorgeous condo. Kenan was entertaining prospective clients and possible production executives three times a week. He had hired a live-in cook and housekeeper to deal with their respective areas of expertise, leaving him free of the worries from entertaining in one's own home.

Kenan had made many new acquaintances in this manner of business and had been included in other social events in the area. His father agreed that he should contact some of their faithful clients and offer them a complimentary vacation to Pompano. The condo was so large it was doubtful that Kenan and the guests would ever cross paths unless they so desired.

Kenan popped the steering wheel with the palm of his hand. "Damn," he said out loud. He remembered he had forgotten to speak with Nathan about a strange conversation he had had the day before he embarked on this trip.

He had been looking through the address file of the company computer to determine which client he might contact next to invite down to Florida in thanks for their long-term business, and had chosen a company by the name of Coastal Transfer. There was no name listed to identify the owner or president of the company. Kenan had recognized the area code and knew it to be that of Washington, D.C. and the surrounding area.

He determined from the beginning invoice date that the company had been with Gray, Inc., for many years. Kenan dialed the number and was surprised when a voice answered, "Paulos residence." He was expecting to hear, "Coastal Transfer", but after a slight pause he took a guess and asked to speak to Mr. Paulos. His call was put on hold during which time he double checked the number and was certain he had dialed correctly.

"Hello," a man answered impatiently.

"Mr. Paulos?"

"Yes, what do you want?"

"I'm sorry to disturb you, sir. Are you the owner or president of Coastal Transfer?"

"Who is this?" the man shouted into the telephone.

"I should have identified myself sooner sir. This is Kenan Gray, with Gray, Inc. I was calling to extend..."

"No one from your company should contact me except Nathan, himself. This is really the clincher," he said in a rage and then hung up the telephone with a bang in Kenan's ear.

He continued to follow the navy Mercedes in the distance and made a mental note to ask Nathan just who this Mr. Paulos really was.

15

Darkness began to fall and Kenan was abundantly grateful for the solution to his most pertinent problem. Just as he expected, the Stevenson's took the shortest route back to Fripp, which meant passing through a small town every thirty to forty-five minutes. If he stayed far enough behind them, hopefully they would not realize they were being tailed through the darkness. When the navy Mercedes stopped for a traffic light, the Audi would make an unexpected turn. Sometimes into a convenient store or the driveway of a local resident, and once into the parking lot of a bar called the Dew Drop Inn. There was a crowd gathered outside the grungy looking establishment and Kenan wondered if he had left with all four of the hubcaps intact.

When he began to feel confident that he had mastered the "tailing" game, Kenan began to speculate on points of gaining lawful entry to the Stevenson's home. He thought of several outlandish ideas that seemed too far-fetched for anyone to believe. It really seemed too nerve racking to admit, but Kenan felt like his best chance was to just bump into these people somehow, someway and strike up a conversation. But, then what would he say? "It's so nice to meet you and may I snoop around your house for a while to look for an item referred to as a seaman's capsule."

The traffic thickened along the road as the passing miles took them closer to their destination. The marshlands were intriguing even in the shadowy darkness and as he drove over bridges the lights of boats twinkled under the big white moon shedding light on creeks joining from every direction to spill their contents into the vastness. Kenan grew anxious for the light of day, which he was certain would present him with even more beauty.

His train of thought was broken when the headlights flashed on a sign that read, "Fripp Island 21". He crossed a long bridge and was welcomed to Lady's Island by a wooden sign with burnt edges and seascape background.

The right blinker of the sedan up ahead flashed in front of him. He touched the brake slowly with his foot and let them make the turn, then drove past and strained his neck backwards to keep them in sight.

Kenan whipped the car into an empty bank parking lot on the right side of the road. He came to a complete stop near the night deposit box and turned the motor off.

Mrs. Stevenson got out of the car and walked toward the Winn-Dixie grocery store. Kenan watched as Mr. Stevenson got out of the car and stretched his legs. He walked around to the rear of the car and opened the trunk and transferred some shopping bags from the back seat into it. His attempt to close the trunk failed and he shuffled some bags around again. Shaking his head, he began to return a few bags to the rear seat. A bag boy rolled an empty cart by and Mr. Stevenson held up his hand in a wave to the young guy and then turned around and leaned against the bumper.

Kenan kept watching and thought of all the shopping Mrs. Stevenson had done today and laughed to himself at how her spouse was dealing with it.

The patient man turned toward the trunk again and leaned deep into it. He emerged with a golf bag in his arms, which he gently leaned against the bumper.

"That's it!" Kenan shouted to no one.

He cranked the Audi and calmly drove the car into a parking space beside Mr. Stevenson and got out. His mouth was dry from his nervousness, but he kept moving. As he rounded the rear of his car and started in the direction of the grocery store Kenan said, "Nice set of clubs you've got there."

"Thanks," Walker said looking over to the stranger in the parking lot. "Do you play?"

"It's a passion with me. I love it."

"Same here."

Kenan was almost beside Mr. Stevenson now. He had to think fast to keep the conversation flowing. Instantly he saw the golf towel hanging from the bag, and in the glimmer of light cast from the lights in the parking lot he made out the words Fripp Island on the towel.

"I see you've played the Fripp Island course," Kenan said pointing to the towel hanging from the bag.

"Yes, many times. We live there," Walker said proudly.

"That's exactly where I'm headed myself." Kenan was relieved not to have to lie yet another time.

"Oh, yeah! Is this your first visit?" Walker asked.

"Yes, it is. Is it hard to get a tee time? I didn't plan far enough ahead to reserve one."

"Well tomorrow it won't be, because a lot of the resident golfers are going over to Dataw Island to play in a tournament. We won't be back until, say, four maybe five. But, now the next day might be pretty tight. How long are you down for?" Walker asked the clean-cut young man.

"I'm not sure yet. I have a little bit of business to take care of but, really a good bit of free time."

Walker held out his hand to the fellow golfer and said, "I'm Walker Stevenson."

"Kenan.... Gray," Kenan said with a heavy tongue, wondering if he should have used an alias.

"Look, we live on Marlin Drive. The number's in the book. I play with a regular foursome and occasionally someone has to renege. Call me the day after tomorrow if you like and maybe we could get together. With your height, bet you can drive a ball to the moon."

They both laughed and Kenan said thank you for the invitation. Mrs. Stevenson joined the two unexpectedly and Walker made the proper introductions then began unloading the bags of groceries from the buggy. It was a tight squeeze, but he managed to get everything, including the golf clubs, back into the trunk.

Mrs. Stevenson asked Kenan where he was staying. "My secretary made all of the arrangements and I'm afraid I've forgotten the name of the condominium complex." So much for telling the truth.

"Is it on the marsh or ocean front?" Mrs. Stevenson asked.

"You know, she didn't say," he replied.

"Well, don't worry. James gives explicit directions. You can't get lost on Fripp. You will fall in love with the island."

"Who is James?" Kenan asked with a worried look on his face.

"He's one of the security guards on the night shift. He'll greet you at the guard gate," Stella explained. "I'm sure there is a guest pass with your name on it and a key to a lovely condominium waiting for you right now."

A guard gate. He should have known.

The conversation was bringing his body temperature to a nervous boil and he could feel the beads of perspiration on his forehead. She explained that he was wise to stop by and pick up a few staples since the Island grocery store was closed this time of the night.

The hospitable couple told Kenan of several restaurants on the Island and filled him in on matters of interest that even the best of travel agents may have neglected to share.

Just before the beads of sweat began to roll down Kenan's cheek, Mr. Stevenson closed the trunk and extended his hand once more. "Nice to meet you. Now, give me a call day after tomorrow."

"Sure will. Thanks for your help." He continued on toward the Winn-Dixie wiping his forehead and breathing deeply. The automatic doors opened and he went inside. He was so perturbed with Nathan right now he could strangle him.

He accepted a buggy that a young woman in a red vest offered him and the sales flyer she was passing out as well.

"A guard gate," he said aloud as he bagged a couple of McIntosh apples.

He knew he had to speak with Nathan. He hurried through the isles collecting the bare essentials and checked out in the express lane. He asked the cashier about cell phone service, or rather lack of, and was informed that it was touch and go on these barrier islands. She told him there were two pay phones just outside the exit doors.

Nathan felt his head turn quizzically to the left and started in that direction. He hadn't seen one of those in years. After two botched attempts at making the call he finally got through after pressing the correct selection to use a credit card, instead of making a collect call, and now he waiting as the phone continued to ring.

Finally, his father's answering service was on the line. Kenan banged his fist on the side of the telephone. "Where is the crazy bastard," Kenan thought as his temper began to rage.

He told the operator his name and she instantly reported that she had a message for him. "Yes, here it is Mr. Gray. Mr. Kenan Gray. Your father wants you to call Barbara at home and she will explain the details."

"That's it?" Kenan shouted.

"No sir. There is a telephone number also."

"Oh great. Thanks a whole hell of a lot," he said sarcastically. "I'm sorry. It's not your fault. Just give me the number please and I'll hang up."

Barbara answered on the first ring. "Hello", she answered in her dignified voice.

"Boy, you were sitting on it, weren't you Barbie?"

"Oh, Kenan, thank goodness. I've been waiting for your call."

"Where's the big guy?" Kenan asked now smiling into the telephone. She always seemed to have a calming effect over him. He and Barbara had a special friendship. He had started calling her "Barbie" when he was just a little fellow and it had stuck.

"He had an urgent dinner meeting, but that's beside the point right now. Where are you?"

"Outside of a Winn-Dixie grocery store a few miles from Fripp Island."

"Good. Your father was hoping that you would call before you got to the Island. He was all in a tither about forgetting to tell you about a guard gate of some sort."

Kenan could tell by the tone of her voice that Nathan had not informed her of his intense concern about this situation.

"Well, he should be. What else did he say?"

"That you are registered under your name and you can pick up the keys, guest pass and all other information required to use the amenities at the guard gate."

"I'm using my own name?"

"Why, of course, Kenan. Don't be silly," Barbara laughed. "Now come on, let me give you the rest of this message so I can get to the theater. I'm certain I've missed all of Act I already."

"Oh, please forgive, my darling Barbie."

"Not to worry. It's part of the job," Barbara said.

"Of a faithful employee," Kenan added.

"Not necessarily. Haven't I told you? I loathe the man. But he pays well."

They both laughed and Barbara quickly asked him to phone his father once he was settled. Nathan should be home at least by eleven.

Kenan picked up his bag of groceries from the sidewalk and moved toward the Audi. He had so many questions on his mind. He opened the door and slid into the leather seat. The parking lot was almost empty. He popped the top on a lite beer and ate some dry Life cereal, then cranked the engine and drove casually into the darkness.

16

She rubbed his fingers, which she held tightly in her hand and looked out the window of the car as it moved past the familiar surroundings. "I do love this place. It is truly enchanting at night."

"Yes it is. I'll bet we see eleven deer between here and the house," Walker said.

"O.K., I'll guess sixteen. Loser makes dinner."

"Deal. Sounds like you're expecting a deer parade tonight."

"The moon's full. You can see more when the moon is full, that's all."

"So now we're giving up trade secrets." He squeezed her hand as he continued down Tarpon Road on Fripp Island.

Standing in the clearing on the right, near the bike trail were three elegant dear. A doe and two little ones. Stella assumed the responsibility of official deer counter.

"That's three and we're not even near the entrance to Deer Lake yet."

They drove slowly along the road, each spying deeply into the dense forest of pines. Walker lowered the windows and the fresh night air poured inside. They both inhaled deeply as if on cue. Four more deer were sighted along the edges of the tiered landscaping at the entrance drive to Deer Lake, a private community on Fripp.

"I was counting on a larger crowd than that," sighed Stella.

"Looks like you'll be cooking," Walker said as he turned left onto Remora Drive and then made a quick right onto prestigious Marlin Drive.

As the headlights lit up the darkness, twenty-eight slender legs stopped abruptly in the middle of the road. Stella and Walker marveled at their breath taking beauty. A large buck was leading the group that now starred boldly into the beam of the lights.

"I win," Stella shouted.

The sound of her voice through the open window sent the animals into a trot and in a flash the last fluffy white tail vanished into the thick of a vacant lot. Deer and other wildlife roam freely about the small private island named for Captain John Fripp, who received the island as a gift from the British in thanks for defending the Southern area from the Spanish. It was only in the past quarter to half century that Fripp Island ceased to be a state wildlife habitat. Only after it was purchased by a private land developer was the bridge connecting it to Hunting Island built. Before, it was accessible only by boat.

Their car neared the end of Marlin Drive and the big white moon shone on their favorite place: their home. Two black and white springer spaniels rounded the white lattice fence in the back and greeted their masters. They too, were enjoying this infinite stay on the coast. Nothing against Georgia red clay, but the sand and salty ocean couldn't be matched. The dogs were a father-son team. Sonny, the father, was thirteen and Ben, the son, was almost four. Their markings were incredibly identical, but they each possessed very individual personalities, due to the age difference no doubt.

The fifth and sixth members of the family followed close at the Stevenson's heels as they ascended the wide Colonial staircase up to the front porch of their home. Once inside, Stella turned on several lamps in the living room and sunroom. She despised overhead lights. Walker began opening the four sets of French doors that led onto the side porches. It was as though they had rehearsed this opening of the house routine before. Each knew their duty.

Without speaking they began to bring in load after load from the car below. Finally, Walker said, "Did we ever consider an elevator when we were building this house?"

"Nope. Not a bad idea though, since Kate and Ely aren't around as much to help with the unloading."

"Why don't you call them while I cook dinner? I think you're back to normal now. The trip really helped things along, don't you think?"

Stella knew she shouldn't say no. Because in essence it really had, although she had thought about the ordeal a lot on the trip home. There were so many unanswered questions roaming in her mind. But, she had to put it to rest like she had pledged to do in the courtroom earlier today. Stella answered Walker by suggesting they postpone the telephone calls until after dinner. She was still preoccupied with the thought of it all. She used a warm tub as an excuse and kissed her husband on the forehead.

She grabbed a worn out Louis Vuitton duffle bag and started for their master suite. She unpacked a few items while the bath water filled the luxurious tub. Relaxing music filtered into the bedroom from the living room where Walker had turned on the sound system. When Stella heard the words from one of their favorite songs, she knew what Walker was thinking. She laughed to herself at his romantic subtleness. Stella reached for a crystal dish that held pastel colored bath oil beads from a shelf near the tub. Her dear sweet Edwina had given them to her for her last birthday. She dropped three in the hot water that filled the bath and watched as they each turned a darker shade of their own hue.

Stella replaced the dish to its position and tossed some dirty clothes into a large wicker hamper in the closet beside the tub. It was already overflowing, but she certainly did not intend to do laundry tonight. She took her foot and packed down the week-old dirty duds to make room for more. Edwina would have a fit if she could see Stella now. She had always been so meticulous about their laundry. When it came to starching a shirt or getting the exact same crease in a pair of cotton twill khakis, she was an expert every time.

Stella undressed and sank down into the slick water. Her thick hair was balled up on top of her head and held into place with a large tortoise shell clip. She closed her eyes and saw Edwina's face. Their last meeting had been an emotional one for each of them. After almost twenty-five years of togetherness twice a week plus weekend babysitting, the void would not easily go unnoticed.

Edwina was her strong, independent self, but the hug she and Stella shared before saying goodbye, lasted much too long to disguise her feelings. Stella remembered the very first day that she met Edwina.

It was near the beginning of summer and she had come to the house in Clarkesville to discuss a possible work arrangement. She waltzed into the house, arms folded and tight lipped. She noticed right away the areas of the house that needed more attention than others and handed Stella a typed list of cleaning supplies she preferred to use. She told the lady of the house all in one breath that Wednesdays and Fridays were the only days she had available and that Stella needed to move her house plant to the other side of the porch because it was getting too much direct sunlight.

That very afternoon Stella moved the plant just as Edwina instructed and had been following her orders ever since, until now. When Walker announced to Edwina one day that Stella was expecting their first child, she threatened to quit, insisting that she had no patience for such. After Stella had an emergency Cesarean Section, she agreed to stay and help with the house, not the baby, until the new mother was back on her feet.

She stood fast to her conviction of not caring for babies until one day when the switch on the electric breast pump malfunctioned and the handy little tool turned into a bosom-eating monster. Kate woke from her nap simultaneously and began wailing in the bassinet beside Stella, who could hardly breathe from the pain, much less think. Edwina walked in the room and surveyed the situation. After denying her better judgment of leaving the house completely, she walked over to the tiny child and lifted her up into her strong dark arms. The crying of the child ceased in moments, but the tears begin to flow from the mother's frightened blue eyes now as the pain increased.

"The batteries," Edwina shouted. "Take out the batteries."

The anxiety of motherhood had made Stella loose most of her common sense. She began to cry uncontrollably as Edwina watched with disgusted eyes. She had patted the baby back to sleep and held her close. Her heart lightened and she sat beside Stella and put one arm around the post-partum wreck of a new mother.

"I'll stay a few more weeks. It's gonna be O.K.," she said.

Stella wept out the words, "Thank you," and reached both arms around the strong woman beside her and held on tight.

Stella blinked back the tears that stung at the corners of her eyes now as she remembered that day. She missed her dear devoted friend, and what hurt more was knowing that Edwina missed her too. She wondered how Edwina was spending her Wednesdays and Fridays now. They hadn't had a chance to talk in several weeks. The last correspondence between them was a sweet letter from Edwina. She had taped the key to their old Clarkesville house to the bottom of the letter apologizing for having not given it back sooner. The key was worn and its smooth edges revealed its frequent use.

The thought of the letter gave Stella an idea. She would have Edwina a key made to this house and send it to her to serve as an open invitation to visit any time, and for any length of time. With that gesture in mind, Stella's mind felt free from any pressing problem for the moment and she sunk even deeper into the tub as the steam continued to leak into the air.

She heard a window being opened in the bedroom and knew Walker was near. He was not necessarily a hot natured person, but he craved fresh air, especially the fresh sea breeze. Moments later he appeared at the bathroom door holding a brandy sniffer partially filled with cognac.

"I warmed this for you," he said, and walked to the tub to give it to her.

"Want to join me? I noticed you played one of our favorite songs."

"Yes, I did. And I would love to join you," he said, kissing her lips, "but, the French onion soup may scorch if I do."

"Yum! You're making French onion soup? Is it almost ready?"

"Yes.

Stella stood up and Walker gazed at his wife's beautiful body before he handed her a towel.

"No harm in peeking," he insisted as he turned to leave. "Dinner will be served on the side porch, ocean view."

"I'll be right out."

Stella grabbed her age old, worn out jeans hanging on a pineapple shaped hook on the inside of the closet door. She opened a bureau drawer in the bedroom and selected a blue oxford shirt with paint stains along the sleeve—it had been Walker's—buttoned a few buttons and tied the rest of the shirt tail in a knot at her waist.

With bare feet and sniffer in hand, she graced the porch with her presence. Walker was bringing the soup out as she sat down at the wrought iron table in one corner of the porch. The aroma was sensational.

"I see you've dressed for dinner my dear," Walker teased.

"Yes, I'm going for the antique look tonight."

"I thought you decided to part with those jeans when we were packing up for the big move."

"Well, I did. But then I changed my mind. I have so many memories associated with these jeans. This is from Ely's first crab cage. Remember?" she asked pointing to a raveled rip near her knee. "And this one is from the oyster roast at the Smith's when I tripped over the drift wood in the dark. Now this one..."

"I get the picture, Honey, but if the pockets are as worn as the trousers are, don't put anything of value into them," he laughed.

"I'll remember that dear. Thank you."

They sipped the cognac and lapped up the rich soup and talked of nothing in particular. A large lamp of crystal and sea-shells was the only light; from the living room it cast a faint light in their direction. The brilliance of the moonlight shining through the screen was an awesome sight and, with the lamp, enough to dine by.

They retreated to the comfort of the wicker rocking chairs over by the rail, propped their feet side by side and continued their nothingness conversation. They made the major decision to plant pansies, instead of those little cabbage type plants, in the flower boxes on the back deck. They decided that they would accept the kind invitation of the Bartletts to attend the Georgia Bulldawgs football game even though Stella dreaded sitting in the Stadium in Athens because it swayed in the wind and made her nervous. They decided that Kate would need a new car by June graduation and that the traditional choo-choo train, which encircled the base of the family Christmas tree, needed a tune up before the holidays. And they decided to make love before they worried with the dinner dishes.

"Well, that will do it for me," Walker smiled.

He reached up and removed the tortoise clip from her hair and brushed the strands back from her face. He stood up and lifted her in his arms all in the same motion. They kissed as he walked toward the screen door leading to the open deck over-looking the beach. She held on to him tightly and relished the romantic moment.

Her eyes glistened in approving surprise as he laid her down in the rope hammock and slipped his shirt over his head.

The knot at her waist in the old shirt slipped loose easily and their bare skin touching heightened their urgency. The moonlight flooded the deck and the crashing waves and sweet sea breeze made the moment even more enchanting. Their kisses were more urgent and mixed with laughter at the thought of the neighbors catching them. Walker felt her breast and more. Their gaze never left one other and an exciting rhythm began as their toned bodies pressed closer and closer. Walker rolled to one side and easily lifted Stella on top of him with his muscular arms. They shared a hushed surprise with their eyes that this maneuver had not landed them on the deck below. As the clouds moved with the gentle breeze the moonlight found them again and in that moment they were one. Their quiet intimacy was a unity of a special kind and reassured her that they were invincible together.

When their lovemaking had ended they lay nestled in the hammock until the telephone rang. "At least they waited until we were through to call," Walker laughed as he stood up to answer the phone in the living room. Stella threw a garment from the deck at his naked butt and followed carrying a bundle of clothing.

"Well, it's not as bad as the time Ely picked the lock with a hair pin because he thought we were locked in our bedroom and couldn't get out. Remember that?" she said.

"Yes, he was only five years old."

And a very quiet five-year-old that night. We didn't hear a thing until he shouted, 'You're free. I've rescued you.'"

Walker was still laughing when he said, "Hello."

"Hey, Dad!"

"Ely, we were just talking about you." Walker winked at Stella. "How's it going?"

"Pretty good. Basketball is great. The studies are a drag, but the chicks and parties make up for that. How's Mom?"

"She's terrific. I'm looking at her right now and she's never looked better," Walker answered smiling at Stella as she zipped her pants. "Want to say hi?"

Stella snatched the telephone anxiously away from Walker and beamed with happiness at the sound of their only son's voice. The only thing that had keep her from crying her eyes out daily, after taking Ely to Clemson to embark on his college career in August, was the actual menial tasks involved in the relocating process. She was consumed by the duties of cleaning out, packing and planning the very day of the move. But, she was grateful to have a project to dive into since she had promised herself there would not be a replay of emotional disorder that occurred when Kate had started classes at the University of North Carolina at Chapel Hill.

Stella and Kate had literally wept in one another's arms on the lawn in front of her dormitory until Walker finally intervened and announced that they had to leave now or get a dorm room themselves. Ely had made some subtle remarks about how Stella needed to control herself when they said their "temporary" goodbyes once he was settled into his room in the athletic dorm.

Both of the men in her life had commended Stella on her emotional behavior that day. The parents of the leading basketball scorer in Northeast Georgia drove away from Clemson University leaving their six foot, four inch, scholarship-bearing son on the brick steps of his new dwelling, free from any embarrassing farewells.

Stella talked with Ely excitedly about everything except Phillip's murder. They discussed Thanksgiving plans briefly and Stella said goodbye and handed the telephone to Walker.

"Why didn't you tell him?" Walker whispered, covering the receiver.

"I can't. Will you?"

Walker lifted the receiver to his ear and after a few sentences, began with dreaded words, "I'm afraid I have some bad news."

After explaining the whole story, he assured Ely that his mother was fine and everything was business as usual with them. Walker, the master of tactful conversation, managed to end the conversation on a pleasant note by asking Ely what he wanted for his birthday.

"A Ferrari will be fine; any color will do."

"Aren't those Clemson alumni supposed to be buying you things like that?"

They laughed a little more and said goodbye. By now Stella was sitting cowardly in the living room in her favorite chase holding a pillow. Walker entered the room and said simply, "Wimp." He sat down on the end of the striped chase and rubbed her feet, then handed Stella the portable telephone and said, "Ring up Kate and I'll tell her too."

Stella pressed some numbers on the phone he handed to her and said, "I owe you."

"I know it. But, this one will cost you a lot."

"Fine. Anything," she said definitely handing the telephone back to him. "Just name it!"

"Another swing in the hammock."

17

She picked up the money from the dresser and counted it quickly. Three-fifty; not bad, he had even thrown in a tip. She folded the bills neatly and slipped them into the side pocket of her tote bag that contained a variety of "office supplies," which enabled her to entertain a variety of clients. She lifted the bottle of champagne from the iced container and walked into the spacious bath. He was still in the hot tub with his eyes closed and didn't budge when she approached and filled his glass to the brim once again.

She turned to leave, she detested overtime even at double rates. It interfered with her set schedule. A gruff voice said, "Leaving so soon?"

"Time's up. Ask for me again sometime."

She was out of sight with no further ado. This part of the game used to be the loneliest. When the heavy hotel room door closed with a bang, the realization that he was still very much alone was ever present. It was easier now since there was no guilt. Priscilla's death had ended the guilt of committing adultery. It was funny how his sinful acts had ceased immediately after her death. But, with the help of a good, expensive shrink, he was back at it.

The emotion that plagued him now was fear. He had one full hour to endure before his dinner meeting with Paulos. What could be so urgent that he insisted on changing the hour of their meeting? They had meet at the same time, in the same restaurant, at the same corner table for close to twenty years. Something was up and Nathan felt confident he knew exactly what it was. The problem started with a "P" and ended with a "P." Phillip. Phillip Dubose. How had Marguerite ever convinced him that letting the boy work on board the shrimp boat was a good idea? Probably with her body, he decided.

But, then he saw the face of the insecure, overweight teenager. Marguerite's only child and she had spoiled him beyond reason. Nathan, too, was void of siblings and knew that a mother's love concentrated on one single child could produce one totally self-centered adult. He was living proof. Kenan had managed to escape that curse with Priscilla's sensible style as a mother. But, Phillip, his bastard son, needed guidance of some kind to overcome the undesirable fate. Nathan knew that although the boy looked nothing like him, their emotional and social characteristics ran along the same pitiful path. But the hell of it was Nathan could never tell his bastard son that he had finally learned the error of his own unkind ways. No heart to heart, father-son conversation could even take place because Phillip had thought his father to be dead.

Marguerite had molded the ugly truth into a blissful love story with a tragic ending, leaving a young mother to raise her fatherless infant alone. Alone, but owning mega-shares of Gray, Inc. stock thanks to her successful blackmail attempts.

She began by phoning Nathan's home in Virginia, which she had never seen, and announced to Priscilla that she too, had given birth to a son. A son whose father was Nathan Gray. Priscilla had remained calm and asked detailed questions that produced answers that were horribly painful for a wife to hear. Marguerite was surprised by the lack of emotion in the woman's voice.

Priscilla had insisted that Nathan gain control over the situation immediately before his parents found out about the matter, thus the first telephone call Marguerite made to Virginia resulted in profits for her of ten thousand dollars.

That was when Phillip was barely a month old. The blackmail continued at different intervals for many years. The stakes grew higher and higher and were always granted on demand. Marguerite's quarterly dividend check alone, from Gray, Inc. was more than enough to pay her extravagant living expenses and lavish shopping habits for the entire year.

Even after both of Nathan's parents had passed away he continued to endure the blackmail from Marguerite. The fear of public embarrassment and humiliation was ever present along with a possible palimony suit that could cost more than her demands. Strangely enough, there had been no further demands since Priscilla's death. However, correspondence to the contrary had occurred. Nathan received a sympathy card from Marguerite with a written promise enclosed stating she would make no more financial demands on him. She asked that he consider meeting his son, who believed his real father had been killed in an airplane crash before his birth. She also had enclosed a photo of her and Nathan taken years ago at the height of their affair in Savannah, Georgia, when Nathan had been sent there to expand the business farther South.

they always did, but Guido was quiet tonight. That was most unusual for the man whom Nathan had joked with for years.

There was no grin on his lips now. Nathan grew nervous and ordered a drink for lack of anything else to say. The burgundy velvet chair that had always been so comfortable now felt like cold, hard steel beneath his tense body.

Maybe it was his imagination, now that he seemed to be in a paranoid state, but even the waiters who were setting up the tables for the night were doing everything possible not to make eye contact with him. There were only two other customers in the place. Two older women who spoke Italian loud and fast.

Guido sent the bartender back with Nathan's drink. He took a long, hard pull on the rim of the beveled tumbler. The vodka was cold and the lime juice left a stinging sensation in his throat. He twirled the tumbler round and round on the glass table top as he studied the candle wax dripping on the candle holder in front of him. The flame flickered very little, unlike Nathan's jumpy stomach. True, this was a situation not to be taken lightly, but it seemed to Nathan that as far as the police were concerned it was an open and shut case. The coroner's report showed cause of death as drowning.

Nathan's mind was in a whirlwind that seemed to change course with every breath. He really needed to lay off the booze until this matter was settled for good. He was having trouble remembering who knew what, and how much, if any. Thankfully neither Kenan nor Marguerite knew anything about his dealings with Paulos or the illegal aspects of their business relationship, so any conversations with the two of them could hopefully be on the up and up. It was getting too hard to lie these days. The truth was effortless and Nathan was tiring quickly, so it appealed to him for the first time in a while.

There were so many unanswered questions. How had Phillip fallen overboard? Had he? What was possibly in the capsule that made it so urgent to find? And why would Phillip have it? Why was the finger pointing at Nathan to handle this mess? Phillip could not have possibly caused this much trouble. He hardly had any sense at all. How could one small object destroy a network that had flourished almost three decades?

Nathan looked up and saw the one person he supposed it would destroy the most, walking toward him in long strides. His bodyguard and "gofer," Calvin, was close at his heels. Anthony began taking off his overcoat as he approached the table and as it dropped behind him, Calvin caught it in one swift motion before it hit the floor. Guido came hustling out of the kitchen wiping his hands on the white apron tied around his waist and greeted Anthony as if he were the godfather himself.

Nathan stood up and extended his hand to Anthony. The men shook hands and sat down as Guido rattled on about the specialties he had prepared for "Mr. Anthony." He turned toward the bar, snapped his fingers and two waiters hurried over with a bottle of red wine and two wine glasses. Guido went into detail about the bouquet, vintage and flavor of the wine but Nathan didn't hear him. He was baffled by the sickening display of attention Anthony was getting tonight. It heightened his sense of fear, which was already overwhelming. It seemed as though Nathan was indeed invisible as everyone kissed up to the overweight, balding, arrogant son-of-bitch who sat across from him. The shit was really getting deep in here and Nathan felt like everyone, including himself, was sitting on eggshells just waiting for the big guy to pop with anger.

Finally, Guido, the waiters and "King Kong" Calvin scurried away and the two men were left alone. Anthony swirled the wine around in his glass as he looked straight at Nathan and said, "Duncan was picked up yesterday on suspicion of murder."

Nathan's mouth dropped open and he felt sick all over, but he appeared amazingly calm on the outside. His black eyes still held the gaze of Paulos. He could not appear weak or he would surely be dead meat. He had seen Anthony Paulos strip men of their dignity before and Nathan was not going to be just another one of his victims. He cleared his throat, threw back a slug of wine and just as he was about to ask what evidence they had against Duncan, he felt cold icy liquid splash about his face and heard Anthony's voice shout, "Wake up you bastard! What are you going to do about this?"

Nathan stood up in a show of rage, knocking his chair over behind him, but saying nothing. Calvin was on the scene instantly and Anthony gave him the nod that everything was under control. He threw a starched white napkin at Nathan and said, "Sit back down, Gray."

Nathan asked the question that had been drowned out by Anthony's ice water stunt and was informed that a syringe had been found in the search on board *The Rennie* with traces of cocaine in it as well as Duncan's fingerprints.

"That's not evidence of murder, Anthony. They'll have to release him in forty-eight hours if nothing else turns up. There were no traces of drugs in Phillip's body. Hell, Duncan uses all the time. We know his habits. I have always wondered what percent of our profits go up his nose."

"I know all that, you dumb shit. They're going for something bigger than murder here. They want our necks. Mine, yours and many others. They're on to us, but they have no proof. We've stopped all operations, of course, and that's costing about a million a day. People on both ends are pissed and I'm holding you personally responsible."

"Why am I responsible?" Nathan screamed.

"Because you are the one who brought the weak link into the operation."

"Well, I have a man down there now working to find the capsule for you. What is in the damned thing anyway?" Nathan asked.

"I know you've got a man down there now, and I know it's your son. Not your dead bastard son, but your legitimate son. So, if he finds the capsule before my men do he can read all about the guts of his Daddy's business. He will see your name at the top of the list of all of the drug dealers from Miami to Maine."

Nathan gulped hard and tried to breath.

Paulos continued on, "Duncan noticed Phillip snooping around his office on the dock several times. He told Duncan he was just trying to learn more about the business. Then his dead body turns up and Duncan takes inventory of his office and discovers a flash drive missing that had delivery schedules, network bosses' information – everything you ever wanted to know about our set up in Beaufort.

Nathan slammed his fist on the table. "Did Duncan have Phillip killed? What about the other guys on the boat; have they been questioned?"

"You are such an idiot. Of course we didn't kill him. Why would we draw attention to ourselves? When we take out someone it's in pieces, not little fish bites. Definitely not our style. More wine Guido," Paulos said as he snapped his fingers.

"Well, if Kenan doesn't find it tomorrow, I'll go down there myself. He doesn't know anything about our business and I want to keep it that way. He doesn't even know you exist."

"Oh, really? Well, why did he call me a few days ago?"

"What?"

"I don't want to get into those details now. The fact is, you sent him down there. He's involved whether you like it or not."

Nathan saw Priscilla's face and thought how he had just decided earlier that day to straighten up his life and start anew. The possibility of that seemed bleak. And it was all because of the puffy little Italian in front of him. Nathan was outraged that Paulos had someone tailing Kenan and he also felt violated because the lard ass knew Phillip had been his son.

"How did you know about Phillip?" Nathan spat the words across the table.

"What? That he was your bastard son?"

Nathan nodded.

"You really don't get it do you? This is no Mickey Mouse Club you're in. I know everything about you and always have. I know you screwed a brunette twice earlier today and you dump every morning at 7:20 a.m. I also know you're nothing more than a spoiled little loser masquerading in a small version of a Herman Munster costume. I should have done away with you when you lost it after Miss Priscilla died and you went nuts. What was the deal anyway? She hadn't given you any in years."

Nathan stood to leave, utterly astounded with the knowledge that he had no private life at all, but Anthony motioned for Calvin and he sat back down for what he assumed to be round two of the meeting. "Look, Anthony, I don't have to listen to all of this. You'll have the capsule or..."

"Or I'll have your son's little blonde head."

"Leave him out of this. I swear to you he knows nothing."

"Well you better tell him this so he'll know the importance of what he's looking for. I am well aware that the seaman's capsule may be at the bottom of the deep blue sea, but it's most unlikely since the body was so bloated it would have been impossible for the seaman's capsule to have slipped over his head. And since we would have already been arrested by now if the police had the flash drive in their possession, that really only leaves one place it might be. With the pretty little lady who found the body."

Nathan was silent. He had nothing left to say and the silence was unbearable. Anthony nodded his head and Guido began to serve dinner. Nathan was incredulous that Anthony expected them to dine after that vicious exchange of words. He shook his head at Guido as he began to serve the pasta onto his plate.

"I've lost my appetite," he said.

Once again Nathan rose to leave and this time Calvin made no effort to stop him.

"I'll call you tomorrow, Anthony," Nathan said in his invincible tongue.

He had been totally humiliated by this man and although he feared for his life, he would not stoop to breaking bread with him. Perhaps Nathan felt he was recouping a small portion of his pride by this insulting act toward Anthony, or maybe it was his childish ways interfering with business. Again.

Regardless of his primary motivation, refusing to have dinner with Anthony Paulos was a bad move. Although Nathan would not realize just how bad until much later.

18

It was high tide and the waves were crashing onto the huge rocks below Kenan. The spray exploded to such heights that, at times, mist reached him where he stood on the balcony and he could taste the salt on his lips. The temperature was mild for this time of year even with the constant rush of the wind off the ocean.

He thought of joining the small group of people gathered at a cabana bar just beyond the kidney-shaped pool, but he had to settle for the six pack he was chilling in the freezer and wait for Nathan to return his call.

Vera, the housekeeper on Ampt Hill, said his father had been waiting for his call, but had just stepped into a hot shower she had suggested to help him relax. "He's very keyed up tonight, Kenan. I told him to stop pacing on my waxed hardwoods or he was going to take the shine right off."

"You've got to keep him in line, Vera," Kenan laughed. "What time did he get home from dinner?"

"He came home a few hours ago, but he hadn't had any dinner. He asked me to make him some buttermilk biscuits like I used to fix when he was a little boy. He ate two of them stacked full of bacon, so I know he was hungry. When are you coming home to see your Vera? It gets lonely around here with just me and your Daddy. I do see Richard every day, but he goes home at night, you know. And your Daddy's not too fond of him, so he doesn't come up to the house too much anyway. I usually go over to the garage to see him. We have a coffee break together and watch 'The Price Is Right' every morning on that T.V. your Momma had put out there for him. He lost the remote control though."

"Well, tell Richard to charge another one and send me the bill. We can't have you two out in the garage without a remote control."

"That's the truth. Now when are you coming home?"

"It won't be long, Vera. We've got a little business to take care of and then maybe I can squeeze a visit in before Thanksgiving. How does that sound?" Kenan asked.

"Like too long."

"You never were a patient person, Vera. Here's my telephone number. My cell phone isn't working well right now. Give this number to Dad when he gets out of the shower please."

"Wait a minute while I get a pen," she said.

Kenan could hear her hard-soled shoes echoing throughout the massive old house as she walked along the wooden floors.

When she returned to the telephone Kenan asked, "Do you ever wear those running shoes I gave you last Christmas? They would be so much more comfortable than those ones you've worn for decades."

"They make my feet look like two big cement blocks. They're still in the box. Now, what's your number? And hush about my shoes."

Kenan gave Vera the number and told the old woman that he missed her, then hung up the telephone. He took one last look of the night sky before he stepped back inside; the moon was big and full, and its beams danced across the water in a way that made him want to buy this corner unit and move here, maybe let this ocean breeze guide the rest of his life. He sighed and turned back inside the condominium to transfer the beer from the freezer to the refrigerator before they began to pop. Nathan had done well with the reservations. Kenan actually thought he would like to return to Fripp soon, when he wasn't on "business." He liked what he saw even in the nighttime hours.

Just on the other side of an octagonal gazebo, Kenan could see the lights of what appeared to be a dining room. The tables near the window were occupied and, judging from the many shadows that danced along the bordering wall, Kenan felt like they must still be serving dinner. A brochure about the island was on the kitchen counter and he picked it up and thumbed through it. He determined that the dining room across the way must be The Beach Club Restaurant and that reservations were required. He sat down at the bar between the kitchen and living room and picked up the telephone. Before he began dialing the telephone number of The Beach Club listed in the brochure, he heard a distance voice saying, "Hello! Hello?"

"Dad?" Kenan said into the receiver. "Is that you? What timing. I had just picked up the telephone to make dinner reservations."

"What? For tonight? Forget it. Lock your door and stay inside," Nathan shouted into the telephone. He had practiced for hours what he would say to Kenan, but those rehearsed words were not spoken. When hearing his son's voice the reality that Kenan could be physically harmed, or even worse, by Paulos' thugs, Nathan panicked.

"What's wrong with you, Dad?"

"Things are tightening up around here, Kenan, and I wish I had never sent you down there," Nathan said.

"Oh, this is a great place. Everything's fine. Fripp Island's a paradise with a lot of class. This condo is terrific. You did a great job with the lodging accommodations. I'm not even going to pick a bone with you about the unexpected guard gate situation. And I've got some great news," Kenan said.

Nathan could tell by the nonchalant air of his speech that Kenan was miles away from any realization of the seriousness of his involvement. He tried to calm himself and asked, "What news?"

"I've met the Stevensons and Mr. Stevenson has invited me to play golf the day after tomorrow."

"Hold it Kenan. You'll be long gone by then. I want you out of there tomorrow. This is not a negotiable request. Do you understand?"

"Not really. I wasn't aware I had less than twenty-four hours to locate the infamous seaman's capsule, Dad. Thanks for all the notice."

Anger whelmed up inside of Nathan once again at the thought of one of Paulos' big oafs laying a hand on Kenan. He breathed deeply like Dr. Minor suggested he do when he felt like he was losing control.

"You're right Kenan. This is not fair to you." Nathan paused and thought of all the danger he had exposed Kenan to for the sake of his own selfish neck. Kenan needed to be informed about the entire situation. Suddenly the thought of confessing the whole ugly story to his son felt like the right thing to do, but Nathan knew it should not be over the telephone. Dr. Minor had said confession was the only way to truly start over, "Honesty will heal your aching mind," Nathan had heard the phrase over and over again. He would tell Kenan, but not now. He would tell him the whole story about Phillip and then admit his involvement in illegal business.

"Dad, are you still there? What are you thinking?"

"I'm thinking I've made a lot of mistakes concerning this matter and I think we need to let me handle the rest of the work. I may be able to handle it all from this end."

"What? I'm already down here ready to go. I'm sorry that it is going to take me a little more time to accomplish our goal, but I can do this," Kenan said feeling as though he didn't measure up to his father's standards like he had felt so many times before.

"No, it's not the time element as much as my concern for your safety."

Well, this was something new. Nathan had never mentioned concern for Kenan's safety in his life. Kenan wasn't sure how to respond to that comment and Nathan continued speaking.

"Tomorrow, get up early and start a vacation. You've earned it. Go someplace and relax; meet some friends, and call me in a couple or three days. Forget about the seaman's capsule and this situation. How does that sound?"

"Like you're not telling me the whole story again. You just told me things were getting tight, now you want me to leave."

"Kenan they are getting tight," my blood is barely circulating Nathan thought. "And that's why I want you out. I can handle this better if I'm not worried about you. I have a lot to tell you when you get back from your vacation.

"And I can't wait to hear it."

"Good. Why don't you come to Richmond after the weekend? Vera would love to see you."

"O.K., I'd like to see Richard, too."

"Yeah, well he's still here," Nathan said as the thought of the yard man and Kenan's close relationship still made him feel jealous.

"Take care, Dad," Kenan said in a worried tone.

"Enjoy your vacation. Spend some of your old man's money. I'll see you next week."

"I have my own, thank you," Kenan said feeling somewhat insulted, but trying to overlook the remark.

"Goodbye. And, Kenan?" Nathan said quickly before his son could hang up the telephone.

"Yes?" Kenan answered.

Nathan hesitated and then said, "I love you." And the line was dead.

19

The sound of the sprinklers on the golf course interrupted Stella's dream of a winding mountain road strewn with yellow and red leaves. She awoke somewhat startled, not because of the continual ticking of the sprinklers, but because of the sudden appearance of a big black bear in her dream. The large bear was standing on its hind legs and held a sign that read, "Feed Mildred More Peanuts!"

Stella rolled over onto her side and lifted her head from the pillow as she smiled. Mildred was the bear at Grandfather Mountain in North Carolina. They had visited there as a family at least every other year in the fall, since the children were old enough to walk. Kate and Ely always pleaded for just one more bag of peanuts to feed Mildred and her cubs. And, of course Walker always bought more until he swore he was penniless.

She'd take a black bear in her dream, no more nightmares. Stella felt good; this was going to be a great day. The sun peeked over the jetty in the distance and even though that was where she had found Phillip's body, she was not thinking of that now and she simply watched the big orange ball swell in the clear sky. It cast a ray of light on the empty pillow beside her.

She was not surprised that Walker was not there. She could smell the brewed coffee as she slipped her feet into the large, white bunny rabbit slippers on the floor and reached for her robe at the foot of the bed. She followed the aroma through the living and dining rooms and inhaled deeply as she pushed open the kitchen door.

A bright red coffee mug sat on the counter waiting for her to fill it full of black coffee. The words, "It's Your Lucky Day," were printed across the front of the mug. She laughed to herself at Walker's choice of mugs for her this particular morning. She watched as the pair of dice in the bottom of the mug disappeared into a sea of coffee. Walker had purchased the novelty item in Las Vegas last year. He loved to buy coffee mugs, but he did not drink coffee.

He had drunk two cups of coffee in his life and admitted that he did not like either one. He did, however, like for Stella to drink it. "You are a much more pleasant person in the morning after you have had your morning coffee," Walker had confessed many years ago. And so began their morning ritual.

Walker made the coffee and selected a special mug for Stella and then he left for his morning run. By the time he returned Stella had usually finished half of the pot and was ready to converse. At a rapid pace.

She picked up the stack of mail from the counter and a quarterly devotion book she subscribed to, and went to the breakfast booth to sit down. Stella sipped the delicious coffee and read the devotion for the day. Each one consisted of no more than three or four paragraphs, but were usually very inspirational.

A picture of a small stone church with stained glass windows was featured on the cover of the current issue. Something about it reminded Stella of her own church in Clarkesville, St. Matthias Episcopal. She would miss the parishioners there more than they could possibly realize. Reverend Davis and his vivacious wife, Linda, had created an atmosphere that captured every heart and soul and for them, Stella was most grateful. She thought of her Sunday School class and how much she would miss the close friendships that had evolved over the years. She had often referred to the forty-five-minute weekly class as her "Bob Newhart Session." It was more of a spiritual therapy class than a teaching class where one instructor presented the lesson. Most of the time, the topic for the day was announced and then the floor was open for discussion. It was always moving and emotional, and someone always cried. Often it was Stella. But most of the time they were good tears.

She walked to the counter and poured herself another cup of coffee. The caffeine was working on her brain and she began a list of things to do beginning with, "Mail Ely's packages" and "Have key made for Edwina." With mug in hand, she went back to the master suite and made the bed, brushed her teeth and splashed some water on her face. She slid into the ragged old jeans from last night, which just always, seemed to be handy, and rummaged through the bureau for an old sweatshirt. Then with walking shoes, earbuds and cell phone in hand, she walked back to the kitchen.

There she found Walker drinking a large glass of water, obviously replenishing the fluids that had left his body and were now dripping from his clothes onto the kitchen floor. But she said nothing, it was his kitchen.

"Good morning my little angel from heaven," Stella said as if she were speaking to a newborn baby. She squeezed his cheek and then his fanny.

"And, hello to you. I see that my choice of coffee mugs has been a positive inspiration once again."

"I'm not sure whether it was the coffee mug, or that last swing in the hammock. It was paralyzing, my dear lover."

"And it can happen again," he said looking at the calendar on the refrigerator. "The moon should be perfect again tonight according to this calendar."

"Sounds exciting to me."

"Why don't we begin with dinner at The Beach Club and work our way back home?" Walker suggested.

"That sounds like a winner. I'll make reservations later today. What time are you leaving for Dataw?"

"In about an hour or so. If you're leaving now for your walk, you should be back before I go."

"That's true, but I thought I might stop by the Marina and have another key made for the front door to send to Edwina. So I may be longer than usual," she said as she picked up the key ring from the counter and maneuvered the door key off and slipped it into her pocket.

"That's a nice gesture. I sure do miss her and her sweet iced tea."

"O.K., I'll try again, but I make no promises. I just can't make it taste the way she does," Stella said in a frustrated voice.

"I'm just kidding," Walker said kissing Stella on the forehead. "I have never expected great miracles from you where the kitchen is concerned. I'm certainly not going to begin now. You more than make up for that shortcoming in other areas, if you know what I mean?"

The corners of Stella's mouth turned up and she hugged her Walker, sweat and all. "I hope you make a hole in one and win the entire tournament."

"I hope you get your wish."

They walked together to boardwalk leading from the porch to the beach. In the distance the shrimp boats were trawling. Overhead the gulls were gliding and the gentle Fripp Island breeze was right on cue.

He kissed her lips gently and placed the small round ends of the cord that rested around her neck, up into her ears.

"Thank you," she said as she started down the boardwalk. "Don't be late for our date," she added, shaking a finger in Walker's direction.

"I would never keep you waiting. Could you wear your new red dress again?" he shouted as the distance between them grew. Stella gave an exaggerated nod of the head and stepped onto the sand.

20

Kenan awoke to the sound of waves crashing. Between each wave that curled down onto the sandy beach, he heard the fizzling and popping of the mounds of salty foam that had been brought ashore by the last retreating wave. The shear drapes were filled with the morning breeze and even though the wind brought in the autumn chill, Kenan still had one foot out of the covers. He had always slept that way. He pulled the icy foot back into the toasty linens and sat up. The sun shone a brilliant yellow from just over the horizon and there was no mistaking this was going to be a beautiful day.

Kenan got out of the bed, pulled on his boxer shorts and walked on to the small balcony off the bedroom. He estimated the temperature to be in the low sixties right now, and the time was six fifty-two, according to his wristwatch. What a day for golf.

The beach, of course, was not crowded at this hour, but there were several joggers out and about. Kenan looked over the balcony at the terrace below. He had left the French doors open overnight. Nathan would not be happy with him for failing to heed his advice. Perhaps he could make it up to him by starting the vacation he had suggested right now, here on Fripp. He saw no reason to waste this magnificent day traveling, and after all, Nathan had not specified where he should take this "vacation." There was one small problem, though. He had no golf clubs.

Kenan walked back inside and descended the spiral staircase from the lofted bedroom. The kitchen was small, but complete, so he made some coffee and sat down in the living room. An island guide was on the coffee table and he thumbed through it and stopped at a quarter page display advertisement for the pro shop here on Fripp. He dialed them up on the landline since cell service was, for sure, hit or miss and asked for information on golf club rentals and tee times.

After a shower and shave, he dressed in khakis, a polo, and cotton sweater and left the condo in search of a newspaper. The newspaper stands were easily found near the entrance to the family, Olympic size swimming pool that was located on the other side of The Beach Club Restaurant and Clubhouse. There were several to select from, but Kenan decided on The Beaufort Gazette and U.S.A. Today. He walked into the pool area and was very impressed with the arrangement. Surrounding the lounging area of the pool were five brightly colored buildings with cupolas of white.

Kenan read a sign that identified them as the Island Shops. With the newspaper tucked securely under his arm, he window-shopped by each one. It was too early for the proprietors to be about, and still too brisk for any swimmers, so Kenan had the place to himself. A cotton sweater in the window of the first shop caught his eye and he made a mental note to return later and check out all the other merchandise inside the coed boutique. Next door was the Fripp Island Logo Shop, which appeared to house everything from snorkels to champagne glasses. On around the circle was an arcade and ice cream parlor, plus a casual dining restaurant called the Fripp Island Cafe.

The last shop Kenan approached interested him most of all. It was an art gallery. He moved closer to the window and peeked inside. He saw several seascapes displayed on easels, and behind them on the wall hung prints of Lowcountry women basket weaving with the marshlands in the background. He loved art; it was something his Mother had taught him to appreciate. He thought perhaps he might find a small print that he could easily carry back on the airplane and then he laughed to himself. This time yesterday he was a bundle of nerves, preparing to hide in the shadows once again and play the private eye role, and now he was vacationing and gingerly window shopping. He definitely preferred the latter, and he was enjoying this morning exploration hour.

He wandered back around the pool and exited through a walkway that was by full beds of begonias, which still held their color. The walk led him to the clubhouse and he took a chance and pulled on the brass handle of the front entry. It opened and he walked inside. The decor was tastefully done. Freshly vacuumed hunter green carpet welcomed his loafers and he felt sort of like an intruder, especially at this hour. As he rounded the corner and smelled the aroma of breakfast being cooked, he guessed that the door was unlocked for a reason.

He followed the short hallway to the restaurant and was seated at a table by the window with a panoramic view. Now this was the way to start a vacation. Kenan was not a breakfast person per se, but considering the dinner of Life cereal and beer, he was prepared for the works this morning.

A smiling waiter dressed in tuxedo attire, minus the jacket, approached him and inquired if he would like some coffee. "No thank you; I already had my coffee this morning, but I will have some orange juice," he said.

The waiter nodded obligingly and moved toward the kitchen. Kenan picked up the menu and decided it would be impossible to choose from the list of mouth-watering selections. Eggs Benedict, pecan waffles topped with whipped cream, hash browns and sausage had Kenan's taste buds buzzing.

The waiter returned, and with his help, Kenan was able to decide on Eggs Benedict with a side order of hash browns for his breakfast feast. He rested his mind while he waited and thought of nothing. And then, when every morsel on both plates was gone, he left a bill on the table and retired to one of the chaise lounges in the gazebo beside the beach.

The entire vicinity around which Kenan had roamed this morning was a part of The Fripp Island Beach Club properties. Kenan gave the developers a star of excellence in the ambience category. It seemed that each portion of the Club he had seen thus far was lacking in no way to create the atmosphere it should. He wanted to check out the rest of the island to see if the other amenities he'd seen in the brochure were up to par with his experience so far.

First and foremost, there was the golf course and a bar and grill adjacent to the pro shop called Hugo's. He reminded himself again to make dinner reservations at The Beach Club for this evening. He should have done it while he was there having breakfast, but his memory failed him. Also, there was the

Marina Restaurant and a more formal bar above the main dining room that looked friendly and inviting.

Kenan heard two distinctive loud clicks and looked over his shoulder to see that the Beach Bar was opening. It was a small open-air bar once the white shutters were lifted and latched to the overhang of the roof above. Simple bar stools were evenly placed around all sides of the bar and one of them seemed to be whispering his name, but he had to let that big breakfast digest before he indulged in anything else. He noticed that the adult pool on the other side of the bar had some true sun lovers already gathered and greased. He wondered if they were from Maine or Canada because to him, the temperature was still a bit too low for a swimsuit. Although, the sights were improving, he thought, as he spied a girl in a string bikini with a cheerful chest.

It had certainly put a grin on Kenan's face. He focused a little more closely and wondered if the swimsuit top was responsible for her voluptuous appearance or had there been some surgical enhancements to her chest? He laughed that he was so relaxed and was pondering trivial details this morning.

It was low tide and the beach was scattered with people. Kenan sat in a lounge chair near the walkway to the beach. The breeze was more placid than the earlier morning hours and the newspaper Kenan held in his hands hardly moved.

But, his eyes did. And rapidly, down the front page of The Beaufort Gazette as he read the story concerning the death of Phillip Dubose. The news story was below the fold on the front page, which Kenan had not bothered to glance at until now. No wonder his father was so uptight last night; the charge was now murder. And the suspect was a man by the name of Duncan. Kenan recognized that name from an earlier conversation with

Nathan. The article was brief and gave no specifics of evidence to constitute the murder charge.

Kenan thought for a moment about calling Nathan and insisting that he give him a chance to meet the Stevensons and look for the capsule, but then he remembered his father's demand that he take a vacation and that surprising "I love you" at the end. "Better to leave well enough alone," Kenan thought. After all, Nathan was capable of a lot of things, but not murder. It was apparent to Kenan that his father had simply made a mistake in hiring this man Duncan. He had been a poor judge of character in this case and now everyone knew it.

Kenan was still not certain where the capsule fit into the picture. His curiosity was nagging him and he wondered what could be inside of it. Nathan had never revealed that information and quite frankly, Kenan had forgotten to ask last night, just like he had forgotten to mention the Paulos fellow.

He looked toward the surf and realized that if he were really going to enjoy this vacation he needed to dismiss the capsule from his thoughts. And with that intention in mind, he turned to page two.

He stopped briefly in the Classified Section to read the Personals. They always amused him. However, the Lowcountry Personals could not be compared to those in the Atlanta paper. Reading that section of the paper had been a great way to pass the time while waiting for the Stevensons to arrive in Atlanta a couple of days ago. They were most comical, but actually left Kenan feeling pity on those who would stoop to such measures to find companionship. He knew some friends in Florida who had an app called Tinder on their phones that could pinpoint a girl within a certain radius from their current location. They kept telling him he was crazy not to download it, but he hadn't.

He was lonely at times, even though he did date several nights a week. Simply having a date did not eliminate the loneliness. Sometimes a disappointing date, one where things just didn't seem to click, could make Kenan feel lonelier than if he had spent a quite night at home alone. Kenan did not mind being unattached, because that was how he preferred it until the dream girl came along. Don't waste time if the spark isn't there.

Anyway, there wasn't a lot of time for loneliness. But, right now he had a few days ahead of him for fun, and he didn't intend to waste one moment.

21

The tide was out beyond the sandbars and Stella's walking shoes were hardly making any tracks in the hard, dry sand. She was listening to the "Oldies, But Goodies" from the playlist on her phone and the voice of the late, great Otis Redding was now sounding into the earphones and she sang along. She knew all the words to every song she had ever heard twice and even after Walker's subtle attempts to tell her that her voice was not particularly melodious; she still always played the sing along game.

Stella pushed the sleeves of her sweatshirt up above her elbows and kept moving. A few houses down she saw Mr. Flannery descending the stairs of his private boardwalk. He was a cantankerous sort who spoke only when it pleased him. Their paths crossed often on these morning workouts.

Stella kept singing and swinging, as her pace was almost a run. Mr. Flannery stepped onto the beach and started toward the North Point. Their paths would cross momentarily and Stella wondered if he would speak, or if perhaps she was invisible this morning. He adjusted his "Go to Hell" hat, the type that Robert Redford wore in *The Great Gatsby*, and snapped his down vest. Stella watched him, only a few yards away now, and thought how the vest was really unnecessary on a beautiful day like today. But then, Mr. Flannery was eighty-nine, and if his blood wasn't cold from that alone, it surely would be from meanness.

She prepared for her casual wave to the island grump, and molded an artificial grin on her face. "Hi," she said as their shoulders passed inches apart. She thought how bizarre it was that he always walked so close to her, even with this whole wide beach, like they were a tag team or something.

"And Hi to you, too. Out looking for bodies this morning?" he asked sarcastically in his Irish brogue.

Stella stopped abruptly, although Mr. Flannery continued his shuffling. She turned the volume down on her phone, and with hands on hips strode up to the shrunken man and said, "Well, maybe I am. But I have a hunch about the south end today. I'm going to start there first."

He continued to shuffle along and Stella continued to follow along with hands still on hips, glaring at the hateful, old man.

"What?" Mr. Flannery stopped and threw up his hands then slightly lifted his hat to scratch his shiny bald head. "Do you wish me to offer you good luck, Mrs. Stevenson?"

Stella drew back her head but continued to hold the man's gaze. "No, Mr. Flannery," she said to the tired old eyes that made her realize there was no use in squabbling with such a veteran of the world. "I wanted to wish you a good day."

One corner of his mouth lifted ever so slightly, and for a minute Stella thought he was going to smile at her. "As long as there is bran cereal in the world, I shall be happy. Goodbye, Mrs. Stevenson."

Mr. Flannery shuffled off leaving Stella standing behind shaking her head. No matter how large or small a dwelling, there must be someone in charge of discontent and stinging words. Mr. Flannery seemed perfectly happy holding that position at Fripp, and better he than she.

She let the gentle sea breeze blow the disheartening remarks out of her mind and turned the volume back up on her phone. *Myrtle Beach Days* by the Embers was coming in loud and clear.

So onward she marched not allowing that interlude to cloud her otherwise perfect day. Stella tried to schedule a walk at least five days a week, weather permitting, and she used this time for mental therapy as well as physical exercise. Once her heels hit the sand her mind was free from all thoughts, she simply enjoyed the music or would daydream. Whatever it took to relax the space between her ears was what she concentrated on during her morning exercise. Reminiscing seemed to be the outlet that worked for Stella this morning.

Two young children to her left were wading in the shallow ponds that formed at low tide, and their mother sat on the edge with sand toys piled around her. The little girl and boy appeared to have the same amount of years between them as her own Kate and Ely. It seemed unthinkable to Stella that hers were both college students.

Her daydreams took her back to a time of sand castle building contests, jumping the waves as they lapped along the shore, and picnics on the beach. They were wonderful times and Stella and Walker had not missed a moment of their children's lives as they soared into young adulthood. Of course, Walker had missed a few programs or basketball games due to work, and Stella couldn't be in two places at one time, but those incidences were made up for three-fold, with family outings. Much of that family time was spent at Fripp Island. Time to learn each child's personality and character traits; time for teaching and sharing and learning to love unconditionally; and time to learn about yourself as an adult through the eyes of your children.

This would be the first year Stella and Walker would not be with Ely on his birthday. If she didn't dwell on it maybe it wouldn't hurt so much. She truly believed that misery lies within one's own soul. It can be controlled and it would be controlled, especially two days from now on that special day.

The Beach Club was up ahead. It reminded her of a massive Southern Plantation with huge white columns and porches everywhere including the second story of the structure. Stella loved the building, especially the elegant navy canopies with the original Fripp Island logo—a front-view silhouette of a sailboat similar to the ones used by Christopher Columbus—in the center. The logo was simple, just the silhouette and a few lines symbolizing the ocean, and she thought the simplicity enhanced its charm.

She reached the boardwalk and took the stairs two at a time, all the way to the top and moved swiftly through the gazebo. It was a fairly new addition to the outdoor configuration of The Club and had been utilized by all. It was so pretty and airy and personal. Hanging baskets hung between each pillar and Stella guessed that the Impatiens, which now tumbled over their edges, would be replaced with pansies in the next few weeks. She noticed a couple of people lounging about the gazebo; one resting their eyes and the other reading.

Kenan had heard the pounding of feet on the stairs and when Mrs. Stevenson appeared on the landing he froze. She glanced in his direction and he managed to slide the newspaper up in front of his face. He listened intently to her footsteps as she moved across the gazebo. Just before he heard her begin to descend the few steps down to the pool area, he heard a soft clanging sound. When he thought her to be safely in the distance, Kenan stood up and moved toward the beach walkway. There on the sidewalk was a single key. He stared down at it for a moment and then bent to pick it up. He rubbed the edges with his thumb as he slid it into his pocket and walked back to his seat.

22

Ely arrived before Kate at the Charleston, South Carolina, airport and despite all his attempts to dazzle the young lady behind the rental car counter, he remained without wheels. The fact that he would be nineteen in two days was no help. He needed to be twenty-one.

Ely made his way back through the terminal toward the gate where the flight from Raleigh-Durham would be arriving at 11:43 a.m. He stopped along the way for a turkey croissant and a soda to kill the hunger pains of a still-growing athlete. There was hardly an ounce of fat to be found on the handsome young man, clad in a denim shirt and khakis with one sole canvas bag thrown over a shoulder. He sipped and chewed all the way back to gate twelve and took a seat.

After a few minutes he pulled a copy of *The World According to Garp* from his bag and began page one of his Contemporary Literature weekend assignment. As with any work of writing, other than those pertaining to sports, the paperback put him to sleep by page three.

He was awakened when his elbow slid from the armrest of the seat and sent his neck cracking down over his chest. He looked up as the words "Wake up little brother," were being spoken into his ear.

Kate, no doubt, had nudged his arm causing the slight muscle spasm he now felt in his neck. Ely accepted her extended hand and she pulled him to his feet. Kate reached high above her head and hugged Ely and insisted he had grown at least two inches.

Ely explained the problem with the car and thanked Kate for being two and a half years his senior. After retrieving Kate's three bags from Carousel two, Ely walked outside like a tired pack mule and tossed the load into the back of a small blue convertible Kate had splurged for.

"You want to drive?" Kate asked.

"Did you list me as an additional driver?"

"We are truly the children of a legal beagle. Yes, I listed your name."

"Then move it over," Ely said as he hurried around the front of the car.

The first half of the short trip from Charleston to Fripp Island passed quickly as they sped along breathing in the Lowcountry splendor. Kate quizzed Ely on his first few months at school, and Ely quizzed Kate on yet another possible brother-in-law that she had put in the wind.

"Is it you or is it them, Snoop?" Ely asked, referring to Kate by a nickname that was so old they had forgotten its origin.

"Both, I guess. Them for screwing up just one to many times, and me for believing that there is a perfect guy in the world whose path shall cross mine at a predestined moment in time. And when that does happen, I don't want to be weighed down by someone with lesser credentials."

"O.K. I see your point, but just how did you know it was time to send Fang sailing. I mean, did he forget to button his collar buttons one day, or did he wear a pair of those god-awful suede slip-on sandals. I know how you hate those."

They both laughed at that comment.

"Two reasons. One, the name was beginning to make me gag. And two, a tall, brawny chick by the name of Beth, I found out he was poking."

"Those are both good reasons. I never liked him anyway."

"Yeah, it was a blessing. I really don't have time right now to be involved with anyone or anything except finding a job and beginning a career and making a living. Which, by the way, is how I got excused from my classes for the rest of the week. I have a second interview Saturday morning with a representative from The Audubon Aquarium of the Americas in New Orleans. I did all right with the first one last month when they were recruiting on campus. Anyway, the recruiter will be in Charleston speaking at a seminar this weekend and we arranged for another interview. The Big Easy; I could live there for a few years anyway."

"Now tell me one more time what your major is, my dear sister."

"I am a Research Microbiologist, with a minor in Economics, or at least I will be by December."

"Everyone minors in Economics. What's the deal?"

"Who knows? Have you decided what you want to do with yourself at Clemson?"

"I believe it's more like, has Clemson decided what they want to do with me? I've played all over the court and still haven't found a permanent nesting spot, but as you well know, Snoop, I am the greatest basketball player of all times, and they would have booted me by now if they didn't have sensational plans for the coolest Freshman."

"So, I suppose the answer to my question is that you're going to play basketball, turn pro, and design your own athletic shoe. I may disown you if you model underwear though."

"What if I give you a share of the profits?"

"You really do have a nice shape. We'll think about it. Hey, how did you manage to get away from practice like this?"

"I told the Coach my Mother found a dead body at Fripp and there was a murder investigation being conducted and she needed me," Ely explained.

"That sounds like Mom is a suspect," Kate said somewhat confused.

"Yeah, that's how the Coach took it, too. But, it got me on a plane, didn't it?"

"You are too much Little Brother. I've really missed you," Kate said as she punched Ely in the arm. "Mom and Dad are going to be so surprised to see us."

"And they're even going to be more surprised when they get the charge card bills for these airline tickets and rental car."

"They won't mind. This is the kind of thing they love. Spontaneity; it's their middle name."

"Well, if they've changed their middle name to 'thrifty' since we've last seen them, my story is that you made me do it," Ely said.

"Not a chance. Our mother doesn't realize the word 'thrifty' even exists, and if she did, she certainly doesn't know the definition."

"You're right. How do you think she's really doing?" Ely asked Kate with some seriousness in his voice.

"I can't know until I see her face and her eyes."

They drove along in silence for a while with the sounds of the wind in their ears and the feel of hair whipping in their face. One could never mistake the two as anything other than siblings. Their dark auburn locks were of the same texture and even had highlights from the sun painted in the precise same locations. They each had profound check bones encasing a perfectly shaped nose, and the clincher was their teeth: the whitest white, behind a killer smile.

Stella had often marveled at their resemblance to one another, even down to each having a mole on their scalp in the same location and one lone mole on their back in the exact same spot too. By the time Kate was seven and Ely was four and a half, people began asking if they were twins. Ely's height always threw everyone off.

They reached a junction where five roads met and weaved a path in and around each other and the marshlands seemed to seep into the convertible and through the pores in their skin until at the exact moment they looked at one another and said, "We're almost to Beaufort."

"Have you had lunch?" Kate asked.

"Not really. I had a little snack at the airport when I was waiting for you."

"Wouldn't some Steamers bar-be-que hit the spot?"

"Yes, either that or a shrimp burger from the Shrimp Shack. But, we pass Steamers first, so it looks like bar-be-que it is," Ely said.

"Yum, I can't wait. I'm going to have the bar-be-que plate with Brunswick stew and cole slaw. Lots of cole slaw. And iced tea. Sweet, with lemon," Kate said.

"I'll go for two sandwiches topped with slaw and extra hot sauce, and onion rings. Ditto on the drink."

Their stomachs churned until they reached the famous restaurant on Lady's Island. The red and white checked tablecloths still covered each table and welcomed them back as did the smell of pork roasting in the rear of the building. Kate placed their order while Ely spoke with one of the cooks in the kitchen who he used to play ball with in the summer. Kate smiled as she watched her brother who had inherited their Mother's way of socializing. They would both talk to the infamous "brick wall" if they discovered that it would talk back to them. She considered ordering the cook some lunch, too, because Ely was sure to invite him to join them. Kate glanced through a Lowcountry Real Estate brochure while she waited for the lunch to arrive. Ely joined her at the table moments before the server approached carrying two heavy Styrofoam white plates piled high with food.

"This was a good idea you had about coming home for a long weekend, Kate," Ely said as he wolfed his first sandwich down.

"Well, I'm sure Mom is fine, but it couldn't hurt to have a little extra support at a time like this."

"True. And when she starts planning my birthday party for Saturday that will take her mind off any unpleasant matters."

"If I were you I wouldn't expect too much until we see what's going on."

"Mom loves birthdays. She won't let me down. But, I understand what you mean, Snoop, we'll wait and see."

They ate every bite and refilled their Styrofoam cups with iced tea then got back in the convertible and continued on. As they passed by the Gullah women in their lean-to shacks selling baskets and the familiar marsh views around each curve, the urgency to be on Marlin Drive at Fripp Island increased. They couldn't wait to see their parents, the dogs, the piano and most of all, the beach. Kate was behind the wheel now and Ely nodded in approval as she pressed the accelerator a little closer to the floor.

23

The old man carefully stepped down from the cab of the pickup truck. The joints in his body seemed to be aching a little more this year with the autumn morning chill. He walked to the wrought iron gate and pressed the buttons on the security switch with his cold black fingers. Gospel music leaked from the speakers in the door of the flaming red truck that Priscilla had surprised him with the year before she died.

He hummed along with the music as the gates opened inward. The breath from his body produced smoke into the air as he sang, "Hallelujah, Amen," along with the recording. Richard tucked his hands into the pockets of his jacket and started back to the truck. He noticed the leaves piled closely around the brick columns on either side of the gate and thought how he better take care of that soon before Mr. Gray barked about it.

His vehicle moved up the winding drive slowly and quietly and came to a stop on the far side of the four-car garage. There was a single door on the front of the garage and Richard put his key in and turned the lock. He walked straight back to a corner of the massive garage that had been made into a small office. His office. He had felt so important when Mrs. Priscilla presented it to him. She had loved to come out and sit with him in the small room when the mansion grew haunting.

She started coming out after Kenan went away to school and on the days when Mr. Gray didn't leave to go to the office. Richard always wondered what Mrs. Priscilla saw in that man. Must not have been much toward the end, but she never said one bad word about that monster. Richard had to respect her for that and for everything else that the grand woman was about.

He opened the door to his office and switched on the light. There was a space heater in the back corner and he turned it on quickly. He rubbed his dry, hard hands together to keep warm for a moment and decided it was a waste with his circulation, so he moved to his second choice, the coffee pot.

Richard pulled a can of coffee from a shelf to his right and dumped four scoops into a filter. Just as he flipped the coffee pot on, he felt an explosion thunder in his head. He fell to his knees. What was happening to him? Was it one of those strokes where a blood vessel bursts in your head?

Richard would never know, because he did not see the man behind him with the silenced gun, and neither did anyone else.

24

Stella could see Sonny and Ben lounging on the broad front porch of their home. They looked distinguished and perfect in that setting. One might guess they were painted there to complete the perfection of the residence. She put two fingers in her mouth and let out a shrill whistle. All four black and white ears perked up and Ben broke into song with his famous howling.

Stella hoped the neighbors were not trying to sleep late this morning as Sonny joined in to accompany his seed. They were such company for Walker and Stella and were treated much like all the other animals on Fripp: like royalty. There was not one pet on the Island that was not cared for to the highest degree or did not appear well groomed at all times. There was a certain unspoken humanizing factor that prevailed among the dog and cat society of the island, which made this a coveted dwelling for anyone on four legs.

The Stevensons' two Springer Spaniels were right at home as the dominoes fell in their favor, and were adapting to the fine, year-round life of leisure with gentle grace. Other than the howling and the crab chasing. They each lost all credibility when it came to the blue crabs. They reverted to the days of roaming the North Georgia mountainous woods and chasing anything that moved, like the great hunters of their heritage.

They met Stella on the drive and sniffed at her feet to decide if she had been anywhere of interest. Obviously unimpressed by her walk to the Marina and back, they walked ahead of her and resumed their positions on the front porch.

Stella meandered around the front yard snapping a few late-blooming weeds from the flowerbeds and wondering where in the world she could have lost that darn key. When she had arrived at the Marina, anxious to have an extra key made for Edwina, she reached into her pocket and felt only emptiness and a small hole in the bottom of it.

She knew there was a good chance that she was locked out of the house, although she continued to avoid the possible realization of the fact by steering clear of any of the doors.

Until the Phillip Dubose tragedy, the Stevensons almost never locked their doors. And then at Stella's insistence, that by locking them her nightmares might stop, it became the new norm to lock them. And lock them all.

She could always pass the six or so hours until Walker returned from the golf tournament on the neighboring Dataw Island by cleaning out the storage room, or washing the cars. The little red MG hadn't had a bath in some time. But since none of these productive ideas really appealed to her, she started up the front stairs and proceeded to turn the knobs of each door. The door to the screened porches was unlocked, but the French doors within them were locked up tight, as was the back door through to the kitchen.

Stella went back down stairs and swept the garage, put some of her gardening pots and tools away for the winter, and brushed the dogs. When her stomach began to growl she thought of visiting a neighbor or walking across the ninth hole over to Hugo's Restaurant next to the pro shop. She could charge lunch there, but she looked pretty casual, to say the least.

About the time she was mulling all this over in her mind, Julie Smith came out of her front door. The Smiths lived in the house to their left and were from Philadelphia. In fact, Stella was not even aware that they were back from their trip home to see some relatives.

"Hello there," Stella said, raising one hand in a wave.

"Well, hello! Are you still tootling around outside? I saw you earlier through the window."

"Yes, but mainly because I can't get inside to tootle. I lost my key somewhere along the course of my morning walk and Walker is on Dataw playing golf."

"Oh, dear, when it rains it does pour," Julie said walking toward Stella and now reaching up to give her a hug.

"So you've heard the news?"

"Yes, we drove in late last night and Dave discovered it as he was looking through some of the back newspapers. Have you talked to Marguarite?

"No, I haven't," Stella answered, "I figured I would be the last person she would want to hear from since I found Phillip's body. And, you know we weren't good friends or anything."

"Sadly, Stella, she has no good friends," Julie sighed.

Come on," she said taking Stella by the hand. "Help me finish unloading the car and come inside for a chat. I was really feeling like making myself a Bloody Mary, but didn't have anyone to enjoy it with me. Dave has gone into Beaufort for some heavy grocery shopping. What do you think? Could you join me?" Julie asked.

"That would be wonderful," Stella said as she grabbed an overloaded tote bag from the back seat of Julie's car and closed the door.

The two women relaxed on the Smith's beachside porch and sipped their drinks. Julie suggested a game of tennis might be more beneficial to them than another cocktail, at this time of day, and Stella agreed.

After changing into a pair of borrowed tennis shorts from Julie; Stella ran next door to retrieve her racquet from the utility closet at her own home. She laughed as she realized there was no lock at all on this door. She backed their golf cart out of the garage and picked Julie up where she waited next door at the end of the drive.

"Are you sure this plan is good with you, Stella?" Julie asked.

"Absolutely," Stella said glancing at her watch. "I have approximately four hours of free time."

25

"Let's see," Kenan said thumbing through his wallet. "Do you accept American Express cards?"

"Absolutely."

"Great," Kenan said as handed the golf shop attendant his card.

"Sure. You'll just about have the course to yourself today."

"Oh, yeah? That's surprising on such a gorgeous day."

"Most of our Thursday regulars have gone to Dataw to play in a tournament."

Kenan acted as though he hadn't heard anything about it. "Really? I think I passed the road that leads to that Island on the way into Fripp."

"Yes, you certainly did. It is halfway between here and Beaufort. It's a pretty place," the attendant said as he handed the credit card back to Kenan.

"I think you're really going to enjoy those clubs," the attendant said. "I've heard they are the best on the market right now."

Kenan nodded and let the fellow keep talking. He knew they were the best on the market and that they did indeed handle well. At least his set back in Pompano did.

Kenan signed the charge slip and picked up his new golf shoes and rental clubs. He smiled at the attendant and thanked him for his help and started out the door.

"Thank you, Mr. Gray. I hope you have a good round."

"I do too," Kenan said and walked outside to cart 19. Moments later he was sliding a tee down into the bright green Bermuda grass on the number one tee box.

The sun was on the back of his neck as he prepared to tee it high and let it fly. The new shoes were a tad tight, but aren't they all in the beginning, he thought. The hole was a par four with water on the left, and between Kenan and the green. He picked up some loose blades of grass and tossed them in the air to determine the direction and strength of the wind. Actually there was not much of a breeze at all on this particular hole.

Kenan stood with bent knees, straight arms and left foot in line with the ball. He brought back the driver and followed through with grace. He had displayed the perfect golf swing and had kept his eyes glued to the ball, so if all went accordingly, his lie should be ten to fifteen yards this side of the lagoon in front of him. With hand to his brow to shield the glare, he looked for the little white object. Yes, there it was. Just exactly where it should be. This truly was going to be a good day. He lifted his tee from the ground and dropped it in his pocket and started back to the cart.

Kenan felt the grooved edge of the key within the pocket of his twill trousers as he walked. He wondered to himself why he had not left it back at the condo. He really should never have picked it up this morning in the first place. Nathan didn't need his help anymore, so he certainly didn't need this key, but still he rubbed it as though a genie were going to pop out and grant him three wishes.

He reached the cart, deposited the driver in the bag and followed along the cart path to his ball. After his second shot the ball was positioned about a foot and a half away from the hole. Par seemed very promising.

Kenan moved through the perfectly manicured course enjoying the solitude and beauty of the nature around him. He saw several deer on the edge of the woods feeding and they never flittered as he drove past in the quiet cart. It seemed to him half of the lots along the course were vacant and still heavily wooded with a mix of hard woods and pines. He thought how this was a very well-kept secret to the vacationing population. If he owned property here, he would prefer little-to-no advertising just as these property owners obviously did. Kenan subscribed to every golf and travel magazine available along with a few others of miscellaneous interest, yet he had never seen this paradise mentioned. He thought that maybe he would check with the real estate office on the island before leaving on Sunday.

By the eighth hole the sun was baking through his sweater and he took it off and placed it in the basket on the cart. With five pars and two bogies under his belt he studied the wooden chart of the upcoming hole.

He was grateful for the thermal water coolers along the course, but he really wanted a beer, an ice-cold beer, an ice-cold draft beer. He was thinking about that and washing his ball on the eighth tee box when he heard the noise. It sounded as though a submarine was surfacing and Kenan looked only three yards to his right and spotted the intruder. He froze when he and the alligator made direct eye contact. His ball fell from the ball washer and rolled down the slight incline from the tee box to the marsh. It was heading straight for the gator's mouth. Thankfully it hit a small rock and veered to the left and stopped in the muck along the edge of the marsh. Kenan did not take his eyes off the seven-foot-long reptile that had proudly showed his teeth, tongue and throat several times already.

Obviously, this fellow was pissed. His tail swung back and forth creating a thunderous noise, however he never moved forward at all. It occurred to Kenan that perhaps the gator was not the intruder at all. It was quite possible that Kenan had encroached into his territory and caught the guy on a bad day. He remembered reading on the bottom of the score-card, "Please do not feed the alligators," but never imagined this.

As the seconds passed, Kenan remembered a bit of knowl-edge he had picked up along the way about alligators or maybe crocodiles. He couldn't remember which. If they were chasing you, you should run in a zigzag fashion, because they will fol-low the same line. However, due to their excessively long tail, it is hard for them to make those abrupt turns and it slows them down. Whether the tale is fact or fiction that is precisely what Kenan did.

He zigzagged the twenty-yard distance back to the cart and applied pressure to the accelerator even before his behind hit the seat. He glanced to his right to see how close by the ga-tor was and felt silly when he realized that the sharped-toothed bully had not even moved.

With his heart still pounding and the need for a cold beer even more urgent, Kenan threw his ball into the number eight fairway and began play there. It was a long straight hole with marshy lagoons all along the left side. Kenan decided he would play it safe and hit to the right. The lavish homes along that side appeared more inviting to him right now.

The wind increase and although Kenan rarely hit woods in the fairway, he chose one now considering the wind and the distance and the lack of strength in his arms after the big fright.

After Kenan hit the ball he remembered why he never used woods in the fairway. He had sliced it hard to the right and even though he did not hear the crashing of glass that would have drawn attention to him, he knew that his ball was definitely out of bounds. His game was going to "hell in a handbag" as Vera used to say, all because of that damn alligator.

He felt a hunger pain mixed in with anxiety bubbles rattling around in his stomach. It was after one o'clock in the afternoon and Kenan entertained the idea of going to the restaurant beside the pro shop for some lunch and that beer, and then starting on number ten with a new attitude. He drove the cart down the right side of number eight fairway not even looking for the lost ball, but marveling at the elegant homes.

He could hear the ocean in the distance and the sound of the gulls laughing.

Suddenly, there it was. A little rectangular sign with the name "Stevenson" painted on it. Behind the short sign was a white lattice fence about four feet tall. There was an inviting courtyard and behind it towered a traditional southern mansion, complete with porches and ceiling fans and a flavor of style and grace that beckoned to him with its hospitality.

Kenan parked the cart on one side of the courtyard, behind a flowering shrub, and slid out of the seat. He peered over the fence into the courtyard and immediately saw a golf ball sitting in the grassy area beside a cement fountain. As luck would have it, there was a gate only a few steps away and without deep concern Kenan moved toward it.

Ten paces took him to the golf ball. He bent down to pick it up and as he did he heard the jingling of what sounded like keys. Two seconds later the truth was known as a handsome pair of Spaniels with dog tags entered the courtyard from a breezeway that probably led to a garage. They progressed into a trot as they saw the interloper and made a b-line for what Kenan thought was his throat. But, soon he realized the two seemed genuinely happy to see the stranger and were greeting him in the receptive manner.

Kenan petted and rubbed the dog's silky fur. They responded to Kenan's attention and even filled the air with a few sporting barks. Considering that Kenan was not exactly where he should be, he felt more relaxed and finally a little less tense about the reptile interlude. Besides, if someone came out to investigate the barking, he had a good excuse. He had hit a wild shot and just came in briefly to retrieve his ball. However, several minutes passed and it didn't seem that there would be an opportunity to see if his excuse would float. Perhaps no one was at home.

Once again he felt the jagged corners of the key in his pocket. Why not live on the edge, he thought to himself. After all, he had met them the night before and it seemed terribly coincidental that his ball should land in their courtyard. How unsociable it would be of him not to at least say hello. That would be his story in the event someone was at home. It had a few holes, but he would fill those as he went along. He had a gut feeling that an empty house stood above him and felt confident about his deceptive story as he climbed the back stairs.

He opened the screen door and tapped gently on the window of the inner door. He waited. He knocked more loudly this time. No one emerged from within to answer the door. He casually pulled the key from his pocket and tried to put it in the keyhole. Almost instantly he knew it wasn't the right door. He closed the screen and walked around the wide porch to the side of the house and continued on past a hammock and big wicker rocking chairs until the front door stood right in front of him.

He questioned his sanity as he approached the white door with a brass doorknocker and matching kick plate. He knocked gently on the window beside the door and waited. Then after glancing from side to side and deciding the coast was clear, he slipped the key from his pocket once again.

He positioned the key near the lock and pushed it inward. It went in easily and Kenan turned the dead bolt lock to the right and heard a click. He turned the knob and opened the door. He had no idea just what was responsible for this massive show of bravery, but he stepped into the house and closed the door behind him.

He considered shouting, "Hello? Is anyone at home?" He could just say that the door was unlocked and he thought they didn't hear him knocking, so he walked on in. Kenan was beginning to clam up and really felt like running back to the door when the telephone rang. He froze in his footsteps and listened as the rings continued. "Four, five, six," he counted to himself. And then an answering machine picked up the call and after a very brief sentence spoken in Mrs. Stevenson's voice and a beep, the caller spoke.

"I thought you'd be at home getting ready for our big date. Just called to check on you and tell you I love you. We just finished a quick lunch and are starting the back nine. See you in a while. I miss you." And there was a click.

After this timely call, Kenan was more confident about his first gut reaction that the house stood empty. He took a brief moment to look around and decided the decor of the home was just as welcoming as the outside.

Since he had never really seen exactly the seaman's capsule he was looking for, he had to envision it in his mind as best he could and search—probably fruitlessly—as quickly as possible. At least he knew that it was yellow and could also estimate its approximate size. He opened drawers and rummaged through them, and then on to closets and coat pockets. There were hatboxes and jewelry boxes and just plain old wooden boxes. He looked in them all. He climbed the stairs to the lofted library and other bedrooms. He stopped and looked at the breathtaking view before him as he entered the room filled with books, a baby grand piano and a bar. He thought momentarily about that beer again, but shook his head and started opening drawers and looking behind some of the books.

He glanced at his watch. He had been in the house for about eight minutes. He decided he would look for about four more and then exit. He bobbed into each bedroom on the second floor and felt as though they had been unoccupied for some time. Everything was in perfect order, not even a hairbrush on the dresser or a garment over a chair like the downstairs room. With the clock running, he thought his time could be better spent in the kitchen.

The doors were still swinging on their hinges as Kenan began the search through the kitchen. It was a very organized kitchen. Skillets, pots and casserole dishes of all shapes and sizes were neatly stacked in the pullout drawers. The smaller drawers were neatly organized, too. No good ole American junk drawer existed in this kitchen. His search task was easier because of the fastidious efforts of the main chef in charge, but the kitchen was also very large, and his four minutes were dwindling. He was searching a large ceramic cookie jar shaped like a pig, when a voice shouted from the front of the house, "Mom? Dad? Are you at home?"

Kenan instantly began to quiver and quickly and quietly put the head of the pig back on its body and started for the back door. Since it was all the way on the other side of the kitchen, and the footsteps were getting closer, he opted for the pantry directly to his left.

A half second after Kenan closed the pantry doors the heavy mahogany kitchen doors swung open. There was a miniscule crack between the two pantry doors and Kenan watched as a young girl stepped into the kitchen. A young, beautiful girl. Her auburn hair was shoulder length and held carelessly into place by a black headband. Her face was incredibly gorgeous and the olive complexion flawless.

His heart was beating loudly and rapidly now, but was it from fear of discovery or intrigue of the girl? She walked across the room to the breakfast booth and looked out the window toward the golf course. As she leaned across the table to reach for a small jar of cashews, Kenan observed that she was tall, slender, and very shapely.

She poured some nuts into the palm of her hand and screwed the top back on the jar. She turned and looked directly at the pantry. Kenan stopped breathing. He watched as she walked toward him in the suede clogs that pounded on the kitchen floor. He breathed in a molecule of air when she stopped right beside the pantry and opened one side of the huge refrigerator. Her slender body dressed in a black turtle-neck shirt and short khaki skirt leaned over and gazed into the refrigerator. Kenan was enjoying the scenery and wished that her black tights were not so opaque, but for now, he was happy just to view the shapeliness of her long legs.

He was sweating bullets in the pantry as the girl lifted a lite beer from the refrigerator and closed the door. She unscrewed the top and laid it on the table. She was so beautiful Kenan dared not blink or he might miss one of her incredible mo-tions. She took a sip of the beer and walked over to a built-in desk near the back door. She looked through a stack of mail and after opening one piece and depositing it in the wastebas-ket beside her; she picked the bottle up and exited the kitchen through the swinging door.

Kenan considered hiding out in the pantry for the next four days just so he could catch a glimpse of this princess a few more times. He shook his head, attempting to return to the land of living, and that of breaking and entering. He had to get out of here. "Get your mind off of the girl of your dreams and get the hell out of here," he told himself.

From the sound of the shoes he felt like she was ascending the hard wood stairs in the front room. Kenan pushed open one pantry door and stepped out. He quietly walked to the back door and turned the dead bolt latch. He stepped onto the porch as the boards creaked slightly and pulled the door closed behind him. He held the screen as it moved into place to avoid any loud bangs and then tiptoed toward the stairs back down to the courtyard.

Still holding his breath, Kenan moved down the stairs ec-static that his clean getaway was nearly complete. Four more steps and then through the gate and away in the silent, electric golf cart. And then he could sit and think of a way to return, on legitimate terms, to meet the girl.

To his astonishment an unexpected springing, bouncing sound drew his attention to the left, and right into the eyes of guy dribbling a basketball. They both looked at each other, speechless, for a second or so. Kenan's mind was racing and interpreted that this young fellow must also be searching for Mom or Dad.

And then, as if he were used to finding a stranger on his back staircase every day of the week, the ball player tucked the basketball under his arm and extended a hand toward Kenan. "Hello, I'm Ely Stevenson."

Kenan stepped down the four remaining stairs and said as they shook hands, "And I'm Kenan Gray."

26

All of the boring tailor-made suits remained in their place in the closet of the master suite on Ampt Hill. Nathan would not need them on this trip. He dressed casually this morning and intended to continue the same dress code until the entire Fripp matter was resolved.

He had called the office and as always Barbara was at her desk by 7:59 a.m. and poised ready to answer the telephone. He knew the coffee was brewed and one empty cup and saucer with two lumps of sugar on the side, sat waiting on the credenza beside the coffeemaker. The blinds were, as usual, pulled high under the cornice board window treatment and would remain there until Barbara returned from lunch at 1:15 p.m., at which time they would be lowered to half-mast. Rain or shine. She was a punctual creature of habit and Nathan's lifeline to the business.

He told her his plans to be away for a few days and gave her authority to handle any urgent matters to the best of her ability. He also told her that Kenan would be leaving Fripp this morning and would be on a weekend vacation, so, he too, would be unavailable, but that he was confident that she could handle anything that came up. She was too, since she always did. Barbara was no novice where Nathan Gray was concerned and after hearing these trite instructions knew better than to annoy the great master of disappearance by inquiring where he might be reached in case of emergency.

More than likely, she thought, he is taking off with yet another floozy for a long weekend in Vegas or Tahoe, or maybe even the Caribbean this time of year. She would check later, as the police would inquire, to see if his passport was in the office safe.

Following the conversation, lasting under a minute, Barbara picked up the coffee cup, returned the two lumps of sugar to the crystal sugar bowl and poured herself some coffee in the same cup. She settled into her seat with a relaxing sigh. It would be nice not to deal with his childish ways for a few days.

Still in the bedroom, Nathan buzzed the intercom button for the kitchen. A second passed and when Vera didn't answer immediately, he pressed the button three more times. Long, impatient buzzes.

"What is it?" Vera's perturbed voice said through the speaker.

"Put my coffee in a thermos and wrap up some of those biscuits from last night. I'll be down in a minute."

"And good morning to you. Can't you say please sometime?"

Nathan looked disgustingly at the speaker on the wall then went to the closet and pulled a zippered duffle bag down from the top shelf. He opened several drawers within the built-in bureau in the closet and stuffed some clothes into the bag. He reached for a pair of black shoes, and dropped them in the duffle along with a tan cashmere sweater. Nathan zipped some hanging clothes into a monogrammed garment bag, snatched his always-prepared shaving kit from the bathroom counter and was down the stairs in a flash.

A disgruntled Vera had left a small brown bag and silver thermos on the large round table in the cathedral foyer and was nowhere to be seen. After pressing the code into the burglar alarm panel beside the massive front door, Nathan flipped three different locks to the open position and made his exit. The large white columns looked cold and lonely as he passed by them and descended the brick stairway from the front porch. The mums along the edge of the walkway looked bright and perky, but did nothing for Nathan's uneasy attitude concerning what would await him as the day progressed.

He turned the corner of the walkway and said a loud curse word when he didn't see his car parked in its usual spot. He cursed again, this time at Richard, who was supposed to have his car pulled out of the garage and ready to go by this time each day. He pressed a button on the side of the garage and one of the doors rolled upward. There was his car. It would be cold as hell in there probably since Richard hadn't bothered to park it out in the sun.

Nathan glanced to the far rear corner and saw that the door to Richard's "office," as everyone but him called it, was cracked and the light was on. He should march over there and fire his ass, but he didn't have time this morning. Instead he tossed the baggage and breakfast into the passenger seat, crawled in beside it and cranked the engine.

Vera watched him through the kitchen window as he peeled out of the garage and down the drive. "What makes him so mean?" she said out loud. Then she wondered to herself if Richard had been the victim of a lip lashing this morning. It wasn't near time for their Price is Right coffee break, but Vera was mad and just had to share her anger this morning. She reached for her crocheted shawl hanging on a hook inside the enormous pantry and wrapped her old bony shoulders up tightly, then walked to the garage.

The wind was blowing with vigor, as though Mother Nature was working quickly to dry the earth for a sunny autumn day. Vera crept across the paved drive lifting one edge of the shawl to shield her face from the brisk wind. She entered the garage through the door from which Mr. Gray had exited and tooled her way past three vehicles to Richard's office.

The door was cracked and when she was about eight paces away Vera said, "He was in a foul mood this morning, wasn't he Richard?"

The smile on her face turned to wonderment when there was no instant reply. She pushed open the door and saw her friend Richard lying on his back in a puddle of blood with one eye open and the other one gone. A pocket of wind blew through the door and blew a coffee can off the table and it fell to the floor with a loud clang. Vera ran from the room screaming, "My Richard! He's done killed my Richard."

When the old woman finally made it back to the kitchen her calves were already aching from moving so fast, or maybe it was from the stiffness of the muscles due to shock. Whatever it was she didn't feel it; she only felt the wet tears streaming down her face and the burning sensation of those to come. With loud heralding cries she picked up the telephone and dialed 911, just as she had done the day she had found Mrs. Priscilla.

She repeated over and over how Richard was dead and what a mean man Mr. Gray had become, or always was. She held the receiver tight in her hand and cried and moved deeper and deeper into the shadows of hysteria. The noise outside became louder with each passing second and Vera had to scream louder to hear herself mourn her devoted friend. And then a man in a uniform came and hugged her as she sat at the kitchen table still holding the telephone. After she couldn't find the words to answer his questions, he nodded to another nice man who spoke kindly to her, but then pinched her arm. She wanted to sleep, but when her eyelids closed there was only Richard's red blood with dry coffee grounds sprinkled in it. She needed to clean up his office for him and she would, just like she cleaned up Mrs. Priscilla's rug for her.

27

Anthony Paulos sat in the dining room of his condominium high atop the stylish Richmond Centre Building in the heart of downtown and only fifteen minutes from the airport. He sat at the long glass table alone chugging coffee and gorging himself on waffles with butter and pecans.

Despite Guido's hard work in the kitchen, Anthony had not enjoyed his dinner last night. The little worm, Gray, had left him with a bad taste in his mouth, but he was making up for it this morning.

The dining room door opened and a young girl in a maid's outfit entered the room carrying scrambled eggs and ketchup on a tray. She walked toward the disgusting man at the end of the table whose gaping silk robe revealed a grossly haired chest. She thought how he looked like an Italian version of Julius Caesar in the film *Jesus Christ Superstar*. She placed the platter of eggs and ketchup down on the edge of the table and hoped his answer to the question, "Can I get you anything else," would be, "No".

The quicker her departure, the less likely it was that she would for the second time, by accident, heaven forbid, catch a glimpse of the Porkers privates through the glass table top. She was only temporary help, called in for a few days from a local service. She must remember to decline if this assignment should ever come up again.

When she arrived this morning a lady, perhaps of the evening, was leaving and she could have sworn she heard her regurgitate as the elevator doors closed. And now, as she stood waiting for his answer, she understood why. No amount of money would justify sleeping with this creature.

But obviously, there was more to him than she realized just yet, because everyone in the plush apartment obeyed him as though he actually owned them. Though the fear in their eyes was faintly masked it conveyed to her the message, "Do as you are told; and do it quickly."

Finally, he spoke. "I haven't seen you around here before," he said with wide eyes and a philandering smile that revealed a pecan fragment on one front tooth.

Gritting her teeth at his nauseating flirtations she said, "I'm only temporary help, sir."

"Well, we'll see what we can do about that," he said reaching one hand down to rub her leg.

She was mortified at his suggestiveness and found herself wondering if she should throw up on him now, or wait until she reached the elevator. The sickening moment was interrupted by a giant—Calvin—entering the room.

Paulos' horny toad routine changed to intense drama at the sight of this man who sat down beside him. The young girl felt most grateful to the unexpected man. Paulos waved the girl back into the kitchen and waited until the door was closed to speak. "Did Gray get our message?"

"Word for word," said Calvin.

"Was it clean?"

"Totally. Except for a little coffee spill," he laughed reaching for a cold piece of buttered toast.

"What are you talking about?" Paulos shouted jerking the toast from Calvin's hand and throwing it across the room.

"Hey, no big deal," Calvin said with hands folded outward. "Ease up."

"Don't ever tell me to ease up, you big idiot. Watch yourself, or you'll end up like Duncan. Careless and caught and of no use to me anymore."

Calvin was big, but he was no idiot. From Paulos' abrupt chastening he deduced two things. First, the Boss was nervous; was it over the possibility of losing his neck or the reality of losing a million dollars a day, he couldn't say. Second, Duncan was on his way out.

Calvin had always liked Duncan. They had started out together, fifteen or twenty years ago, loading the refrigerated trucks and hauling their mixed payload—just enough frozen shrimp to hide keys of coke stacked floor to ceiling. In those days they could pack the white powder in just about anything from frozen pizza boxes to fish sticks. No one suspected a thing. And then the Rin-Tin-Tin dogs came along with their PhD noses and they had to move from the big cities to places along the coast where smelly shrimp was more readily available.

That was all right, since both he and Duncan had moved up to higher positions because of that change. It stinks on those docks when the heat is right and the shrimp are lying in the sun waiting to be packaged and frozen in with the stuff. He was much better off working closely with The Boss and his sharp tongue.

The productivity level was much higher now and that meant more money coming to him more frequently. It had been a good move for the network, but now his friend Duncan was about to be history. Calvin only hoped he wasn't the one to have to do it.

Paulos pushed his chair back from the table and snarled something to Calvin about meeting him in his office in a few minutes when he had finished his shower. Calvin was puzzled. Usually The Boss's mood was a little better than this after he had just been laid. He must really be worried. Calvin knew he didn't need to be late for their little meeting, but he felt like there was time for a morning snack. He walked into the kitchen and all eyes turned his way. When they saw it was Calvin, the room bellowed of sighs of relief that it wasn't Mr. Paulos.

"Good morning," one of the cooks said to him.

"Hello," he answered.

"Can we get you something this morning? Some coffee, maybe?"

"No, no coffee this morning," Calvin said rubbing his forehead with one hand, as the vision of the black man's blood and the coffee aroma filled his head.

The cook looked at the huge man and awaited his answer and wondered why Calvin wasn't having his usual morning snack of coffee and four Danishes.

A moment passed and Calvin said, "How about some hot cocoa? It was a little chilly out this morning. Bring it to me in Mr. P.'s office."

Calvin was on his third cup of cocoa and deep in the comics when Paulos made it into his office. "Listen up," he said as he popped Calvin on the shoulder and walked around behind the big onyx desk to have a seat. "We've got a lot more to do today. Now I want you to remember every last syllable I tell you. There will be no notes made whatsoever. That's where Duncan blew it, you know. Making notes on the computer. He wrote down every last name of the network members and every stinking place along the East coast where we make drops or process the goods. Damn, he is stupid."

Calvin drew the curtain a little more closed over the mental picture of Duncan he had in his mind.

Paulos continued on, "The kid took his flash drive and put it in that damn capsule. And that's what we've got to find to save our necks. Even if it did fall to the bottom of the ocean, it could wash ashore one day. I'm not going to feel any relief until I'm certain every search possibility has been exhausted. I'll give Gray a couple more days and then I'm not sure what I'll do with him, and that son of his, if they come up empty handed."

Calvin looked straight at his boss trying not to blink and trying to remember all of this lengthy dissertation. True, he was no idiot, but neither was he blessed with mounds of common sense.

"Calvin, I want you to get in touch with our men who are following the Gray kid. I want to know what he's been doing. Have someone sit, round the clock, and watch the monitors in the Ampt Hill house. The cops might find something if they start searching things and I want to know about it. Tell Mark to start tailing Gray again. Then call my pilot and tell him to get the jet ready. I want to leave Richmond this afternoon. Now don't screw up, Calvin. And, hey, send in that new little maid from the kitchen."

"O.K. Boss," Calvin said with a contemplating look on his face. He was trying to decide where to start.

"Well get going," Paulos shouted.

"Right," Calvin stood to leave. "What are you going to be doing?" he asked.

"What's it to ya? Get out of here."

While Paulos waited on Calvin to return with an update, the bulky Italian plugged numbers in his calculator and became increasingly frustrated. This snafu was costing him a ton of money. Operations were closed down tight and the goods had all been moved to new locations by now, so in essence they were paying double overhead costs. Profits were not coming in since inventory wasn't going out. He thought about "Dollar Signs Gray" and how he ought to be concerned with this aspect of the mess he had created, but all he seemed to worry about was his kid. And why, now, after all these years.

The telephone rang several times and it was other members of the network calling to express their feelings. The group census was to take Gray out if for nothing else than to prove a point. Tempers were boiling and money was virtually flying out the window. Paulos agreed with all the callers. They should all pay for this blunder, both of the Grays and Duncan too.

He lifted the receiver and pressed some numbers. From the middle desk drawer, he pulled a new fat cigar while he waited for an answer. After several rings someone said, "Hello."

"Geno, my friend," Paulos said in a quiet, but enthusiastic tone.

The voice on the other end said, "Paulos, it's been a while. Who is it this time?"

"Having any bargains today? Say, buy two get one free?"

"Afraid not. In fact, I've gone up on my prices. Units are sixty each now, but if a few pounds of shrimp were thrown my way you might narrow the margin," Geno laughed.

Paulos thought how this was all getting expensive, then of the lady at Fripp Island who had found the body and contemplated adding her name to the list when there was a knock at his office door.

"Stay put," Paulos said. "I'll be in touch."

Paulos' sexiest smile curved across his face in case it was the young girl, who was really trying his patience with her tardiness, as he said, "Come in."

It was only Calvin, but he seemed full of fervor and very anxious to speak.

"Where is she?" Paulos grunted disappointedly.

Calvin looked bumfuzzled and a deep, "Huuhh?" spilled from his lips.

"The maid, you shit for brains."

"Oh. She got sick and threw up right after breakfast. The cook said she vomited all over the place; that he'd be cleaning all day," Calvin said.

"All right, all right. I get the picture."

Calvin paced back and forth in front of Paulos' desk and began to dismiss items from his small memory bank one at a time. He touched his two index fingers together as if to say, "First of all," but didn't. He got right down to the guts of it all.

"Gray's skipped town so Mark can't tail him," Calvin said.

"The cops are all over the mansion. House, grounds, garage, everywhere. My man watching the monitors planted inside is worried they might find our cameras," Calvin said looking toward Paulos with a questioning eye.

"And, your pilot says the plane, excuse me 'JET.' He gets real upset when you call it a plane. Anyway, it won't be ready until late, late afternoon. They were working on it when I called. Just a tune up, but it will take 'em a while to put it back together."

It appeared to Paulos that Calvin was about to continue, but he could take no more. He stood up angrily and the leather chair beneath him was thrust backward.

"Don't you have any good news?" he hissed, hands in the air in a pleading way.

"Yeah, I do, as a matter of fact."

"Well, please enlighten me," Paulos said as he stroked the countable hairs on his head back into place.

"The kid hasn't moved. He's had a real vacation of a morning. A little breakfast, newspaper and now he's playing golf according to our man."

"Any contact with the broad?"

"You mean the Stevenson lady?

"Yes, I do," Paulos said impatiently.

"Not much, but he talked to her husband last night in a grocery store parking lot. Just walked right up to him like he knew him. After all that hiding around in Atlanta. Strange, isn't it?"

"Yes," Paulos said quietly, rubbing his chins and wondering if he was getting screwed.

Were they all in it together? Did those Stevensons have the capsule and Nathan and his kid were going to double cross him? Maybe that's why Nathan had the balls to get up from the table last night and leave before dinner. But, it still didn't make sense about this lady. She was just walking on the beach. If she were in it with them, she wouldn't have wanted the body found either. It was getting too confusing. Paulos had no patience for playing this game of ifs and suppositions. His methods were more to the point; get rid of the problem and anything near it. It had worked for over twenty years. Why change now? But before he had Nathan or any of them killed, he had to make sure that they weren't hiding the capsule. He would wait for one more conversation with Gray. That son of a bitch better call like he said he would.

"What are you thinking, Boss?"

"I'm thinking a lot. Tell Mark to get to Fripp. That's gotta be where Gray's headed since his son is still there. He's trying to win Father of the Year all of the sudden, so he's probably going to help the kid."

"Well, I wouldn't be so sure about that," Calvin said as if he were Sherlock Holmes himself.

"And why the hell wouldn't you, asshole?" Paulos spat back at him.

"Because, according to news from Richmond, the police think Gray may have had something to do with the murder of his groundskeeper." Calvin laughed out loud like a child who had just gotten away with stealing candy. "It seems the house-keeper found the body and went into hysterics. While she was there she kept mumbling something like, 'Mr. Gray's done it now. He killed my Richard.'"

"That was on the news?"

"No, that was on our monitor."

"The official word is that Gray is a possible suspect, but could not be reached for comment. This little trip to Fripp could be costly. Going out of town makes him appear a guilty man. Do you think I ought to phone up the cops and be an anonymous caller and drop the hint of his whereabouts?"

Paulos rubbed his freshly shaved chin and spoke with certainty, "No, they'll find him on their own, but when they do I want him to be real dead."

28

Kenan stuttered as he looked at the young man and said, "My golf ball landed in your courtyard." Then feeling like an already convicted criminal, he tried to explain to Ely Stevenson, why he had been upstairs instead of in the courtyard. The handsome young fellow who stood before Kenan had many of the girl's fine features. Kenan was certain they had to be siblings. He might be able to use him to get to the girl, but first he must get out of this situation.

Following a minute-long explanation of meeting the Stevenson's in the grocery parking lot noticing the sign on the golf course, the ball in the back yard and stopping to say, 'Hello,' Kenan finally allowed the tall guy to speak again.

"Do you play basketball?"

The perspiration instantly ceased pouring from Kenan's armpits as he realized that this member of the Stevenson family was not in the least bit threatened by the mouthy stranger who stood two feet away from him. Kenan tried hard not appear so nervous, now that the conversation had changed drastically and was on a less stressful key.

"Yes, I do. Not seriously since high school, but an occasional backyard game every now and then."

Kenan usually did shoot a few hoops when he was on Ampt Hill into the near shredded woven basket, but it was a game with imaginary players. And he always won. It would be interesting to see how he would perform in a one on one game with a real opponent.

"How about a short game?"

"Sure, my golf game has turned sour any way."

Kenan followed Ely through the courtyard and out of a gate on the opposite side of the courtyard from which he had entered. He stepped onto an asphalt surface and knew immediately he was going to get creamed.

He laughed and said to Ely, "You must play a little bit of ball."

"What makes you say that?" Ely asked in jest.

"Well, anyone with a court that runs the width of their home on the coast, with a goal at either end is probably pretty serious about basketball," Kenan said as he looked at the private court enclosed by a white lattice fence to match the courtyard.

Ely blushed a little and told Kenan about all of the scholarships he had been offered last year and how he finally decided on Clemson.

"Could I have a minute to warm up?" Kenan asked.

"Sure. I need to go get my shoes on anyway."

"Now wait a minute, I'm not exactly wearing the appropriate footwear either, you know," Kenan said pointing to his new golf shoes, thank goodness, shy of the metal spikes.

"You do have a point. I'll spot you three points and that should even up the odds."

"I'll take that."

"O.K., I'll be right back."

Ely picked up his bag from the back of the convertible parked in the drive and walked up the front steps. He found Kate listening to the answering machine. He caught the last few words of his Father's message.

"Dad's at Dataw playing golf, but I don't know where Mom is," Kate said questioningly.

"The golf cart's gone, so she's probably scooting around the Island," Ely said sitting down on one of the matching sofas in the large living room. He unzipped his bag and pulled out two long, black high top shoes.

"Did you have room in there for anything else?" Kate asked astonished at the size of the shoes.

"Yep, I have a pair of jeans and three t-shirts."

"And that's all?" Kate said, shaking her head.

"Well, I've got some clothes here, and besides the Polo shop is always open. And better yet, it's my birthday this weekend. No problem, Snoop."

Kate picked up one of the black leather blobs by the tongue of the shoe. "So why are you putting these on now?" she asked.

"I found someone to play a game with me."

"You did? So quickly? Where'd you find him?"

"Coming down the back stairs."

"What?" Kate asked, silently refusing to give him the other shoe until he explained himself.

When Kate had all the facts and accepted them as truth, she gave Ely his shoe.

"You are so fastidious," he said looking up at his sister who sipped on a beer.

"That's a big word for you, jock," she kidded Ely whose brain power excelled way beyond that of most athletes and all but one member of his graduating class.

"May I have a slug of that please?"

"It's almost gone. I'll bring you and your new buddy one down in a bit. That is if he's old enough," Kate said with a nod that insinuated the need for an answer to the unspoken family rule."

"Yes, from the looks of him, I believe he is legal in his own right."

The "legalities" of the drinking age had been a topic of conversation since Ely turned eighteen last year.

Stella was adamant in her belief that if the government could draft "her baby" at age eighteen and send him off to war, then he most certainly could drink a beer within the boundaries of his own home. Walker's interpretations of the law did not seem to float with his lovely wife on this issue, but he made no argument, because it did seem to him that she had a point.

Ely found Kenan dribbling the ball down to the back goal. "He has a pretty good lay-up," Ely thought to himself. "Ready to play?" he said.

"Ready as I'll ever be," Kenan answered. He actually felt very at ease with Ely, despite their miscalculated meeting.

"We'll play to fifteen, one point at a time. Win by two. Sound all right?"

"Sounds like a work out for me. Don't forget my three points."

The two pounded the asphalt for only five minutes and Kenan was left breathless while Ely whistled a Globe Trotter tune and spun the ball on his middle finger. Final score, fifteen to four.

Through short, deep breaths Kenan suggested they play again. Ely commended his determination and they began to dribble and block all over again.

Kate heard the familiar bouncing sound resume outside and sat back down at the piano bench to play a while longer. She had stopped to fulfill her promise and serve the boys a beverage after their game, but from the sound of things they were at it again. After playing a couple of songs from her favorite music book she decided to go on down and watch the guys play ball and catch a glimpse of any new moves Ely may have learned at Clemson. She grabbed three beers from the refrigerator and moved to the back door. Thankfully it was unlocked and she did not have to fumble with the door and cold drinks simultaneously. Kate walked through the courtyard, opened the gate and stepped onto the basketball court. The two players were at the opposite goal and she crossed the court and sat on a small bench in the grass that her Mom always called the cheerleading section. She put the cold drinks down beside her and heard Ely shout, "Game," just as the ball swished through the hoop.

"What good timing I have," she shouted in their direction as she popped the tops on the refreshments.

She could hear footsteps and heavy breathing approaching her and picked up two beers and stood to deliver them.

That's when she saw Kenan Gray for the first time. His blue eyes were hypnotic and his blonde hair was gorgeous, even with the edges trickling in sweat. Ely's voice freed her from his trance. "Well, let go."

"What?" she responded, shaking her head slightly.

"Let go of the beer," Ely said in slow distinct words as if he were speaking to an imbecile.

"Oh, sorry," Kate said in what Ely recognized as her "cutesy" voice. He had heard it many times before with many different boyfriends. But, why was she using it now on this guy? She didn't even know his name. That thought reminded Ely of his manners and he introduced the two who were already staring at each other.

"Nice to meet you," Kate said in that voice again.

"And nice to meet you, too," Kenan said accepting the beer she offered to him. "I have wanted one of these for a couple hours. Did you come out to beat me in basketball, too?"

"No," Kate laughed, "Tennis is my game."

"Oh, now that's a game I've played a little more frequently than basketball in the past five years. Maybe I could go for golf, basketball, and tennis all in one afternoon."

"That would make for a full day," Kate said smiling.

Ely recognized Kate's flirtatious smile too, and he quickly turned his back to Kenan and looked straight at his sister while sticking a finger down his throat and pretending to gag silently.

It didn't seem to faze her. Ely was a little disappointed since it usually was good for at least one of her eat-shit-and-die looks. Kate was in another world.

And his new friend Kenan seemed to be accompanying her. Ely felt like he should leave before he really did get sick.

He told Kenan that he enjoyed the games and that he hoped to see him around. He told Kate that he was taking the convertible down to The Beach Club to scout out their Mom and maybe catch a pickup game of basketball. There was no response, because no one was listening to him. Ely turned to walk to the car and as he turned the corner of the house he shouted, "Remember, you're too busy to get involved with anyone."

Kate and Kenan sat on the bench for a while and chatted about how he had met her parents, what had actually brought him to Fripp, where she went to school and other seemingly insignificant matters. This was all a prelude to the in-depth discussion that was to follow in the next three hours they spent together.

The sound of the ocean eventually beckoned them to the beach and they walked toward the sun on the wide stretch of sand. After a while they found it hard to walk and look into one another's eyes at the same time, so they sat down on the Crowe's boardwalk steps. Kate said they weren't usually down this time of year, but they wouldn't mind anyway.

The conversation delved deep when Kenan said, "You really do love this place don't you?"

Kate's eyes seemed to sparkle even more as she looked out at the water. Kenan watched the reflection of the waves breaking in her eyes and without warning, a tear edged its way out and rolled slowly down her cheek. Instinctively he touched her face to wipe it away. Her skin was soft, just like he knew it would be.

"What's wrong, Kate?"

"I do love this place. It's been our family retreat for almost all of my life. We had summer rental cottages until Mom and Dad finally built a dream home on our lot. But, now," she paused and her lips quivered as she tried to speak again. "Oh, I just hope things can be the way Mom and Dad always wanted them to be."

"I don't understand," Kenan said genuinely, for at this point he honestly did not.

Kate told Kenan all she knew about her Mother finding a boy named Phillip Dubose dead on the beach. She admitted that the tears were selfish ones over her concern for the incident ruining her parents new beginning here at Fripp. She explained how her Dad had called them last night and told them about the tragedy and how he insisted things were getting back to normal for them, but she and Ely had come to surprise them regardless.

Kenan sensed the obvious closeness of this family that had suddenly become very important to him. He felt remorse that his family business had caused them such a disturbance and possibly more turmoil if a murder trial should be in the making.

It surprised him to feel so hurt watching Kate cry. "Maybe this was it," he thought. He was uneasy with the thought that the time was now. Was this love? Was this what had changed all of his friends? Silent moments passed as he dealt with this new realization of love.

Kenan brushed back the hair that blew in Kate's tearful eyes and touched her cheek. He kissed her gently on the lips and she kissed him back. It felt so natural, like they had been together forever.

A parade of sea gulls circled overhead and sang a tantalizing tune, as if poking fun at the two lovebirds perched on the steps. Kate looked up at the beautiful white creatures with outstretched wings and began to laugh.

"Talk about a mood swing," Kenan said laughing along with her and placing an arm around her shoulder to pull her nearer him.

"I have never kissed anyone that I have only known for an hour. Especially like that. I must admit, though, I wanted to kiss you the moment I looked up to hand you that beer. You are rather gorgeous, you know."

Kenan wanted to be as honest as Kate, but somehow he didn't feel like the sentence, "And I wanted to kiss you the moment I saw you as I was peeking through the pantry doors," would fit in right now. He would find the right time to tell Kate everything that had happened in past few days and how he was connected in the situation. He would not allow there to be any skeletons in the closet at the beginning of this love that he had waited and wondered about for so long. But now was not the time.

"Then we should make a perfect couple because you are absolutely the most beautiful creation I have ever seen. Could I perhaps have that kiss now that you wanted to give me back at the house?"

Before she could answer their lips met again. When they parted and Kenan looked into Kate's eyes once more, he noticed that some tears still hung on to her thick eyelashes. He reached into his pocket and pulled out a handkerchief and wiped the tears away.

"Thank you, how gallant," Kate smiled. "Most guys your age have never heard of real handkerchiefs, especially one as lovely as this." She took the handkerchief and opened it to see the monogram more clearly. The stitches were very detailed and Kate recognized that it must be his family crest. The name "Gray" appeared on the bottom of the shield in distinctive letters.

"I suppose you're right, but my Mother gave it to me the Christmas before her death, and it's very special to me."

Kenan's eyes squinted as he looked directly into the sunlight and away from Kate. She could sense his grief and said, "I'm so sorry."

"It was all so senseless," Kenan said, allowing himself to really think about his Mother's death, and not pushing it to the back of his mind to escape the pain it caused.

Recognizing that Kenan was completely focused on his mother, Kate said softly, "Would you like to talk about it?"

"I think I'd like for you to know about it. I seem to want to tell you everything and to know every little detail about you," Kenan said, looking deep into her eyes. "But I don't want to scare you off." He smiled.

Kenan took a deep breath and began. "My Mother was murdered in our own home by burglars, so they say. I don't understand how they determined it was thieves when nothing was missing. I have accepted that I may never have a more thorough explanation. She was my best friend, Kate. My father never had much interest in me until she was killed, so she and I were especially close."

Kate listened with sympathy building in her heart. She could not imagine losing one of her parents, especially in that way. They were so incredibly close; it was unthinkable to her just how she could ever manage the suffering of a loss comparable to Kenan's.

"She was shot once in the back of the head, and the family doctor assured me that she felt no pain, as if that were a consolation. No one heard any shots and none of the help was around. They say Mom walked in while the burglary was in progress, but it just doesn't add up. Vera, our housekeeper, never leaves the house. And on that day someone called and told her that her granddaughter had fallen at school and needed to be taken to the hospital. They couldn't seem to get in touch with Vera's daughter so Richard, the groundskeeper, took Vera to the school. They found Vera's granddaughter sitting happily in her classroom and no one knew anything about a telephone call. When they returned, they found Mom on the living room floor."

"The police just ignored all of these obvious happenings that would point to murder?" Kate asked in astonishment.

"They did investigate, but just not enough to convince me," Kenan admitted.

"Was your father satisfied?"

"He had a nervous breakdown. That's a story for another day. Or another week, maybe. It would take me a long time to explain Nathan Gray."

Kenan reached for Kate's hand and suggested they walk for a while. "Thanks for listening," he said.

"Thanks for sharing."

They stood and Kate handed Kenan the handkerchief.

"You know you never return a handkerchief that has been used," Kenan kidded her.

"What? Do you think I have cooties?"

"If you do, I want to catch all of them."

He lifted her in the air in flash and carried her down the steps before placing her safely on the sand. "And if you take it with you, I can be assured that I may call on you again to retrieve my possession."

They were laughing and smiling and spinning in their love struck world, where neither had expected to be. They walked and talked and held hands, and even kissed some more. The conversation seemed to steer away from most serious subjects that might hinder the fun they were having, but they did speak of one very serious matter: the fact that they had fallen in love.

"I am totally responsible and usually try to analyze everything, and always where guys are concerned. Maybe this really isn't happening. Maybe I am still on the airplane asleep, and this is just a dream. Oh, I would be so sad if it were only a dream," Kate said disappointedly.

"Does this feel like a dream?" Kenan kissed her again and lifted her off the ground while they held each other tight.

29

After Stella dropped Julie off at her house, she parked the golf cart back in its special little spot in the garage and silently praised Walker for always leaving the key in the ignition. She had been hopeful that his car might be in the garage when she returned, but no such luck.

Stella had declined Julie's kind invitation to come to their house and wait for Walker. She was beginning to feel like a bug that just wouldn't go away. She planned to stretch out in the hammock and listen to her stomach growl while she imagined Walker saying, "I told you those jeans should have been disposed of a while back. Look what a mess they got you in to." It was already two thirty so he should be home any minute.

She laughed to herself at Walker's inability to pass up a chance to say, "I told you so." But then, to be such a success in the legal field, one had to believe that they were always right, she supposed. It was a laughable characteristic to her, and so it never caused any annoying feelings.

She let the dogs come in the screened porch with her and gave their long ears a nice scratch. The sound of iron meeting a golf ball told Stella that someone had made a nice chip onto the eighth green just to the right of their house. She walked around to the back porch and turned another corner onto the side porch. A pleased golfer was approaching a ball that appeared to be merely ten inches from the hole. He popped it in and rested his hand on the flag post preparing to pull it out should his unfortunate opponent ever get out of the sand trap.

As she turned around to start back for the hammock, Stella noticed a golf cart parked beside the lattice fence enclosing their courtyard. That seemed strange to her. And as she looked around a bit puzzled, Stella heard a faint familiar squeak. The screened door on the other side of the old Gullah table was moving slightly from the suction of the gentle breeze. She moved closer and saw, in frightened amazement, the inner door standing open.

After reliving the entire episode of Phillip for Julie earlier today, Stella felt a bit uneasy to say the least. She looked down at her canine protectors. Apparently there were no unusual scents since there was no serious sniffing going on. But who was she kidding, the only way they could kill an intruder would be by drowning them with saliva.

Maybe she was over reacting again. No, the doors were definitely all closed and locked tight earlier, she was certain. She took a deep breath and went inside.

30

"**I** know what you mean, though," Kenan was saying to Kate sarcastically. "Things like this just don't happen in our generation. We didn't even meet in a bar or online. This will probably never work out."

"It very well may not," Kate said, "but I'm certainly going to enjoy this feeling while it lasts."

"I was only kidding," Kenan answered in astonishment. "Personally, I think we should go ahead and decide on the style of rocking chairs we prefer for when we're old and gray and sitting on those rambling porches back at your house."

"Back at my house," Kate said alarmingly. "How long have we been gone?"

"Oh, just a few hours," Kenan guessed looking at his watch. "Or maybe all afternoon."

"I really need to see my parents." Kate said anxiously. "I need to see how Mom is doing."

"And I guess I really need to return the golf cart to the pro shop. They may start to think an alligator ate me."

Kate looked a little confused and Kenan told her about what had happened earlier that day. He explained how the anxiety of it all had led to him hitting a poor shot right into their courtyard. Which had led him to her. Simple deduction told them they owed the alligator living in the lagoon on the eighth tee box a hearty steak dinner.

They reached the boardwalk to Kate's house and the conversation that had been endless seemed to cease.

"What do we do now?" Kenan asked. "It's really too soon to get married I guess," he said laughingly, still in disbelief of how their afternoon had transpired.

"Not really. I've always planned on wearing Mom's wedding gown and it's waiting in my closet upstairs, all boxed up," Kate said through a big grin on her face. "But, why don't we just plan a day that requires a few less details for tomorrow, like tennis. You really need to see me on the court. I'm pretty good."

"Changing the subject, huh? You're probably right though. O.K., tennis it is." Kenan smiled. "Do you think we could have dinner tomorrow night, too?"

"Yes, I do. That will be our first official date. Better make it special," Kate warned as they started up the steps toward the house.

"Can you come in for a minute?" Kate asked.

"I could but I think it best that I shouldn't. At least right now. You need to be with your family. I'll reserve a court for around eleven tomorrow morning, how's that?"

"That's good, but come over earlier so you can have time to get to know everyone."

They had reached the point along the walkway from the beach where their paths would part, for now. Steps led downward to the front drive and steps led upward to the side porch. Kate stood on the first step of the stairs leading to the porch and looked at Kenan, eye to eye. And lips to lips, and chest to chest and so on. They parted silently after Kenan kissed her more tamely on the forehead.

Kate floated up the stairs and around the porch to the back door. She heard voices inside and tried to disguise the passion, she knew was written all over her face that Kenan's last kiss had conjured up within her once again.

She subdued herself as best she could and opened the screen door and walked inside. Everyone was sitting at the breakfast booth and Kate surmised that they had not witnessed that last heated kiss and she felt a little more at ease.

The screen door closed with a soft pop, and all eyes turned to Kate. Her Mom screamed and shouted and shooed her father out of the booth so that she could get up herself.

Walker and Stella hugged Kate simultaneously with a grip that lasted forever it seemed, and she held on tightly in return and enjoyed every moment of it.

"All right, break it up, break it up," Ely's deep voice thundered through the huddle. "You've got some explaining to do, Snoop. Where have you been all afternoon? Mom was getting ready to call security about you, too."

"About me, too? Who did she call about the first time?" Kate asked as the huddle disassembled. Her answer looked as though it would come in normal Stella fashion. Only after the details were told.

Stella began to talk fast and unfold the scenario of her day. The lost key; the locked door; the unlocked door; Ely pulling into the drive in a convertible; Walker finally home from Dataw chastising her about losing the key. Anxiety, excitement and then worry over where Kate could be all afternoon. She was talking with her hands and very theatrical as though she might cry at any minute. Then she stopped and stood still, opened her arms and said, "But it's all fine now because here you are and what a glorious surprise visit you and Ely have gifted to us." And then Stella breathed, finally.

The telephone rang as if to signify the end of a play and her mom answered it and said, "Thank you so much for checking into things. In the meantime, Ely has returned home and explained everything to me. I should have called you back to let you know what had happened." Stella paused then said, "Yes, things are fine."

"I suppose I jumped to conclusions, once again," Stella admitted, looking to Walker for forgiveness.

"Well, after the ordeal you've been through, a little suspicion is in order," Kate consoled her Mom.

"We've lived through the 'little suspicion' phase, and it looks like we're entering full blown paranoia," Walker laughed hugging his wife from behind.

Stella knew he was teasing her and thought nothing of the comment.

"Mom always was one to rely on security guards and policemen to help with her problems. Remember when she dialed 911 about the black snake on the patio in Clarkesville?" Ely said.

"Now wait a minute, you guys were just babies. I couldn't go out chasing a snake and protect you at the same time," Stella said in her own defense.

"But, the Animal Control Man, two Police Officers and two Sheriff's Deputies could. Right?" teased Ely.

"It took me a long time to live that one down," Walker said. "Every time I went in the courthouse for the few weeks after your mother's 911 call, someone would always ask me if I had seen any snakes lately."

"I was a little more courageous this time," Stella said patting herself on the back. "I walked right through the open door and .."

"And walked straight to the telephone and called Security," Ely said.

"I don't understand?" Kate said. "Why would you call security because the door was open? You never lock doors around here."

Stella explained to Kate that they had begun locking the doors more frequently since she had found Phillip on the jetty. She went on to tell her about losing the key and being locked out all day. "I'm just glad you had your key, Kate, so you two weren't locked out when you arrived," Stella said to her daughter. "Oh, enough about that. Tell us about 'Mr. Gray,'" Stella said dreamily.

Kate did not seem to respond the way they had all expected. She had a puzzling look on her face and appeared to be in deep thought.

"What's wrong?" Walker asked, knowing his daughter well enough to see her wheels were turning in confusion.

Kate spoke softly and slowly, "I didn't bring my keys with me. The front and back doors were unlocked; I'm certain."

31

Marguerite had spent most of the morning sorting through Phillip's room. The cardboard boxes she had brought home from the grocery remained empty. She just wasn't ready for this yet. How could this have happened to her son just when things were starting to materialize for them? They could have been a happy family; she was certain of that. Nathan was really warming up to Phillip and Marguerite felt that the time had come that she should tell Phillip the truth about his father.

She sat Indian-style in the middle of Phillip's bedroom floor, clutching his pillow, and daydreamed that the three of them were in Richmond, living in the mansion on Ampt Hill, which she had never seen. She would finally be the wife of the affluent Mr. Nathan Kenan Gray, Jr. and the lady of the lovely estate. The dream that had filled nearly two decades of her life would culminate in grandeur and elegance. She would have proven that she was a masterful artist of taking what one wants.

Marguerite remembered how the only problem for so many years had been Nathan's wife. Her laugh was now near crazed as she thought how things have a way of working out if they are planned just right. She looked down, rubbed Phillip's pillow, and broke into tears once more. She certainly hadn't planned for this tragedy and now nothing seemed to matter at all.

Nathan had phoned several times to console her, but they were aimless attempts. She wanted to scream and shout at him for not coming to be with her. She needed someone to hold her, not just phone and send flowers. But she knew she could never act that way with Nathan for he was the only one she had left to love.

Marguerite stood up and laid the pillow back on the bed and smoothed it in to place. She left the room and closed the door. She walked down the hall and into the living room of her ocean front villa beside The Beach Club. The clock on the mantle tinged daintily twice and forced Marguerite to be aware of the time of day. Since Phillip's death there had been no beginning or end to each day.

For the first time in days, Marguerite walked over to the picture window in the living room and pulled the drapes open. The sun flooded her pale face and her eyes squinted instinctively. It was a gorgeous day. She opened the sliding door and stepped onto the balcony. To her right she could see people sitting by the pool and also around the cabana bar.

The sound of the waves forced her to look at the ocean, which she had avoided since the day Phillip's body had been found. As her eyes scanned the horizon, chills ran up her spine at the thought of seeing a shrimp boat. Luck was on her side and the only vessel visible was a sailboat. It was inevitable that she would see the trawlers, boats she had once thought so graceful but now despised. She had to hate something or blame something or someone for Phillip's death. It had crossed her mind that Nathan should be that someone, but then that vicious Duncan had been apprehended and charged with murder. She often wondered if Nathan suspected her secret and would retaliate.

She walked back in the house leaving the door open for the breeze. Marguerite sat down in a chair in front of the reflecting glass door and saw herself. She looked down at her hands and saw the chipping nail polish; as she surveyed the rest of her body, matters didn't improve. What would her endless collection of suitors think of her now?

Even though she had not had her true love, as her own, for all these years, she had others. Marguerite had always tried to take care of herself. She was aware many thought her appearance to be a bit seductive. Everyone needed a style and that was just the one she had chosen years ago.

She walked back to the master suite and turned the shower to scalding hot. After a long while she emerged and began her ritual with face creams, nail polish, and the trusty old curling iron. She shivered with fright as the telephone beside the bed rang loudly and startled her. The silence in the villa had been so constant that any noise at all seemed deafening. With one eyelash on and one off, she moved through to the bedroom and answered the call, "Hello."

"Marguerite? Is that you?"

"Yes," she said with excitement building in her voice. "Yes, Nathan it's me, of course. Please tell me you're coming to see me soon."

"I'll do better than that. I'll tell you that I'm in Beaufort."

"You're kidding," Marguerite squealed.

"But, listen carefully, I need your help."

Nathan told Marguerite that he had some auto trouble on the trip down and that she needed to pick him up in Beaufort. He explained that the mechanic was located near Bay Street and that he would walk down and wait for her at their favorite restaurant, Gatsby's.

Marguerite hung up the telephone and screamed with delight. One glance down the hall at the closed door of Phillip's bedroom brought her screams to a halt. Her method of dealing with misery had always been to find someone who needed her, if it were only for one night. Sex had been a temporary answer to the misery of being without Nathan. Perhaps sex with Nathan could mitigate the pain of living without Phillip. She knew it wasn't a cure-all, but it was the way her twisted mind worked.

Marguerite knew she was a little crazy, or why would she have been so obsessed with the same man for all these years. Why else would she have fallen to such desperate and evil measures two years ago to finally try and make that man hers?

She walked over to the closet as the urgency to have him in her grew unbearably. From her very large lingerie drawer she chose a pair of black, fishnet panty hose and then grabbed a black short skirt from the closet. After a little decision making a white shear blouse with pockets over the bosoms won over a bustier and jacket set. After weighting down her body with costume jewelry she was ready for the hardest selection of all: the shoes. Marguerite peered into a closet at the endless array of labeled shoeboxes. She carefully pulled out a pink box from the third shelf and opened the lid. Inside, a pair of black high-heeled sandals sat waiting for her.

"These will be perfect," she said out loud to the empty room.

She clip-clopped out of the villa for the first time since the funeral and just as she was about to get in the car, she decided to unbutton one more button on the already gaping blouse. "It was time she felt better," she assured herself.

32

"I'd like a beer and a shot of Wild Turkey American Honey on the side," Nathan told the bartender at Gatsby's. "And let me have an order of these fried grouper strips," he added, twirling the stand-up brochure on the bar around and round with one finger. He felt a little better now that he had arranged for his car to be hidden. He had given Reb, the backyard mechanic on Bladen Street, two hundred and fifty dollars cash, to keep his car in the garage behind his home until further notice.

If it wasn't enough to be worried about Paulos and his band of gunmen, now he was a fugitive, running from the Richmond Police. The bartender placed Nathan's beverages on the edge of the shadowy area of the bar where Nathan had chosen to sit while he waited for Marguerite. It was most unlikely that his face should be flashed across any television screen in the Lowcountry, but no need to chance it either. The dark side of the bar would do for now, even as the sunny terrace called him.

Nathan attacked the cold beer and slugged down the whiskey with a jerk of the head. It burned just enough to feel good. He motioned for the bartender to bring another shot, and without warning the news report from his car radio roared in his ears once again. It had nearly paralyzed him the first time he heard it, now, recalling it here, he was simply numb.

"Top news story this hour: A man was found shot to death this morning on the property of Richmond's renown businessman, Nathan Gray. Details are sketchy at the present time, however, Mr. Gray is a suspect and cannot be located. If you have any information concerning his location, please call the Richmond authorities".

The announcement had shocked him beyond belief, but it only took him about half of a minute to realize what was going on. Paulos was speaking to him in his sickening language. This was a threat, a scare tactic to get Nathan moving just a little more quickly. Kenan would be devastated with this news.

Nathan understood Paulos' message, but the strange twist was that he should be a suspect in Richard's murder. That was obviously a development Paulos hadn't planned on, because he knew Nathan needed to get to Fripp to further the search efforts, and by all means did not need to be apprehended by the police. Everything is such a mess, Nathan thought.

In a short while, the bartender brought the steaming grouper to Nathan and he pointed to the empty beer mug and shot glass, asking Nathan if he wanted another round. Nathan did, and he was relaxing more and more with each drink he downed. It was good to relax, but it clouded the reality of the situation he was in, filling his head with one thought: Marguerite and her massive mammaries and the fact they were in route to rescue him.

It wasn't long after he had finished the grouper appetizer that those same massive mammaries he had been dreaming of jiggled into the restaurant, shielded only by a doubled layer of sheer fabric, and joined Nathan at the bar. Their greeting was more heated than either expected would occur in a public place, but the dark corner of the bar proved to enhance their first few moments together.

Nathan's hands were drawn to her breasts like magnets and as they kissed forcefully, he squeezed them with equal strength. Leaving one sandal on the floor, Marguerite slid a fishnet leg over the top of Nathan's legs. His attentions were drawn to the warmth pouring out from under her skirt and his hands roamed lower. Without speaking, Nathan threw some bills on the bar and led Marguerite and her bouncing bosoms out of the restaurant.

Marguerite was on top of the world as she paraded out of the restaurant on Nathan's arm. She felt incredibly sexy and the aching inside of her became more intense and vast with each step they took. Once in the car, they engaged in more foreplay, though the console got in their way.

Nathan cranked the engine and pulled into traffic on Bay Street. After crossing the bridge to Lady's Island, Nathan made an unexpected right hand turn onto a sandy road. He made another turn and sped along with the moss filled trees flying past them until they reached another bend in the road. It seemed to Marguerite that they were in a secret enchanted forest as the sun peeked through the dense brush in long, narrow rays. What a perfect place for some of her passion games.

Nathan stopped the car and pulled Marguerite on top of him with urgency. He pulled her blouse off and threw it in the back seat and played once again with the chest he had bought a few years ago.

Close to an hour later, Marguerite's white sports coupe drove away from the enchanted forest and continued on toward Fripp. The two finally spoke to one another in idle chatter rather than body language. Admittedly, neither wanted to spoil their first hours together with talk that would most certainly lead to tears. There would be time for that later.

Nathan lied and told Marguerite that while he was here he was going to try to find a buyer for the shrimp boat docked at Johnson Creek. In order for Nathan to have time to snoop around for the capsule, time away from Marguerite was necessary, but not easy to obtain. He knew Marguerite would not go near the docks, so selling the shrimp boat should prove to be a successful lie. He merely explained that he wanted to get rid of as many bad memories as possible, for her benefit, as well as his own.

Marguerite thanked him for his considerate thoughtfulness and they drove in silence for a few miles.

"Why don't we stop at one of these seafood markets and pick up some shrimp or crab for dinner?" Nathan suggested.

"I'm ashamed to say we would need more than seafood to put together a meal from my kitchen. I've lived off of cereal and toast for the past week or so, and my cupboard is bare. But, I've got a better idea. Let's go to The Beach Club and have a romantic dinner tonight. How does that sound?" Marguerite asked.

She saw the look of disappointment on Nathan's face and was about to give in, when Nathan said, "O.K., if you can promise me a romantic table in a dark corner, so I can have you all to myself." He knew he couldn't stay cooped up in her villa every night, so better to get the dining-out over with early.

Nathan had no plans or schemes at the present time for searching for the capsule. He knew he needed some time to develop his strategy, but he felt as though it were a waste of time. This was like looking for the proverbial needle in a haystack. A light went on over his head, and he suddenly felt stupid for having not thought of it before. He could lie. He could lie to Paulos and tell him he found the capsule, but nothing was inside of it.

True, it may be a temporary solution to the problem, but it would be a solid answer for Paulos at the moment. Which hopefully would make him call his bullies off, and relieve Nathan's fears of any further killing. Kenan's face popped into his mind and he shook his head as if to completely erase the horrid thought.

As the tension lines in his forehead relaxed Marguerite's painted nails crawled up his thigh.

"I have better things to do this afternoon than think about Paulos," Nathan thought as he enjoyed Marguerite's handiwork.

33

"Are you going to finish your shrimp bisque, Mom," Ely asked Stella as he moved a little closer around the table toward her and dipped his spoon into the gold-rimmed bowl.

"Yes, I was. But, if you promise not to turn the bowl up and drink it like you do at home, I'll let you finish it for me," Stella smiled at her son.

Kate hurriedly ate the five remaining scallops she had chosen from The Beach Club menu as her appetizer, before Ely started grazing in her direction. She watched her parents as they watched Ely eating. They had always loved to see him eat. Once, when he was three, he ate a six pack of chocolate ice cream sandwiches in half an hour. The baby-sitter, Robin, was unaware that he could open the freezer by himself and was shocked to realize that the ice cream he had been nursing for thirty minutes-was actually one of many. He hadn't even gotten a stomachache over the incident. The big guy could eat.

The shrimp bisque disappeared quickly and with the beautifully set table absent of anything edible at the moment, Ely began bouncing his knee nervously and Kate thought at any minute his Achilles tendon may experience a sudden turbo spring and send the table sailing across the room over the heads of the well-dressed members.

Thankfully her dad suggested that he and Ely check the score of the football game on the television upstairs in the bar. She watched as her dad and younger brother, who indeed did clean up very well, exited the dining room obviously in an intense conversation about the probable score of the game. They were both clad in navy blazers and gray slacks, an unplanned coincidence, and moved across the floor with an identical stride.

Suddenly, Kate found herself imagining Kenan dressed in a navy blazer and necktie. She knew he would look incredible, but she really needed to concentrate on her family now. She tried to focus more surely on some quality time during dinner rather than daydreaming of a guy she had met only a few hours ago.

"I am glad Ely left some of his clothes down here at the end of the summer," Kate laughed to her Mom.

"No kidding. He popped into the house this afternoon just as I was looking through his bag that I found lying on the living room floor. Even in my confused state of the situation; I thought it was a very light load," Stella laughed.

"You know, the whole locked or unlocked door situation really puzzles me, Mom."

Stella felt her muscles tighten at the uncertainties that existed in her mind over the strange occurrences of the afternoon. There was no doubt in her mind that all of the doors were locked when she returned from her walk. It was a complete mystery to her as to how they became unlocked by the time the children arrived on Fripp. Walker's suggestion that as the day grew warmer, perhaps the doorknobs and locks loosened up somewhat. That theory was believable since the doorknobs were very hard to turn at times due to the salty air. So, for now, that would be the explanation for this weird occurrence and Stella was determined to enjoy every moment of this surprise visit from her children. She tucked all the doubts and questions she had about the matter back in the corner of her mind where she had stored her doubts about the strange man with the base-ball cap at The Ritz. There they could rest together, and hope-fully, vanish from lack of substance and never plague her again.

Suddenly Stella felt as though she needed to stretch her legs. She touched Kate's hand and said, "Sweetie, I'll be right back. I'm going to the ladies' room."

She moved in and out of tables toward the other side of the restaurant, smiling at acquaintances as she passed. Stella disap-peared around the corner and walked down a short hallway to the restrooms. Upon approaching a dark green door marked with a brass silhouette of a woman's profile, Stella reached for the shiny door handle and stepped inside.

The two painted doors on the other side of the double basin counter were closed, thus occupied, so Stella waited patiently and primped in the mirror. She noticed a black quilted clutch purse lying on the end of the counter, with a handkerchief resting on top of it with a striking monogram of a family crest. Stella took one step closer to read the small letters at the bottom of the crest. She couldn't quite make the letters out. Was it G...R... or no, maybe S...H... she con-templated. She made a mental note to start carrying reading glasses along with her.

The sound of a toilet flushing and a door opening drew her attention to a person standing in front of her. It was Marguerite in the flesh and Stella's mind and tongue were frozen. It went unnoticed in the midst of Marguerite's babbling on about ruining their dinner date with tears of Phillip, and how was she ever going to get through this, but she hoped she hadn't made a mess of his handkerchief with mascara, and just look at her face. She was a mess, inside and out.

"Oh no, Marguerite, you look lovely tonight. I am glad you feel like getting out."

Stella tried to console her with concerned eyes and a gentle pat on her clammy bare shoulder, but she knew her words were not making it past Marguerite's earlobe. In a fleeting attempt to be kind, Stella handed Marguerite a tissue from the box on the counter and the woman tucked it into her quilted purse along with the monogrammed handkerchief.

Stella breathed a sigh of relief as the woman exited the bathroom. She had no earthly idea how she would handle such a tragedy herself, so she certainly wouldn't pass judgment on this woman.

After a moment, Stella moved back through the crowded dining room where Kate waited for her. She watched her beautiful daughter as she approached their table and could see by her facial expression that she was deep in thought of Kenan Gray.

Kate was shocked back to earth with the sudden appearance of her Mother, and she sat up straight and tall in her chair and suddenly said without any prefacing, "So, how are you really feeling, Mom? Do you need to talk about anything? That's why Ely and I came home, just to make sure you are really handling this horrible ordeal in a healthy way. You know, get it all out and then put it behind you." Kate was shaking her head in affirmation as if she had been pondering this situation the entire time Stella had been in the restroom.

Stella burst into laughter and moved over into the chair beside Kate. "I realize why you came home, honey, and I appreciate it more than you know."

"I feel a 'but' in there somewhere," Kate interrupted.

"Buuuuttt," Stella said slowly as to not disappoint her. They both laughed and Stella reached for her daughter's hand and said, "Let's talk about him."

Kate's face blushed in all of its normal places, and then some, at the mention of Kenan.

She paused and at the insistence of her Mother's glare, she said, "It's crazy. It's absolutely crazy, but I'm sure I'm in love. Completely in love," she professed squeezing Stella's hand tightly and nodding her head in assurance as she so often did when she spoke.

"Mother, it scares me very much. This has never happened to me so suddenly before. Please don't have a stroke when I say this, but I would marry him tomorrow, and," she looked pleadingly at her Mother for help or advise, or maybe permission, Stella was not sure which.

"And?" Stella said.

"And, we've talked about getting married. I mean he hasn't really proposed," Kate said with exaggerated nods to the left and right now. "But, we just touched on it in passing. I told him about your wedding gown in the closet just waiting for the big day." She lapsed into love land again as Stella sat speechless in total disbelief.

Stella reached for the bottle of Cabernet on the table and poured each of them another glass. Stella lifted her glass toward her lips, hoping that perhaps this reserve vintage might numb the shock of Kate's admittances. Just as Stella was clearing her throat and preparing to speak words of advice, including slow things down, take it easy and really get to know each other, the spot lights under the pear trees outside the picture window beside them became aglow. Dusk had turned to darkness. The almost bare limbs were highlighted as well as the red leaves that puddled beneath each individual tree. Their color was brilliant. Just as brilliant as the leaf Walker had surprised her with only a week or so ago at Gatsby's, back when things had been unblemished.

Their kiss on the deck of the Tiger Den was once again upon her lips and the realization that they in fact did name their son Ely was ringing clearly in her mind. Those two young college coeds had taken a chance with love at first sight and it had worked emphatically. How could she deny her own daughter a chance at that same happiness by saying those trite words that mothers are supposed to say to their impulsive children, especially where love and passion were concerned.

Stella looked at her Kate with tears in her eyes and was silent.

"Oh, Mother, please don't do this. Don't cry. I don't want to be the cause of any more tears," Kate pleaded quietly.

"These are happy tears my darling." Stella raised her glass and waited for Kate to poise her own. "Here's to my intelligent and sensitive daughter. Always follow your mind and your heart, not necessarily in that order, and if that leads you to Kenan Gray, then I wish you the best of love." They touched their glasses.

"Oh, Mother, that was beautiful," Kate said as she caught the spilling tears with her napkin. "I'm going to have to write that down so I can always remember your words. I'm so very touched and happy and impressed."

"Me, too," Stella agreed. "That was pretty well said on such short notice."

They toasted their glasses together again, with more zeal this time.

"Now sit back," Stella insisted. "I have a story to tell you. Once upon a time, in a little college town," she began.

Kate looked at her Mother as though now was a strange time to share a fairy tale, but as she listened the message became unequivocally clear. When Stella had finished, Kate asked, "Why haven't you ever told me that story about you and Daddy before?"

"Well, I suppose we just always started from the wedding. You always used to look at our wedding pictures and ask a million questions. But there were never many questions about our first meeting, so I guess I forgot to mention it.'

"Or maybe you were saving it for a special time like this," Kate smiled proudly.

Kevin, the waiter, appeared beside Stella and politely asked if there was a problem with their salads. Kate and Stella looked down at the table and saw the Hearts of Palm salads staring back at them.

"No, Kevin dear. There is not a thing wrong with our salads. The presentation is excellent. We simply have been busy gabbing and honestly didn't realize you had served them. Please go ahead and bring our dinner out if it's ready. We'll just eat everything together. Oh, and would you mind getting Walker and Ely from the bar, please?"

"I don't think you'll have to, Kevin. Here they come down the stairs now," Kate said.

Before Walker and Ely sat down at the table, Stella said quietly to Kate, "Now, I'm not going to mention all of this to your father right now, I'll let you tell him, but, please don't tell him tonight. You do realize that he still has high hopes that you'll become a nun one day?"

"You ladies didn't have to wait for us. You should have gone ahead and started on your salads," Walker said in his gentlemanly tone.

"Why we wouldn't have dreamed of starting without you," Stella said to Walker patting his hand and smiling tactfully at Kevin as he served the bread.

A similar smile was returned to Stella with a bonus wink of the eye that only she could see. "Your dinner will be out in a moment," he said as he turned to leave.

Talk of all of the possible ways the Stevenson Family could celebrate Ely's birthday dominated much of the conversation during dinner. The sautéed oysters that sat atop each of their entrees as a garnish helped them to make the final decision. They would have an oyster roast on the beach Saturday night.

Stella insisted that they have The Beach Club handle all of the food and spirits for the party, leaving them more time to spend together since this was a short visit. "And, not to mention," she said quietly, casting a thoughtful eye toward Walker, "You never have really enjoyed digging the oyster pit anyway, Honey."

"Now wait just a minute," Walker protested.

"No, she's right, Dad," Ely said, finally coming up for air from his double order of buttermilk flounder. "You always insist on doing it, but you really hate every minute of it. It's kind of like the deal with the Christmas tree every year. You always put it in the stand and twirl it around while we say, 'A little to the right or a little to the left,'" Ely laughed as he moved his hands to either side. "And then you have to get it up the front stairs, in the house and hope and pray it doesn't fall. Now, you can't tell me you enjoy that."

Before Walker had a chance at a rebuttal, Kate chimed in, "Remember the year Dad nailed the whole tree stand to the living room floor?"

"If you guys want to wash dishes to pay for your dinner, just keep it up" Walker threatened. They proceeded from there into a series of hilarious family stories.

The man at the corner table with his back to the Stevensons had heard just about all he could stand from the All-American-Family for one night. He had learned some interesting details to report to Paulos and he needed to phone him before it was too late in the evening. It seemed to him that the conversation had turned to mush anyhow. He signed the check in one of his many aliases and left the dining room, moving so closely beside their table that he could smell Mrs. Stevenson's perfume. Duncan was right about the lady being a looker, he thought. But, then Duncan didn't have much time left for women, did he? Mark walked through the French doors that led from the restaurant down a sidewalk to the gazebo. As he breathed in the salty air he thought how this little beach party was really going to make Geno's job easy.

Now that he knew Nathan was on the island, if he could just get him to this birthday bash, Geno would really love him. He could be done in a matter of seconds. That was a stretch though since Nathan and his legit son didn't seem to be comingling on the island. He better make a separate plan for Nathan. Mark had done some pretty good work for the boss during his few hours on the Island. The Beach Club proved to be a central meeting place and he was able to take care of several things at once.

He wished he had been able to hear what Nathan and the dead guy's Mother had discussed over dinner, but from the position of her foot during their meal it was doubtful they spoke of anything other than what they were having for dessert.

It was most unusual that he and Nathan hadn't met over the course of the years of their involvement with the network. They had indeed spoken over the telephone, but never had they seen one another, face to face. He wondered if Gray had sense enough to realize he was being followed. Surely he did, but just not by whom.

He turned away from the dark sea thinking of the good news he had to report to Paulos. He walked slowly down the path and across the lawn where he had seen a group enjoying a casual game of croquet late this afternoon when he arrived. This was a real nice place. Maybe he could bring the family down next summer. Things around here were getting ready to sizzle now, but by then everything should be back to normal.

34

The breeze left a definite chill on Nathan's cheek this morning as he stood on the balcony of Marguerite's villa. He supposed the Indian Summer the Islanders had been enjoying was coming to a close.

The noise leaked through the door behind him that he had purposely left cracked, in hopes of replacing some of the stale oxygen inside with the exhilarating ocean air. Nathan had not realized the extreme loneliness Marguerite was feeling until they reached the villa yesterday. It was obvious to him that she had chosen to mourn the death of their son in seclusion. True, it may not have been by choice, considering she had not acquired many close friends over the course of the years living on Fripp.

Nathan knew the type of woman Marguerite was and this new awareness of the situation did not surprise him. Her interests did not lie in befriending other women, maybe their husbands, but not them. He was almost certain she was perceived about the Island, and probably Beaufort too, as a flirtatious, dangerous and loud woman. She was all of those things and worse, but last night they had shared a new emotion between them.

Last night after dinner, two people who had, for years, only shared passion, grieved over a son whose life they had never united in until now.... after death. Needless to say, Nathan's feelings for Marguerite had broadened. None could be mistaken for love or any sensation of that depth, but it was more than completely sexual now.

It was probably a crazy idea, but maybe he could take Marguerite back to Richmond with him to meet Kenan next week and tell him the whole truth. Suddenly he remembered the hard cold facts. Yes, it was a crazy idea, with the police looking for him in connection to Richard's murder. The tranquility of this island had started to slow down his brain waves. He had so many things to worry about he wasn't sure where to start.

Paulos was probably as good a place as any. He had to make that telephone call to the big guy today. He dreaded it, but at the same time was most anxious to get it behind him. He would do it when Marguerite showered. Surely she would shower sometime this morning.

A voice from the kitchen shouted, "Brunch is ready."

Nathan walked back inside and was amazed at what he saw. There was a white tablecloth over the dining room table that was set for two, complete with what appeared to be real china and crystal. Why shouldn't it be; he had given her plenty of money over the years. Marguerite directed him to the tall buffet against one wall, handed him a plate from the table and said, "Help yourself."

He thought how her little trip out to the Island Market had proven to be very beneficial to his growling stomach. He picked one of several croissants from the tray and took a bite of it before placing it on his plate. "This really looks good. You haven't cooked a meal for me in quite a while."

"Well, this should make up for it," Marguerite said stepping into line behind him.

Nathan loaded up his plate with link sausages, cheese grits, poached eggs and fresh asparagus. He sat down at the table and picked up one of the melon balls from a bowl placed near his chilled orange juice.

They ate everything on their plates and went back for seconds. After commending Marguerite one more time on a job well done, Nathan suggested that she retire to the shower and let him clean up the kitchen. "It was the least he could do."

She kissed him and said he was spoiling her, and then walked to the back of the villa. When the bedroom door had closed safely behind her, Nathan went into the living room and picked up the telephone. With undependable cell phone service on the island, the landline was the best choice so as not to agitate Paulos with a possible dropped call. He was still unsure of exactly what he was going to say as he dialed the number of Paulos' condominium in Richmond.

The call was answered on the first ring, and the familiar sound of the housekeeper's voice said, "Hello.

"Let me speak to Mr. Paulos," Nathan said.

"Who is calling, please?"

"He's expecting my call. It's Nathan Gray."

"Mr. Paulos is unable to come to the telephone. Please give me your telephone number and he will return your call in a moment," the housekeeper said.

"Just let me hold a minute. I don't want him to call me back," Nathan said insistently.

"I'm afraid that is not an option. Please give me your telephone number or get lost."

The people who worked directly with Paulos had a way of adopting his undesirable temperament. Nathan spat the telephone number of Marguerite's villa into the receiver and slammed the telephone down.

The housekeeper telephoned Mr. Paulos' suite at his favorite hotel/casino in Atlantic City where he had chosen to "weather the storm." The telephone rang as he was about to step into the hallway in route to the high rollers crap table. He shoved the door closed with his heel and walked through the plush suite to a telephone in the living room.

"Yeah?" was all he said when the receiver reached his ear. "Hold on," Paulos said.

He reached in a drawer and retrieved a pad and pen.

"O.K., got it."

He hung up the telephone and dialed the number he had just written.

The ringing in his ear lasted only one half a beat, and then there was Gray's voice speaking quietly.

"What have you got, Gray?" he shouted into the telephone.

"Something that you really want. I found the capsule last night. I'll mail it to you on a rush delivery, but the best part is that it was empty. No flash drive or anything inside. If there had been incriminating evidence inside of the capsule the police would have it by now and we would have been arrested days ago. You know that. So, it looks like your worries are over, Boss."

"Where'd you find it?" Paulos asked with no excitement in his voice at all.

"It was a piece of cake. I didn't even have to break in the house. It was in the garage wrapped around the arm of a beach chair."

"How can you be sure it is the one that belonged to Dubose and not just one like it?"

"Easy," Nathan said, trying to maintain composure in his voice, "It's got his name written on it in black marker."

"Get it to me fast," Paulos said, granting more credence to Gray's story.

"It will be on its way today. Relax, and tell everyone else to relax. Duncan should be released very soon on insufficient evidence and the whole mess will be cleared up. I think we should start operations again on Monday," Nathan said with feign confidence.

"What you think doesn't matter anymore to the members of the network. You've got a lot of reconstruction work to do on your image, Gray."

"I realize that, and I plan to begin working on that right away," Nathan said pointing his middle finger at the receiver.

After Paulos gave Nathan a mailing address, the conversation ended. Now all he had to do was to find another capsule, write the name on it and mail it to Paulos. It sounded very easy, but Nathan knew he was probably being watched, so he would have to sneak around a bit. And another problem occurred to him. If he had supposedly already found the capsule, then he certainly couldn't be seen by Paulos' men snooping around the Stevenson's place again.

It was time to trust someone else's instincts rather than his own. Kenan believed that this whole search was ridiculous and that the silly capsule was at the bottom of the ocean. Nathan would believe that too, and from now on, he would consider the capsule that he would purchase later today, as the original one. Perhaps he could convey more convincing remarks to the network members during future conversations on the matter if he truly believed it himself.

Nathan still wanted desperately to escape the hold of the network, but now was not the time. One mention of anything other than complete support and commitment would surely lead to his bloody death. The Richard melodrama plagued his mind momentarily. He didn't know enough details about the murder to even make a calculated judgment on how the police could think he was involved. "One thing at a time," he said quietly. "Beginning with the kitchen, and then a little shopping, followed by a visit to the Post Office."

Nathan stood and surveyed the mess through the arched threshold of the kitchen. He hadn't cleaned up a kitchen in years. The bedroom door at the end of the hallway opened and Marguerite appeared in a red corset and garter outfit, with matching heels and a feathery cape of some sort. She motioned to him with the feathers and Nathan floated down the hallway, past the kitchen. It didn't look like he was going to have to break his abstention from cleanup record after all. A little change in schedule shouldn't hurt. He had the hardest part of his day behind him now that he had talked with Paulos. He deserved a reward, and it looked as though it would come to him in the color of red.

35

The pewter wind chimes hanging from the Gazebo Bar played an original melody as they talked quietly and sipped on frozen Margaritas that Beth, the bartender, had prepared for the early afternoon crowd around the pool. Kate followed the lines in the grip of her racquet with her finger while the sunshine blazed down on their heads.

"I feel a little guilty for not having warned you about my incredible tennis ability until you witnessed it first hand," Kate smiled at Kenan harassingly.

"You certainly should. I wish I had seen all of the plaques in the tennis shop with your name on them before, instead of after, our games. I just can't trust you anymore. One day into the relationship of a lifetime, and I already have my doubts about you."

Kenan looked at Kate as he laughed. He reached for her tanned hand still resting on the racquet and squeezed it tightly.

"The sun really is shining directly in your eyes, Kate. Why don't you move over here next to me so you don't get wrinkles?"

"What a splendid idea," she said, laughing.

The sarcasm between them was playful as well as their constant touching. Kenan moved her chair next to his and they leaned their heads back on the chairs, closed their eyes and held hands as they continued to talk.

"How old were you when you started playing tennis, anyway?" Kenan asked.

"About six. I started here at Fripp. I can remember riding my bike over to the courts every weekday morning in the summer and waiting for Lewis, the tennis pro, to pair me with a child who was vacationing on the island."

"Weren't there other kids living here during the summer that you could have played with?"

"Yes, there were, and I did sometimes, but they were really no challenge for me. You see, I was great from the beginning," Kate snickered haughtily.

"From now on, I will do all of your boasting for you. I will stop people on the street and tell them how wonderful you are."

Their games were slanting to the romantic zone, as they stared at each other and then kissed. Kenan's hand lurked on the edge of her short pleated tennis skirt as they kissed, holding tightly to the smooth leg that had been hidden from his sight the first time he had seen Kate.

"I don't want our life together to begin like any of the other relationships I've ever had. I want to know everything about you, and you me," he said knowing he would have to confess the snooping around masquerade. "I love you entirely now, and I can wait for you. But, do you think we could combine a wedding with Ely's birthday party? I'm not sure I can wait too long past tomorrow night?"

Her eyes said, "Are you serious?"

"Only kidding. I wouldn't share our day with anyone. But I think it should be soon. Don't you?"

"Yes, I do," Kate said smiling up at Kenan's handsome face. She brushed a blonde lock from his eyes and said, "Thank you for making our beginning so special. I think the waiting is a very romantic idea."

"Now, remember there are some stipulations in the time frame of this waiting period." Kenan spoke like a businessman submitting a contract for approval.

"You are so perfect in every way, so I can only imagine that you will be incredible in bed. And what you don't know, I'll teach you," Kenan said pleasingly.

"Or, vice versa," Kate stated.

"Now, wait a minute," Kenan cajoled.

"I can't let you start this relationship off with the upper hand," Kate protested. "Whether I have or haven't, or what I know or don't know, is beside the point. We are equals and I am so in love with you. Why don't we talk with Mom and Dad Sunday?"

"You are absolutely right, Kate," Kenan said somewhat apologetically. "I will never be chauvinistic toward you, I promise. My father treated my mother that way and I swear I will never ever let that happen with us."

"Kenan, I was only kidding," Kate said lifting his hand to her lips. I know you would never do that." Her smile brushed the unpleasant memories of his parents' marriage from his mind.

"Let's finish these margaritas up and go over and take a look at that sweater you said you saw earlier at the Island Shops," Kate suggested.

"That sounds good. Let me go and pay the bar tab. I'll be right back."

When Kenan returned they walked hand in hand over to the Island Shops. They passed two different couples along the way that Kate knew so they stopped for her to introduce them to Kenan and also for her to invite them to Ely's birthday party. They purchased more than just the sweater at the clothing store and Kenan met Jeannie, the owner, and they shared loser side stories of playing tennis with Kate. Then they went over to the Fripp Island Logo Shop to buy Ely's birthday gifts and met Sylvia, the proprietor, there. Kate had no problem deciding to purchase a thick, navy terry cloth robe with the logo in white on the lapel for her brother.

"Let's walk back to the Gazebo Bar and relax in the sun a little longer. Maybe the same chairs are still available," Kenan suggested. He folded Kate's hand into his own and they peacefully strolled back toward the beach. "What a difference a day makes," he thought.

36

Hours later, the sound of water running and the smell of sausage grease greeted Nathan as he meandered down the hallway buttoning his shirt. Marguerite stood at the sink with plastic yellow gloves on her hands scrubbing a cast iron pan.

"You know you should never scrub a cast iron pan with an abrasive pad," Nathan offered.

"Oh, yeah?" Marguerite said teasingly. "Since when did you become the authority on household chores? You probably haven't been in the kitchen of that huge mansion in Richmond in months."

"And you're probably right, but somewhere along the way I picked up that bit of knowledge."

She turned the water off and for the first time Nathan heard the small clock radio in the corner of the kitchen as it whispered an easy listening tune. Just as Marguerite was suggesting that he carry a sweater with him on his errands, Nathan heard a voice say, "Top of the Hour News." Nathan placed a finger to his lips and a loud, "Ssshhhh," came out.

Marguerite hushed instantly and they listened as the news broadcaster announced that investigations had failed to produce further evidence necessary to continue to hold the man charged in the murder of Phillip Dubose of Fripp Island.

"D.B. Duncan of Harbor Island will be released today," the radio said. "Two local men were arrested and charged with vandalizing...." Nathan turned a knob on top of the radio and it clicked off.

"How can they do this?" Marguerite shouted.

Nathan turned around to find Marguerite's face turning even brighter than the shade of red of the feather boa that had been so much fun in bed only an hour ago. Quite frankly, he was rejoicing with relief that Duncan was going to be released. Paulos would be happy as hell about it and perhaps this news could prove to the fat bastard that Nathan really did know what he was talking about when he suggested resuming operations on Monday.

But, that aspect of the matter was beside the point now. He had to control Marguerite. Nathan had seen her madness rage only once before, many, many years ago. Over what, he could not remember now, but he didn't want to experience it again.

"Now wait a minute, Marguerite. Let's sit down and think this through," he walked toward her hurriedly and led her to the sofa in the living room to sit down.

Before he convinced her to sit and talk calmly, she pushed his hands away from her waist and looked at him with conviction. "This investigation was our last hope to discover what really happened to Phillip." Her eyes were dropping tears, but they were surely from the exorbitant rising temperature inside her body. This woman was not crying, she was boiling.

She paced back and forth behind the sofa, rubbing her face and neck, thinking and wondering how this all could have happened to her. To Phillip.

"There is a piece of this horrible puzzle missing," Marguerite said in a concerning voice. "And I will not rest until I know what it is, even if I have to spend the rest of my life searching." She marched toward the telephone and lifted the receiver. "I think those half-ass detectives in Beaufort should know my intentions, and they also need to know just what I think of them and their worthless investigations." She began to dial a number.

Nathan's heart was beating in his throat. He knew Marguerite meant what she said and if Paulos got wind of this motherly maniac causing more trouble, he knew he would be the next one with a bullet in his brain. What could he do; what could he promise her or buy for her that would settle her down. The wheels in his head were spinning, but no solutions were popping out.

He reached for the telephone in her hand and spoke at the same time, "Honey, put down the telephone. At least for now. You are not rational. Please let me help."

The crazy woman's eyes lightened faintly of the rage within them, and her neck turned ever so slightly to the right in wonderment. She reminded Nathan of the puzzled look of an innocent puppy and he believed for some reason she was momentarily vulnerable.

She released the telephone to him without any struggle, holding his gaze all the while. "You've never called me 'honey' before, Nathan."

Nathan took this inviting opportunity to cease the moment. "Marguerite," he began, "Our relationship is changing, darling." He threw another one in; the first had worked so remarkably. He led her to the sofa and they sat down. "There is nothing standing in our way of spending the rest of our lives together. It is a terrible tragedy that we have lost our son, but can't we share the grief and try to move along with our new life together?"

"Do you mean together, like husband and wife?"

Choosing between death in forty-eight hours by a hit ordered from Paulos, or death from too much sex, Nathan said, "Yes, honey, that's what I mean."

"Could we buy a huge diamond, pear-shaped, I've always wanted that kind, and we would live in Richmond and I would be the wife of the affluent, Nathan Kenan Gray, Jr.?" she asked dreamily with a far-away look of a psychotic woman.

"Yes, that's right," he said, thinking how his shrink, Dr. Minor, would love to get Marguerite in his chair and study her multiple personalities. They could get group rates.

Marguerite jumped up off the sofa with what appeared to be overwhelming joy. She rushed to the balcony doors, pulled back the drapes and the sunshine rushed in the room. Marguerite turned around quickly, startling Nathan and his confident hopes of having solved yet another problem today.

"But, I want to keep my villa here, on Fripp. Even though it is where this terrible tragedy happened, I couldn't bear to leave this beautiful island forever."

"Certainly, you can keep this, my love. I would never ask you to do anything you didn't want to do," Nathan said, nearly gagging. It was really getting deep in here. He rose and joined her at the balcony doors.

"I just feel like shouting for the whole island to hear, that I'm going to marry you."

"Well, do it," Nathan said and opened the door in front of her.

Marguerite stepped onto the balcony and the wind blew back her hair. Nathan watched her and contemplated how eerie it was that the woman who stood before him could experience such universal mood swings in a matter of seconds. But, obviously he had mastered the reins by which to guide her. He was silently reveling in the fact that he was truly a genius, as Marguerite turned her eyes toward the great Atlantic. Her focus was on the inevitable. Her insides shook as her brainwork became tunnel vision into the madness of Little Phillip's death. Marguerite's eyes did not blink even as the wind blew strong into them. She watched as the shrimp boats in the distance danced along the white caps, singing the teasingly cruel childhood song, "La, la, la, la, la," expressing that they had something that she did not. And that was the knowledge of what really happened on board *The Rennie* that dreadful day.

"Well?" Nathan said. "Go on, shout it out."

"I can't," she turned and said to Nathan. "I've got to have some answers to my questions about Phillip. What kind of mother would I be if I let this go without demanding more investigation?"

"Is this a quest to right the wrongs for the whole world to know, or just for you to be certain within your own heart and mind, Marguerite?" Nathan asked, trying desperately not to lose control of the situation. Perhaps he would have to confess his involvement and disclose all of the facts to Marguerite in order to keep her from conducting her own public investigation. Her love for him was obvious. She would forgive him and they would live happily ever after in the house in Richmond, which she had obviously dreamed of being the "lady" of, for many years, and Kenan would accept it, somehow, some way. Nathan's mind was a minefield, with explosions occurring one after the other. "Worry about Kenan later and Marguerite now" he told himself.

"A little of both, I suppose," Marguerite spoke after a moment of intense contemplation. "I feel so responsible. I was the one who pushed him and encouraged him to try and learn about shrimping. It was a part of my intricate plan." She looked deep into Nathan's cold dark eyes that were inspiring her to continue this honest expression of her feelings.

"I knew how you were intrigued with the shrimping industry and I thought how wonderful it would be for your son to be involved with you. After you helped him get a job on *The Rennie*, I really had high hopes. And now this happens. I have planned and worked for so long to have us together as a family and it can never be. Not now with my precious Phillip dead and ultimately I am to blame. There is just no escaping it, Nathan. It is my fault."

Nathan knew from her words that she was suffering inside. She would love him even more for taking away the guilt that engulfed her and ate at her heart. He took her hand and led her back inside the villa and closed the door.

"I have something to tell you, Marguerite. Please sit down with me while I find a place to start."

They sat beside each other on the sofa and Nathan spoke sincerely, but yet dramatically. "You are not to blame, my dear Marguerite." He held her hand now, and looked down at the sofa and not into her eyes.

"What? What do you mean?"

"Please," he shook his head. "Please let me explain the whole story and then hopefully you won't feel so responsible."

Amazingly, Marguerite closed her mouth as instructed and listened intently while Nathan told his story.

"I'm not sure where to begin, and I only found out this information myself two nights ago. I think it might help you understand the situation surrounding Phillip's death better. I mean, I don't know who killed Phillip, but I believe I know why he died."

Marguerite's eyes insisted on more. "Tell me who did this and what you are talking about," she screamed in confusion. "I what to know who murderer my son."

"There's not just one single person, Marguerite. It's a network of people. You see, Phillip was snooping around where he shouldn't have been. He was making some people real anxious and these people are not accustomed to being nervous for long. Phillip must have been suspicious that the shrimping on board the boat wasn't on the up and up. I don't have any idea who or what tipped him off."

Nathan stood up and moved around the room hoping that the motion would help him to explain things a little easier. Telling Marguerite was much harder than he ever imagined it would be. The words weren't coming out of his mouth in the same order as they were running through his mind. Marguerite's eyes grew wider and wider as he continued to speak, more quickly now, as if it could help him from falling in the abyss he feared was forming between him and Marguerite, one growing deeper with each word he spoke.

"If I had known that he was in any danger I would have jerked him off that boat myself, I swear to you. They thought he had taken a flash drive with all of the members' names on it. If he had turned it in to the police we would have all been nailed."

"We?" Marguerite shouted accusingly.

"Yes, Marguerite," Nathan said definitely, "I am involved with that group. But, how could I have known anything like this could possibly ever happen?"

"You should have never agreed to let him step one foot on that boat with such horrible people. Who are these people anyway?" Marguerite demanded.

"Business partners."

Her questioning stare insisted on a more thorough explanation. He could feel himself growing angry with the idea of humbling himself to her intimidating looks, but he had to keep her on his side, otherwise she could destroy him.

"O.K., Marguerite. It's the mafia. Organized crime; drugs. Phillip discovered the whole set up. He was my son, too. Don't you think I feel badly about this horrible mess?" Nathan looked at Marguerite asking for forgiveness.

She stood up and walked over to the fireplace where a picture of Phillip rested on the mantle in a dark mahogany frame. She lifted it down and rubbed her finger over his face. Nathan watched with fearful eyes.

The silence was unbearable. Should he continue to plead his case? He waited a few moments, attempting to choose his words with caution. She spoke first, easing the tension only less than one degree.

"Maybe that's it?" Marguerite turned and looked at Nathan, who was still standing beside the sofa.

"What?" he asked.

"Maybe you wanted to get rid of our son. You've never acknowledged him in the past so why should you consider starting now. Was I pushing too hard about getting you two together? Did it make you nervous? You sure look nervous now, Nathan."

Nathan's head was spinning again. What could he say to gain control of her again? Ideas were clicking quickly through his head, but with each revolution problems seem to surface as well. Suddenly, something hit him in the temple that brought all thoughts to a halt and stars to his eyes. He fell to his knees in pain and delirium as another object flew past him and crashed into what sounded like a million pieces behind him. Nathan lifted his head slightly only to see Marguerite reaching for yet another object from the mantle to throw in his direction.

"You crooked son of a bitch," she screamed, "And murderer. You are just as guilty as the rest of them. I hope you burn in hell, but I may be right beside you because I hope to kill you myself." An alabaster bookend grazed Nathan's nose and landed with a thud on the floor. He wondered if he could make it down the hallway and into the bedroom without being bombed in that wide-open space. That would only be a temporary answer to the problem since she was sure to follow him. He saw the complete hysteria in her eyes and knew she was near the point of collapsing. He moved toward the woman who was now holding her head in her hands, sobbing the name "Phillip" over and over.

Nathan reached down and wrapped his arms tightly around the small woman in misery. Two weak fists beat against his broad chest in a fleeting effort to resist him.

Marguerite lifted her face to meet his. "It's really so pitifully ironic, Nathan. I've plotted and outlined every move I made for the past couple of years, beginning with the day she was finally out of the way."

"What?" Nathan asked, shaking her in his arms and waiting for her to expound on the subject. Now he was the one with unanswered questions and his patience was nearly gone. "Speak to me." He shouted and shook her some more.

"Since we're being so honest," she said in a deep scary voice looking at Nathan through droopy eyelids, "Let me tell you about my little secret. I am a very cunning woman, Nathan Gray, and that should never be forgotten. I became tired of waiting for you to see that I am the only woman for you. The one who should be by your side, always. So I just helped matters along by removing the obstruction between us."

Nathan realized what this lunatic was suggesting, but he said nothing and listened with horrifying dismay.

"Like I said, it's so ironic, I had Priscilla killed so that you would be mine alone, and now I don't even want you."

The panic within Nathan turned to rage, and he threw Marguerite onto the floor. Her head hit the edge of the slate hearth and Nathan saw her eyes roll backwards. He slapped her face and shouted, "Wake up you bitch. Wake up." He lifted her head from the floor by her shirt's collar.

Marguerite did not move. The pool of blood under her head began to spread and Nathan saw it as it reached the molding of the hearth and streamed down toward him. "I won't let you die before you've paid for killing Priscilla. Wake up!"

Nathan laid two fingers on her throat and checked her pulse. She was still alive. He lifted her in his arms and blood dripped in large drops on the cream carpet. A small cotton blanket hung across the back of a rocking chair to his right and Nathan reached for it and wrapped it around Marguerite's head. "Good, I didn't want to look at your face any way."

He marched down the hallway, carrying Marguerite with the force of an army, but with the madness of a maniac. The door to a closet beside the bathroom was open and Nathan looked inside. He laid Marguerite on the floor and reached into the closet with both hands and removed four shoeboxes. He threw them across the room and reached inside for more. When he had emptied the closet of the bottom four shelves of shoes, he pulled out those same removable shelves.

Nathan checked for a pulse again, found one, then rummaged around in the bathroom until he found some bandaging tape. He taped Marguerite's mouth closed and put her hands behind her back and taped them together. After a brief examination of the wound on her head, Nathan decided she wasn't going to bleed to death. He shoved her into the closet, threw the blanket in with her and closed the door.

The blood stains on his hands and forearms were clogging his pores and his head was swimming. He needed air. This whole villa needed air. He walked to the living room and once again opened the door to the balcony. He stepped out and the sun blinded him, though it felt good to close his eyes. If he could just keep his eyes closed and forget about all his problems and the many mistakes he had made over the years. If he could go back, he would go back to that day when he returned home to Ampt Hill and found Priscilla and Kenan on the ridge beside the mansion. He would roll in the leaves with them and hold hands and laugh.

Oh, how he would laugh, and love, and hold on to what he could have once had. Priscilla would have forgiven him. He knew now that she had loved him then.

But, he had blown it, and started a game with that beautiful woman. Nathan's intentions had substance at first, trying to make her jealous to win her back or some screwy scheme. But, as they say, "The road to hell is paved with good intentions," and he was traveling that freeway now at breakneck speeds.

Nathan knew he had to gather himself and stop thinking about days gone by. He just couldn't shake the picture from his mind of Kenan and Priscilla sitting together in the leaves laughing loudly. If only he could hear it, one more time.

Saddened by the realization that it was impossible, he tried to focus on what had to be done. The search for an identical capsule had to begin, and then he had to get it in the mail to Paulos. After that he would deal with Marguerite and then Richard's death. He looked down at his bloody knuckles as they grasped the iron railing, and saw that the blood had dried in the intricate grooves of his gold family crest ring. Cleaning up himself would be the first order of business.

He didn't want to leave the warm sunlight, but he turned slowly away and moved to the living room. At that instant, a familiar laugh bolted up from below and exploded in his eardrum, bringing a smile to his face which he thought had probably left his countenance forever.

He peered over the railing at two people sitting at a table near the Gazebo Bar. Their conversation was quieter now and he couldn't make out any distinctive voices. He squinted his eyes and stared at the young man and woman below him, with tennis racquets and beverages in front of them. The gentleman laughed again and the sound twisted his heart in a knot until tears rolled down his cheeks.

If there was any way Nathan could have doubted his first notion of the identity of the young man at the table, the flashing ray of sunshine that struck the man's ring finger and sent a piercing glare into Nathan's eyes, was clear confirmation. Only one other person in the world possessed a ring identical to the huge gold mass on Nathan's finger, and that was Kenan.

37

He sat in his car parked near the dock at Johnson Creek waiting for Duncan to arrive. The temperature was in the low sixties and the sky was blue in all directions. It was a beautiful day, especially for someone who was used to tall buildings surrounding them with only a patch of noticeable sky straight overhead.

Mark got out of his car and leaned against the hood. The marsh was beautiful as the sun's rays created a golden pathway through the center of the greenish blue waters. There were no horns beeping or motors rumbling or people shouting. The only sounds were those of the inlet waters lapping against the big poles of the dock adorned with oyster shells, and a glitter of noise as the breeze lingered between the marsh grass. He thought once again what a well-kept secret this area of South Carolina was and how he wanted to come back when it wasn't business related.

Mark had worked with the network for many years and was one of the official troubleshooters. Which meant a lot of his work entailed some nasty business. He knew when he left New York City a few days ago, that this trip would be no different from the others, but he was happy to hear Paulos say last night that Geno would be in charge of the finishing strokes. Geno was on his own payroll and was a perfectionist besides. The most important item of concern to Mark was that if there were any mishaps, the burden was not going to be on his shoulders. There had been enough of them already and Paulos' frustrations were stacking up.

The Boss had been happy, though, to discover from Mark that a little party on Saturday should provide the means to an end for some of the cast of characters on his list. Mark enlightened Paulos on Gray's location and felt Geno would have no trouble getting to him, since he would probably be in the bed with the short buxom woman. His orders were to call Atlantic City when this task at hand was complete and the whole inexcusable snafu was behind them.

The Boss was also adamant about finding Phillip's killer. No one takes out a man without his order. Someone had over stepped their position and Paulos aimed to right that wrong as well. Mark understood why Paulos would want to get to the bottom of the mystery and rid the field of those aspiring to move up in the ranks behind his back.

The sound of footsteps on the dock interrupted Mark's peacefulness. Geno came into sight and stopped when he made eye contact with Mark. He turned his forearm over and pointed at his watch. Mark gave a shrug of his shoulders in return and Geno turned and walked back to cabin cruiser parked at the end of the dock beside *The Rennie.*

Duncan was more than a half hour late for his meeting with Mark. He had said he would come straight from the jail to Johnson Creek and they would collaborate at length on possible ways to fix this mess.

Mark reached into the car through the front window and picked up his sunglasses on the front dash. He adjusted the dark shades perfectly over his eyes so that Duncan couldn't look into them and suspect the truth.

Finally, a minute later, the sound of tires rolling over the crushed oyster shells turned Mark's attention from the panoramic view to the vehicle approaching him with Duncan behind the wheel. Duncan hopped out enthusiastically and walked toward Mark.

"Hey, Mark, sorry to keep you waiting. The exiting paperwork took longer than I expected, then I had to stop and get some cigarettes. Man, I couldn't smoke in there. I was about to lose it," he said as he inhaled deeply through the filter of a fresh smoke.

"How about joining me?" Duncan held the pack toward Mark.

"I'd love to. I could smoke a cigarette the length of that shrimp boat, but I promised my wife I wouldn't. She's bitched at me since we were in high school about quitting. It took a few serious chest pains to make me do it, though. But, don't let that stop you, man," Mark said, thinking how Duncan should enjoy his last moments. "You deserve to smoke after what you've been through."

"No kidding man, I'd forgotten how damned confining those cells are, and these new rules about smoking are going to create more trouble than they're worth. I wasn't the only guy suffering. Seems like all of the bad guys like to smoke." Duncan laughed and Mark laughed along with him.

"Hey, Duncan," Mark changed the subject. "I'd like to take a ride out and see exactly where the kid washed ashore. Sort of snoop around through my binoculars," he reached through the car door once again and picked up the case on the seat. "What do you think? Just to get the feel of things."

"Sure, come on. My cruiser's parked over there." Duncan pointed to the boat on the end and Mark acted as though he had just seen it for the first time. "A boat ride is just what I need after being cooped up in that place," Duncan said stepping onto the old plank stairs leading to the dock.

"This is really a scenic spot," Mark said opening his arms wide.

"Isn't it though," Duncan answered proudly. "You're still in New York City, aren't you?"

Mark answered yes, and the small talk continued until they reached the boat and then the conversation turned toward the capsule. Duncan backed the boat out of its space and followed a path through the marsh grass leading to the open waterway. They sat for a while in silence taking in the view and Mark almost forgot why he was here, until the door to the cabin opened slightly. Duncan was on a platform above the cabin so could not see Geno as he stood in the dark cabin below.

The boat moved across the water with the sun directly overhead. Mark shouted trivial questions up to Duncan over the roar of the engine, about islands they passed along the way. He pointed to one on the right in the distance and Duncan pulled the throttle backward gently.

"Now, that's a piece of history, there," Duncan nodded in the direction of the island.

"Tell me about it." Mark said half genuinely and half wondering when Geno was going to make his move.

"It's called Horse Island. Back when the Spaniards were trying to acquire these parts, Captain John Fripp was the fellow in charge. He stationed most of his men at the South tip of what is now Fripp Island, and they bombed the Spanish as they passed through the inlet. Their ships were filled with lots of treasures including horses. As the ships sank, the surviving horses swam to that island. Thus, Horse Island. There are still wild horses there. I've seen one or two. If I pull a little closer, you could look through those binoculars and maybe see some yourself."

The door to the cabin opened a little more and a nod in the affirmative from Geno brought the words, "Yes, that's a good idea," to Mark's lips.

The boat moved at a slow speed toward the barrier island with tall pines and only a slither of beach. "Why is the beach so small?"

"Erosion. The state really needs to address the situation soon. The water is so deep all the way to the Island that I could drop anchor and almost jump to shore."

"Well, I don't guess we need to do that today," Mark kidded. "Just pull up sort of close. Come on down and have a look through these babies yourself," he suggested.

Duncan turned the engine off and jumped down from the skipper position to stand beside Mark near the edge of the boat.

As Duncan was looking through the binoculars, Mark began to feel the dread of what was to happen next. Trying to drive the guilt from his mind, he slapped his long-time buddy on the shoulder and said, "Way to go getting out of jail with no charges."

"Yeah, that sure was a surprise."

"What do you mean?" Mark asked with astonishment.

"We've known each other since the beginning Mark, don't tell me you are one of those guys who follows the Boss's rules to a tee. He wants results and doesn't really care about details."

Mark patted Duncan on the back and nudged his shoulder in a jovial way and said, "Keep talking, man".

"Right after I got here," Duncan began, "Here in the Lowcountry, I realized I was going to need a little expert help to get set up. This isn't exactly Chicago where we have plenty of colleagues, right man."

Marked nodded in agreement and listened intently.

"So I started talking to a boat neighbor back at the dock. I was trying to learn the backroads of Beaufort County to get our trucks in and out of here and back on the interstate fast. You won't believe my luck." Duncan smirks at Mark.

Mark's eyes widen, "Tell it, man".

"Turns out he's a Sheriff's Deputy. A very disgruntled, underpaid, over-worked deputy. Can you believe it? So, after a few beers one night, I asked him if he'd like to make some easy extra bucks. Who wouldn't, he says to me. So, just like that, I've got myself a local informant. Miller, that's his name. Miller, tells me the weekly schedule for speed traps, license checks, detours or anything like that, ya know," Duncan said proudly and continues. "Once we were all set up and organized we start running ahead of schedule. The Boss is happy; I'm happy; Miller's happy. Good deal, right?"

"Yeah, right," Mark said rubbing his head, "But I'm not making the connection between Miller, you and Dubose."

"Well, if Dubose wouldn't have kept snooping around and making Miller all paranoid, none of this would have happened. It was all so senseless. Miller thought Dubose was close to understanding that he was helping with the transporting schedule for the 'shrimp' and would soon be asking more questions about the smaller packages that went into each ten-pound box of seafood. He kept studying the chart in my office, too. It has names and locations on it. Asking questions right and left."

Duncan paused to light a cigarette then continued, "It's hard enough hiding drugs from the cops, but having to hide it from a worker who really shouldn't be here anyway, is even tougher. It started getting ridiculous. I mean, the kid is here thinking he is an apprentice or something stupid like that; and we are trying to keep everything out of his reach like he's a toddler who could hurt himself. What's his connection with us, anyway? Who's his Daddy? Must not really care about him too much to involve him in this kind of business without telling him the truth."

"His Dad is in Virginia; been around a long time. I don't know the whole story, but in the end look who got hurt. So keep talking. What happened next?"

"One day last week, a crewman was laid up with a bad back, and another was at the hospital with a wife in labor having a baby. You probably never realized human resources was such a large part of my job, now did you Mark?" Duncan said with a laugh.

"That leaves me and the kid. Truly, a total waste of time to even pull up anchor. Then Miller comes strolling down the dock and hears my sob story. Jumps onboard and offers to help out. Just after we cast the first net, I shared with Miller that my flash drive was missing and asked if had he taken it because he was pissed I had his name on it? He got all puffy and angry. Started saying we were all going to land in jail. The next thing I see is Miller punching Dubose in the stomach.

The kid lost his footing and fell overboard before I could say a word! Man, he sank like a ton of bricks. Such a big guy. We had no chance of finding him, even if I had stopped the boat. We waited until dusk to head back in so that no one would see Miller get off the shrimp boat. I went home and laid low until the cops came knocking because Dubose's mom had reported him missing."

"That's quite a story," Mark said. "One with too many loose ends to suit me. The Boss is right, Duncan. We need to tidy things up around here."

It was quick and easy. Duncan never knew what hit him, so he didn't have time to feel betrayed or worthless. Mark was grateful for that. Rule number one in his book was to never get involved, but that was not so easily followed when you had known someone like Duncan for such a long time.

Geno had crept up the few steps from the cabin and fired two bullets into the back of his head. Mark stood ready to catch Duncan as he became lifeless. The impact threw him forward and Mark held him tightly around the waist as his bloody head hung down over the side of the boat. Blood dripped into the water in several steady streams as Mark watched Geno attach an anchor securely to his leg with a rope.

Geno mumbled his first words of the trip, "O.K., dump him over," and then tossed Mark a cloth to wipe both sides of the boat free from any stains. "You're gonna near more towels for clean-up," Geno mumbled as he opened latches of storage areas around the sides of the boat. As he found them, he threw them in Mark's direction. Mark made a mental note to ask the Boss what services Geno's fee included. He was sure clean-up was on the list, but he wasn't going to get into it with Geno. He was tired of him already.

"I'll be below. He's got some good Whiskey on board this boat. How about a blast?" Geno asked.

"No thanks," said Mark. He didn't feel like celebrating and besides he had to try to navigate his way back through the marsh to Johnson Creek. He had tried to pay close attention on their way out so maybe he could retrace their path now. He cranked the engine and left Horse Island, and his friend Duncan.

It wasn't an easy task, but Mark managed to return to the dock at Johnson Creek. His worry of anyone seeing them as they returned was thankfully in vain, and soon after they secured the boat to the dock and double-checked for any stains, they got in Mark's car. They drove slowly over the oyster shell drive and turned right in the direction of Fripp Island.

Geno smelled of whiskey and still held the source in his hand. He turned the decanter of Wild Turkey American Honey up to his lips and swallowed a large gulp, followed by a loud, "Aaaahhh". Mark supposed this was what hit men do when they finish a job. He hoped Geno would just get wasted and pass out. He didn't particularly enjoy his company.

When Mark picked him up earlier today at the airstrip on Lady's Island, Geno was smug and condescending. Mark had no use for his type. But after another twenty-four to thirty-six hours their ways would part, so no big worry. Mark drove over one bridge and then another as the sun poured in through the glass of the car and helped the temperature inside rise to perfection. That along with the booze sent Geno to wonderland. Mark was happy about that for a lot of reasons, but mostly because if he was asleep he couldn't make any stupid drunken remarks to the security person at the guard gate entering Fripp. The security was tight and it was hard to gain entry without guest or visitor passes. Property owners had special decals displayed on their front windshields and could pass through the gate without waiting in a line, but without the decal you had to personally speak to the guard each time. They were quick about their business, but thorough. The top security was just another reason for Mark to return and bring his family for a vacation next summer.

As he started over the Fripp Island bridge, he slowed his speed to twenty-five miles an hour as the speed limit sign demanded. There were only two cars in front of them as he approached the guardhouse bordered with Palmetto trees. Mark eased his car forward as the two in front of him continued on their way. He lowered the driver side window and looked up at the smiling security guard.

"Well, hello Mr. Rogers," the man said to Mark as if he actually lived on the island. "How are you enjoying the Tennis Villas?"

Mark was dumbfounded at the guard's memory. He stumbled over the words, "Fine. Thank you. Have a good day," and drove on.

Almost an hour later, the telephone rang in Mark's villa near the tennis courts that overlooked the marshlands. It was Paulos returning his call.

"Phase one is complete," Mark spoke calmly into the telephone.

"Good. I feel better already. Look, I spoke with Gray earlier and he swears he found the capsule. He is supposed to mail it, overnight mail, to me today. He should be mailing it right now. If that son-of-a-bitch is lying to me about this damn capsule, I'll kill him twice. Did you tell Geno about the little birthday party planned for tomorrow night?"

"Yes, we spoke briefly about it when I picked him up at the airport. He's, um, resting now. We'll go over the details at dinner tonight." Mark doubted that would happen but he said it any way.

"Look, I, um, I learned something from Duncan before Geno did his work. It looks like Duncan had a helper in the Beaufort County Sheriff's Department. A guy by the name of Miller, and he is responsible for Phillip Dubose's death. It is a bit of a tale. Do you want the whole story?"

Just as Duncan had said earlier, Paulo's was not interested in details – just results. "No," Paulo's replied, "just add him to Geno's workload. Don't worry with him until after tomorrow night though. What about the Gray kid?"

"That was my next point of conversation," Mark answered. "As luck would have it, I passed them on my way to the villa after our meeting with Duncan."

"Them?" Paulos asked.

"Yes, the Stevenson's daughter was with him. Remember, I told you last night she's in love with the guy. I know all about the inside romance," Mark laughed mockingly.

"They had on their stylish tennis outfits and he was carrying both of their racquets like a real gentleman. It looked as if they were headed to The Beach Club across the street. I thought I might wander over and take a look."

"Yeah, you do that," Paulos blurted into the telephone, laughing along with Mark. "Try to determine which side of that little blonde head of his will be the easiest for Geno to focus on through the scope tomorrow night."

38

It was all so strange to both of them that they were really and truly in love after only a day. Kate shared her dream wedding idea with Kenan and even if he had abhorred the suggestion he would have never spoiled a chance to make her dream come true.

Kate wanted a wedding ceremony on the beach in the middle of the day. The time, of course, would depend on the tides. It would be similar to a garden wedding, except on the beach.

"I've solved all of the possible problems that could arise with a wedding of this sort," Kate explained to Kenan who said nothing yet, but listened with a smile.

"Dad and I will walk down the boardwalk from our house and step onto pieces of wood that have been covered in white cloth, maybe velvet that would serve as the aisle. People will be sitting on either side of the aisle in folding chairs blanketed in white seat covers. Perhaps we could have some type of lattice arbor over the alter, all finished in white of course."

Kate looked at Kenan for approval.

"Oh, yes, of course," he said quickly.

"And, how do you feel about tails as opposed to a tuxedo?" Kate asked.

"Which ever you feel will look best, is exactly what I will wear." Good answer, he thought to himself.

Kate's thoughts flew right on to the music. "A small brass band would be perfect; don't you think?"

Kenan nodded. "Yes, perfect."

"And then when the ceremony is over and we've pounded back down the aisle to the tune of 'Dum, dum, dee, dum, dum, dum, dee, dum' the band can start playing dancing music and we can take off our shoes and tie up the long train of my wedding gown and start the party."

"Are we going to share all of these plans with your parents on Sunday, too?" Kenan asked wondering when he was going to throw in all of his confessions.

"Probably not. One thing at a time would be our best strategy. You know, Mom already knows how I feel about you. She could see it last night at dinner. She'll be happy as long as I'm happy. We had a really nice talk."

"What about your father?"

"He'll be happy to, I'm sure. But, you've got to remember, he's been used to the legal system pace. We have to move a little more slowly with him," Kate laughed.

The two relaxed in the sunshine for a bit longer and then decided to go back to Marlin Drive and see what the rest of the family was doing.

They got out of the golf cart and went up the back stairs only to find Walker sitting in a chair beside the Gullah table reading a golf magazine. Kate's eyes told Kenan to sit down with her father, so he did. "Mind if I join you?" he asked.

"Not at all," Walker said closing his magazine. "How was the tennis?"

"Murder. Did you teach her how to play like that?" Kenan smiled over to Walker.

"What I couldn't teach her, I made sure a tennis pro did. Kate is very serious about her tennis, though. She never tires of practicing. It was, and is, a great source of enjoyment and exercise for her."

"And don't forget, a great way to exercise her competitive spirit as well," Kenan added.

"She does love to win. I can't imagine where she gets that from," said Walker with a laugh.

"I might have an idea. Kate tells me you are one heck of a lawyer."

Their conversation sailed smoothly through subjects such as work, golf, Kenan's business, golf, Kenan's family, golf, Kenan's education and more golf. Walker was so tactful in bleeding the information a father would like to know about a guy his daughter is interested in from Kenan, that Kenan hardly realized he was being tested. They actually got along very well and Walker felt good about Kenan.

He and Stella had met Kenan briefly this morning when he came to pick Kate up for tennis. They all had a laugh remembering their meeting in the grocery store parking lot only two nights ago. Stella remembered telling Kenan that night how he would fall in love with Fripp Island and never want to leave. She had no idea how right she would be and that her beautiful Kate would be the reason why.

The screen door opened and Kate and Stella emerged with a tray full of shrimp salad, Brie and crackers, and toasted bagels. They also had a tub of cold long neck bottled beers.

Walker and Kenan stood up and helped them empty their arms of the luscious lunch and place it around the table.

"I'll be right back," Stella said. "I've got to get the plates, napkins and forks. Walker, honey, will you please tell Ely lunch is ready."

"After we help our own plates," he said jokingly. "Then we can just give him all that's left."

"Now, don't be silly. Besides, I've made him a turkey sub, too."

"The perfect, Mother," Walker announced walking over to the edge of the railing and calling Ely's name in the direction of the basketball court. The bouncing noise that had been the backdrop for Kenan and Walker's conversation ceased and moments later the sound of feet on the stairs beside them yielded a sweaty Ely.

Stella appeared in the back doorway holding a turkey sub and the other items she had gone back inside for. One look from his mother and Ely said, "Excuse me while I clean up a bit."

"Thank you, sweetheart," Stella said approvingly.

Lunch was terrific and it was incredible how everyone seemed to accept Kenan like an old friend they had known forever. Stella was so happy for Kate that being with Kenan was effortless for her family.

The late afternoon turned out to be a time for separation of sexes, so to speak. Walker, Ely and Kenan played nine holes of golf while Kate and Stella discussed what Kate should wear to the interview in Charleston tomorrow, then changed subjects and compiled a list of Ely's favorite side dishes to be served at the party tomorrow night. There were still a few islanders Stella had been unable to reach, so they made a few more telephone calls as well. Marguerite was one of them, but there was no answer at her villa that afternoon. Stella felt odd about inviting her any way. It would be terribly painful to attend a party in honor of another boy after your own son had been found dead. But, Stella also knew Marguerite's need for socializing and certainly didn't want to hurt her feelings by not including her either. It was a Catch 22. Damned if you do, and damned if you don't. Kate had told her Mother not to worry about it, at least she had tried to reach her.

Kate told her Mom that Kenan was going to Charleston on Saturday with her and that they would leave around 6:00 a.m. She wanted to show him the Market and some other historical spots, but they would be back in time to help start the party.

When the boys returned from the course, their industrious women-folk had already prepared Ely's favorite: mashed potatoes with cheese and a monstrous Caesar Salad, and the steaks were soaking in garlic powder and ground pepper.

Following a candlelight dinner in the dining room and much laughter and good conversation, Kenan admitted that it was probably time for him to go back to his villa. Kate needed to be her best for the interview tomorrow, although he wondered why she was even going if they were in fact going to get married, she certainly couldn't move to New Orleans. However, that was not brought up, so neither did he mention it before he said goodbye to Kate.

After a quick shower Kenan crawled into the big bed in his condo and was asleep almost instantly. He awoke, startled, when a familiar voice said, "You could have at least locked your doors, even if you didn't follow my instructions to leave the island."

He sat up quickly and instinctively reached to turn on the lamp beside him. An arm attached to a dark shadow stopped him from doing so. He was frightened even though he recognized the voice to be that of his father.

"What is going on," Kenan demanded.

"Leave the light off. They're probably watching and I don't want them to know we have talked. You could be in a lot more danger if they think you have met with me."

"Who is 'they'?" Kenan asked, his voice flecked with anger.

"I can't tell you and don't ask me any more questions that I can't answer for you right now," the dark figure sat down on the bed now and the hardness of Nathan's face and worry in his eyes was clearly seen in the moonlight.

"Kenan, we have to talk. I want you to know everything that I have kept a secret from you for most of your life. But, now is not the time. Right now, you have got to leave this place."

"No. You told me to take a nice vacation and I happen to be doing just that. Tell me what you're talking about. You look awful. Are you all right?" Kenan asked.

Marguerite's insane words rang in his ears, but Nathan answered, "Yes, I am alright. I am almost finished with my work here and then I will return to Richmond to face matters there," he said without realizing Kenan probably knew nothing about Richard's murder.

"What's going on in Richmond?" Kenan said quickly.

Nathan covered it up well with business as an excuse.

"I saw you with that girl today. There are plenty of women for you, son. Pack up and be gone by morning. She wasn't that special anyway."

Kenan could take no more. He pounded out of the bed and ordered Nathan to leave.

"What? You have no idea what you're talking about? She's...I won't let you ruin another chance at happiness. Out," Kenan pointed wildly at the door. I want you out now. Take your vague threats and those shadows you keep jumping at and get out."

Kenan was pushing his Father now toward the spiral staircase. He wished there had been a door to the bedroom that he could have slammed in Nathan's face, but the single lofted room did not possess one. Instead he shouted the words, "I don't want to talk to you again until you are ready to tell me everything; the whole truth. I am tired of waiting and wondering."

Nathan kept whispering, "I'm sorry, I'm sorry," over and over as he left the condo.

39

The next morning, Stella sat at the kitchen booth organizing newspaper clippings and photos of Ely in action on the basketball court to put in a scrapbook for his birthday. She had saved so many things that they would all never go into just one book, perhaps this could be Volume One of her son's basketball career. Stella laughed and smiled to herself as the keepsakes brought back memories of the past. She had almost been able to tune out the rumble of the washer and dryer in the laundry room, which she detested, but it had to be done sometime. The basket in their bathroom was literally packed to the gills and most certainly some of its contents would need to return to school with her children on Sunday.

By 9:00 a.m. she had completed half of the scrapbook and the third load of laundry was spinning. A loud clanging noise suddenly came from the laundry room and Stella went inside to investigate. Walker had probably left a golf ball in his pocket and it was banging around in the tub of the washing machine.

Stella turned the dial from the spin cycle to the off position and lifted the lid. The load of laundry clung tightly to the sides of the machine and in the bottom laid the culprit. Stella lifted a cylinder shaped object from the machine with a nylon rope attached to the top. She turned it around in her hands until the name Dubois came into full view. The same sickening chill, which she thought gone forever, showered her body as she remembered finding Phillip's body. She picked up what she knew to be called a seaman's capsule from the bottom of the machine. The nylon strands of the rope had broken apart from the rubbing of its tightly wound twine against the rocks.

She remembered watching it wash back across Phillip's body down toward his feet. She had reached for it instinctively before the next wave carried it away to sea. It was covered in seaweed and almost slipped out of her hand. She had quickly put it in the front pocket of her hooded jersey and ran back to Walker on the beach screaming the whole way.

There had been no doubt that Stella was in mental shock by the time she reached her husband. No wonder she had forgotten about the capsule until now. She wondered if she ever would have remembered it, had it not surfaced on its own.

The top was screwed tightly onto the bottom and Stella hit it a couple of times on the washing machine to try and loosen the hold. Finally, the top twisted off and inside she found a shrimper's knife and a flash drive. Stella felt as though she was losing control. Her hands began to shake as she turned to go and find Walker.

40

Kenan had decided on the drive to Charleston that he wouldn't mention his father's visit to Kate until he knew the whole unblemished truth. All he really knew right now, anyway, was that his father was the same insensitive man he had been for all the years before and that he appeared to be on the verge of yet another breakdown. But, Kenan was determined that he would not be taken down with his father and lose his happiness with Kate. He wished the interview were over now since he felt like he could hardly wait another minute to tell Kate his secrets.

"It can't be all that bad," Kate said as she approached the armchair where Kenan sat in the lobby holding his head in his hands.

Kenan looked up alarmingly into eyes that he knew trusted him completely. He stood up slowly and reached out for both of her hands. "How was the interview?"

"I think it went really well. I learned a lot about the company too. How are you?"

"Kate I need to tell you a few things. Do you think we can go into the coffee shop over there," he nodded behind him, "and talk for a bit?"

"Sure," she answered with obvious unease about her.

They walked hand in hand over to the arched entrance of the hotel coffee shop. Close to an hour later they emerged from the coffee shop still hand in hand. Kate had not been happy to learn about Kenan secrets, but she kept an open mind, like Kenan had asked her to do from the start, and she had been understanding. Her main concern was the safety of her parents. Kenan assured her that his father was no murderer; he was strange and self-centered, but no murderer. Kenan wondered if the "they" his father had mentioned last night were murderers, but did not say anything to Kate about it. He made a mental promise to tell her who "they" were the second he found out himself. He had assured Kate by saying that if her parents were in danger that they had been in that state since her mother found the body, and no harm had come their way thus far.

"Kenan, it appears to me that you were sort of a victim of circumstances. I really believe that, I do. But, I also really believe that we need to go back to Fripp and explain things to my parents. We'll have many other days we can share together in Charleston. I just have to be honest with you. I really need to see Mom and Dad right now. Do you understand?"

"Yes. Yes, I do," Kenan answered. "You relax on the drive home and I will get you there as quickly as I can."

Kate reached for her cell phone to turn it back on and Kenan touched her hand. "Don't. You need time to think and process everything that is happening. We'll be home before you know it."

Kate could see the disappointment in his eyes and she could sympathize with him because she was feeling disillusioned herself. She couldn't help but wonder in the back of her mind if she had been existing in a fool's paradise for the last day and a half. All of the emotions she had been feeling since she laid eyes on Kenan were totally uncharacteristic of herself. She had known that from the beginning, yet had dismissed it as how it felt to be truly in love. The doubts were flooding her brain and then Kenan stopped and stood still in the middle of the parking lot where they had left the convertible. He placed both hands on either of her shoulders and looked deep into her eyes.

"I can feel you slipping away from me. You can't let this happen. I won't let this happen," Kenan said with conviction, turning away from Kate now and seemingly searching for some way to vent his anger, then settling for pounding his fist into the other hand's palm.

"My father always seems to win. Don't you see? He is causing more pain in my life and he doesn't even know your name. You've got to know I would have never hurt your parents over that ridiculous capsule. Kate, I am the person you fell in love with so suddenly. I am not a fake or a crook or any awful person."

When he turned to face her again there were tears in his eyes. Kate could not deny how completely she loved him, but she was having doubts.

"Mom told me to follow my heart and if it leads me to you, then she would be happy for us. I love you Kenan Gray and we'll get through this. It just may take longer than we thought."

Those words from Kate seemed to be all that Kenan needed to feel secure with their relationship for now. He would not push her for anything more. After all, he had told her some pretty shocking details. Hiding in the pantry, following her parents in Atlanta and chatting in the grocery parking lot like it was all so spontaneous. He was ashamed.

They drove in silence for a while, each recovering in their own way from the emotional fatigue that suppressed the joy of the day that could have been. The silence didn't seem so uncomfortable since they were driving along with the convertible top down, and it was hard to talk above the wind noise any way.

They hadn't touched since leaving the parking lot. Kenan was trying to give her space. He wanted to put his arm around her or hold her hand; just something as the yellow lines on the road flashed by like the seconds on a clock and moments in their life together.

Without notice a tingling sensation moved through his body. He turned his eyes to the console of the car where his forearm rested. Kate had intertwined her fingers in his and was holding them tightly. Perhaps their hearts were still united and the scars from this fiasco would indeed pass.

41

The old mahogany rocker creaked each time Stella rocked forward. It was the only sound in the house as she rolled up and back in the familiar motion of the family heirloom. The noise was no nuisance, any more. It provided a sense of comfort to Stella as she stared out at the crashing waves through the picture window of the library upstairs.

The rocker had been Walker's Grandmothers and she had been rocked in it as a baby. Kate and Ely had also drifted into dreamland in their mother's arms, and father's too, by the gentle sways of the sentimental antique. Stella wondered if the stalwart women before her who had rocked a million miles, ever had the type of worries that now caused such discontent in her mind.

She looked across the room at her favorite picture of Walker and the children placed among a diverse collection of framed snap shots on the baby grand piano. Walker sat on the beach with his legs crossed as Kate and Ely, barely out of diapers, clung to his neck from behind. At that moment in time there was absolutely nothing that could hurt those children, guarded by their invincible Father. And now, Kate was in Charleston with someone she had known for only hours and wanted to marry, and whose name kept popping up in all of the wrong places. First, on a file from the flash drive she retrieved from her washing machine this morning, and now from a monogramed handkerchief on Kate's bedside table that was identical to the one Marguerite had used to wipe her tears away only two nights ago.

Stella's suspicions were running high and her nerves were a wreck. Walker knew she felt unsettled about letting Kate go to Charleston anyway and now the knowledge of the new found capsule and its contents. He had immediately plugged the flash drive into his laptop to investigate. Miraculously, the flash drive uploaded with no problem; the water-tight seal on the capsule had done its job. Lists of names and addresses flooded the screen. There were many maps with exit numbers marked along major freeways and interstate highways. Spreadsheets and timetables labeled "drop" dated back to two years ago.

Among the names was Nathan Gray, but that proved in no way that there was any reason to doubt Kenan Gray was anyone other than the man he claimed to be.

Stella hoped that Walker would feel as certain about that assumption when she told him about the matching handkerchiefs when he and Ely returned from their run. After Walker called the police, Stella had gone into Kate's room to tidy up and exhaust some nervous energy and worry. There she found the handkerchief starring her in the face. She had no idea why Kate would have the handkerchief, but it had to be Kenan's. She was almost hysterical with this realization. The frightening aspect of the situation was that Kenan was related to that hard, mean looking man Marguerite was with at dinner. It was the same man that Stella remembered so vividly from the Water Festival last summer. She dared not look across the room more than once at dinner the other night, in the direction of the man with the cold eyes and stern jaw, for fear of being spooked. It was crazy, she knew, but it was true.

"How does the mind work?" Stella said aloud to no one. She had started out worried about her daughter and now two minutes later was thinking about a man who would most probably never come into contact with their lives even momentarily.

She was so confused and frightened. She had to calm down. "Breath," she said out loud several times. When Kate finally did turn her cell phone back on after the interview she would find at least twenty missed calls from her mother.

The clock nestled between two rows of books on the bookshelf alerted Stella that it was almost ten. There was no longer any coffee in the mug. More caffeine wasn't what she needed, but it was what she wanted. Ely had obviously chosen her mug this morning, it was adorned with John Wayne's photo on either side. A classic cowboy photo of him with the pale red shirt, tan vest and distinguished cowboy hat. Stella and Walker had brought the mug back to Ely from their trip to Laguna Beach, California, over ten years ago. They had flown into Orange County Airport to avoid the Los Angeles traffic and had been surprisingly greeted by a life-size photo of the actor who had been Ely's hero since the age of three. Some children had enjoyed Sesame Street or good ole Mr. Rogers. And then there were those, like Ely, who went straight on into the cowboy classics like *The Train Robbers* and *True Grit*. Strange, but true.

Stella decided that the "mug message" from Ely was "Be Strong". She stood up with as much courage as she could muster and went downstairs to fill her cup one more time before she showered and dressed to be ready for the detectives Walker had alerted. They were to arrive from Beaufort around ten thirty. She hoped Walker and Ely would come straight home from their run together so she wouldn't be alone when they arrived. She knew their questions would be endless even when some of the answers would be the same. Stella was afraid of a repeat performance of their badgering on the day she found Phillip.

The sun was shining through the palladian window on her face as she ascended the stairs to the bedroom. She closed her eyes and held onto the railing as her bare feet touched each wooden riser, one step closer to the warm shower at a time.

Just as the steam began to circle around the shower door and Stella was pinning up her hair, the telephone rang. She reached for her robe and walked to the telephone on the bedside table.

"Hello?" she said.

"My I please speak with Mr. Stevenson," a polite voice said.

"I'm sorry; he's not in just now. This is Mrs. Stevenson; may I help you or take a message?"

"Hello, Mrs. Stevenson. This is Abner at the Ritz Carlton - Buckhead."

"Well, hello there. What did we leave behind this time?" Stella laughed.

"Oh, no it's nothing like that, Mrs. Stevenson. Actually, I was calling with some follow-up information on the incident involving the mysterious gentleman in the Atlanta Braves baseball cap."

"Really!" Stella said with surprise in her voice. "Yes Mam. It seems that one of our housekeepers on staff found a cap fitting the description given by Mrs. McFee, stuffed underneath a mattress. The room was last occupied by a gentleman named

Mr. Kenan Gray. This information may be of no use to you, Mrs. Stevenson, but I felt I should inform you never the less."

Stella's knees buckled and the tall bed did not assist in breaking her fall. She slid down the side of the bed until her knees were touching her throat.

"Thank you very much, Abner," she paused, "Yes, thank you. We'll see you soon, too."

Suddenly she was cold. She was so cold. Her long, slim fingers felt like icicles as she reached up to the bedside table and lifted a small porcelain frame with Kate's picture in it down to her eye level.

"Dear God above, I pray that you will watch over my Kate."

42

"O.K., Stella. I understand your view point and you have a legitimate reason to panic, but…"

"But, what, Walker?" she interrupted.

"But, you need to consider things other than the obvious. So what if he was the mysterious man in the baseball cap in Atlanta? Don't you think he would have hurt us by now?"

"Dear heavens above, that is my whole point. He is out with our daughter. Aren't you worried that he may hurt her? I can't even think until they return. And then I'm going to get some answers. Or do you think we should let the police handle that? I'm going to tell the Sheriff all about this when they arrive. They really should be here by now. Maybe they could have the Highway Patrol look for Kate's little rental car and just pick him up on the road. Her phone is turned off. It is going straight to voicemail," Stella said as if she had just struck upon the most brilliant idea of the century.

"And what do you think that would do to Kate. Seeing the man, she thinks she is in love with handcuffed and hauled away?"

"How did you know she was in love with him?" Stella asked stunned.

"I'm not blind, Stella. It happened the same with us, you know. Maybe it's in her genes. My point here is that I don't feel like she is in any danger. She could be, but my gut instincts tell me she couldn't be in better hands. That boy loves her. Please realize how very hard this is for me to say. Kate is my daughter and I don't want to share her with anyone, especially with someone she will grow to love more than me. That's a whole other feeling for me to deal with on another day. But, now, waiting is what we have to do. Please remember, Kenan had no idea, just as we did not, that Kate would even be on Fripp Island this week. I talked with him, Stella. He loves Kate, and besides that he really is a good kid."

"He's not a kid."

"Oh, give me a break here. Don't you trust my judgment? Haven't you always?"

"Walker, look what this is doing to us. I hate it," she screamed. "I just hate it. We never fight, or hardly even disagree. Of course I trust you. This is not about me second-guessing you. It's about our safety; my family's lives. I feel so threatened. First the capsule, then the handkerchief and now The Ritz. It sounds like a script from one of those television mysteries. The plot is thickening and then someone usually dies, Walker."

"There's just no reaching you right now, Stella. You are determined to think the worst and I can't change that right now. Please gather yourself before the Sheriff and his deputies arrive."

Walker left the bedroom and Stella felt worse than she did when he had found her minutes ago in a heap on the floor beside the bed. How dare he be so dismissive. When was this ever going to end, she wondered.

After a quick shower, she dressed and sat in the sunroom watching and waiting for the detectives. The capsule and the flash drive once contained inside of it laid on the coffee table in front of the wicker sofa where she fidgeted impatiently. The tinkling of ice in a glass alerted her that someone was near. In the doorway stood Ely. A smile appeared from somewhere on Stella's worried face and Ely moved closer to his Mother.

"Snoop is fine. You really don't think she'd ruin my birthday by getting hurt or anything, now do you, Mom?" Ely said jokingly.

Her attempt at a humorous response failed and Ely sat down on the sofa beside her and gave his Mother a gentle hug.

"I just want to see her. I want to know she's all right and then I can regain my senses. I can approach the entire situation with a clearer mind, like your father is doing. But, until then, I'm nothing more than a wreck. I'm sorry you have to see me so out of control, sweetie."

"It's all right. Just don't forget to wrap my gifts." He smiled and winked at Stella then walked back into the living room and she heard him talking with Walker.

Walker suggested that Ely drive the golf cart to the Marina and check on their boat. "Have them gas it up if you think you'd like to take a ride after lunch," Walker called to Ely as he descended the front stairs. Stella was furious at his thought of a boat ride. Their world is crumbling and he is going on a boat ride?

Before he could close the front door, the sounds of car doors slamming in the drive warned him that the dreaded moment was upon them. He hoped the detectives were more considerate this time around.

Walker greeted them at the door and showed them into the sunroom where Stella waited. Three detectives sat down in various chairs and Walker sat beside Stella, then squeezed her hand and cast a supportive look in her direction.

After explaining how she discovered the capsule she handed it to the detective closest to her and gave the flash drive to another who stood and moved nearer to take a better look. Walker had already emailed them many of the files on the flash drive at their request. The third man joined his fellow crime busters in the middle of the sunroom floor. She wondered why she had even bothered to offer them a seat.

The detective who held the drive said, "This is all we need."

"All you need for what?" Walker asked.

"Let's just say this is the missing link of a big..."

"Real big," another detective interrupted.

"Ring of crime," the original detective continued, "Police forces along the Eastern seaboard have suspected these guys for a very long time. We just weren't sure how they were connected. Now we have a clear picture."

"There's one other thing," Stella said, as she looked up at the detectives whose eyes seemed so void of concern for her.

Walker's hand slipped from hers and she felt the distance grow between them as she was about to spill her guts about their daughter being in the company of someone possibly related to the list at this very moment. Her empty palm was a catalyst for more mental anguish. She knew it would be a mistake to soil their perfect record of trust within their marriage. Even when she was so certain that things were not as they should be.

"Just please let us know what happens. That's all. I just would like to be informed," Stella said as the words came out of her mouth in pieces, revealing her uncertainties.

"You can count on that, Mrs. Stevenson. Hopefully we'll have a good bit to report by early afternoon. This will be national news. The story will be breaking fast."

Stella did not move from the sofa as Walker showed them out. He returned to the sunroom moments later and starred at the window at the wide stretch of beach in front of him.

"This is really great," Stella said in deep disgust. "Our daughter's future in-laws are a part of the biggest crime ring on the East Coast."

"Stella that is all speculation. You really need to go and take a walk, anything to attempt to clear your head. Kate said they were going to spend the entire day in Charleston, Honey. You have a long wait ahead of you," Walker said.

Stella looked at her watch. It was only ten-thirty. Walker was right once again. She pulled herself up from the sofa and walked over the window and stood beside Walker.

"Will you please hold me?" she asked her husband.

"Always," was his only reply.

They stood at the window holding each other until Stella loosened her grip around Walker's chest and looked up into his eyes.

"I'm sorry, Walker. I am just so worried. Why is Kate not picking up my calls? The interview has to be over now. This whole thing is so incredibly crazy. We should be out playing golf now or planning a winter cruise. That's what you worked so hard to achieve. You deserve more than this and I'm not helping matters. I promise to improve ninety-five percent, when I lay eyes on Kate."

"What should I do with you in the meantime?" Walker asked.

"I suppose you could lock me in my room."

"Not a bad idea. Or I could drive you down to the Club and let you go over the details for Ely's party tonight with Andy, the greatest chef in the Lowcountry."

"Good idea I suppose. I'm ready as I'll ever be."

They drove to the clubhouse and found Andy in the kitchen ordering his assistants around. When he looked up and saw the Stevensons his round face grew into a round smile. They went into the dining room and discussed once again the menu, which included roasted oysters, of course, accompanied by other appetizers such as shrimp tortellini, scallops in wine sauce, tenderloin of beef with horseradish sauce, and lobster dainties.

Andy suggested serving lighter appetizers when the guests first arrive such as imported cheeses and a vegetable tray. They all agreed starting the party at five o'clock rather the original time of six o'clock was a good idea due to fewer hours of daylight.

"The guests will be able to enjoy the beach for at least an hour and stand around the roasting pit if they choose," Andy explained. "And, of course the Gazebo will be set up with tables and chairs for those who wish to be on higher ground.

"How will the bar service be arranged?" Walker asked.

"If it is to your liking, we were going to use the Gazebo Bar. You've invited practically the whole island anyway, and we need that size bar to accommodate everyone so there will be little waiting."

"Sounds good to me," Walker said.

"Everything should be perfect," Andy smiled. "The only problem would be the wind. It's pretty breezy today. I have two gentlemen digging the pit right now, and I've instructed them to dig it a foot deeper due to the windy weather."

"Thank you, Andy," Stella said standing. "You know, Walker loves to dig the roasting pit. Do your helpers need an extra hand?"

Andy looked bewildered. "It's a family joke, Andy," Walker smiled. "Don't pay any attention to her. We'll see you about four-thirty this afternoon."

Walker and Stella left the dining room and walked to the car. They had parked in the circular drive in front of The Beach Club, near the Pirate Cove-themed playground. A huge wooden pirate ship, complete with a gangplank slide and climbing ropes up to the highest mast, stood on the right side of the playground. Adjacent to the ship, which you could enter into the hull if you were four feet tall, were swings that made you feel you could touch the tall mast with your toes.

Kate and Ely used to climb inside and pretend to be Captain Hook and Tinkerbell and many other characters. They would climb on top and play as well, before sliding down to the ground and running from the swings to the merry-go-round and usually stopping at the park bench where Mom or Dad, or both, supplied the hidden treasure of chocolate candies.

That had been a very special part of their early days on Fripp. The park still was special, but in a different way. It also had a basketball court on the left side. As they approached the car they heard the sound of a bouncing ball. Walker peeked around the corner of the hedge and confirmed that it was Ely. The sound of more than one set of feet made Stella know that Ely was in the midst of a game.

"Hey there," Ely said when the two appeared in the opening. "Been doing some shopping for my birthday?"

"You are incorrigible," Stella laughed.

"How's the boat?" Walker asked wondering if he had made it to the Marina yet.

"Great, but Edgar says it's too choppy for a pleasure cruise. And it's supposed to get worse," Ely reported.

"Are you hungry?" Stella asked, realizing that was a silly question. Ely was always hungry.

At the mention of food, Ely stopped dribbling and threw the ball to his opponent. He walked over to his parents and said, "You know what I've been thinking about?"

"Birthday gifts?" Walker said.

"That, and Mom's spicy chili, with sour cream and cheddar cheese on top."

"Well, think about an hour and a half longer and then it will be ready."

"Oh, Mom you're great."

"I know it. Bring your friend if you like," Stella said as they walked to their car.

As they turned onto Marlin Drive they passed their postman, and they all exchanged a friendly wave.

"Maybe he brought us a million dollars today," Stella said.

"Why do you always say that?" Walker asked.

"I guess because Mom always did. And still does. She never loses hope."

"Well, you need to take a few lessons on hope from her about now," Walker teased.

"I think I have improved a good bit. Now, don't be hard on me."

"I suppose you're right," Walker said as he pulled the car into their garage. "I'll go get the mail and you get started on the chili."

Stella said, "Sounds like a good plan."

"I know you were half way hoping that they would be here when we got back, but don't get discouraged. You're right, you are doing better, so don't worry. She's fine." Walker reached over the console and kissed his wife on the check before they got out of the car.

It tore his insides apart to see her hurt and tormented. She was right; this is not how it is supposed to be. As he walked to the mailbox at the end of the drive, he thought how their relationship had been over the years. Stella was also correct when she had said that they didn't fight, or hardly argue. She had told him many years ago that it was impossible to argue with an attorney, out of the courtroom or even between the sheets. Thank goodness Stella was not the stubborn type or their relationship would have never worked.

That point left Walker hedged on the gate of consideration that perhaps Stella's view of the situation had substance. The simple fact that Stella felt strong enough to disagree about it with Walker, was the cardinal point of his interest. He couldn't let Stella realize that his convictions were wavering or all hell would break loose. He had to remain patient, which was one thing that the legal business had procured in his demeanor over the years. To become impatient, lends to the loss of one's cool. And to lose one's cool results in the surrender of authority and an illustrious reputation.

And so, with that mental check on his own senses, Walker opened the mailbox and pulled out several magazines, or wish books as Stella referred to them, two probable bills, some junk mail and four other cards or letters. They always had a full box. Walker walked back to the front steps and sat down of the third step from the bottom. After a brief glance at the topics of interest in a golf magazine, Walker reached for the cards and letters, as an alternative to the bills. Always good news first.

In this case, that wasn't necessarily true. Enclosed in an envelope with a Clarkesville postmark, was the photograph of Walker and Stella taken at the Buckhead Diner by Lois. It was a photograph Walker thought would look very nice in a frame on the piano, until he examined the backdrop of the snapshot more closely. Behind the wheel of a gray car parked outside the window behind them, was Kenan staring directly into the camera.

His blood was scalding. The feeling of helplessness was more than Walker could manage. This man was with his child, his daughter. He was not in a courtroom and quite frankly he didn't care about his reputation of distinction, or who witnessed the uncontrolled behavior he felt engulfing his soul at this very moment. He wanted his daughter. Now.

Kate beeped the horn of the convertible as she turned into the driveway and smiled and waved at her father on the steps. She waited for a wave in return, as did Kenan, beside her. The two in the car exchanged a bewildered glance as Walker strode toward the car in giant steps and opened the car door.

Walker lifted Kenan out of the convertible with Herculean strength. He shook Kenan by the shoulders and shouted, "Who in the hell are you," before he punched him hard in the stomach with one fist, and in the jaw with the other.

Kenan sunk down to the cement. Walker looked at Kate still in the car unable to loosen her grip on the steering wheel and said, "Are you all right?"

She answered, "Yes," as her father walked around and opened her car door to help her out.

"Go in the house, Kate," Walker said flatly.

Kate walked up the stairs, practically backwards, still uncertain if her father would display more of this behavior she had never before witnessed. She saw her father extend a hand downward to Kenan and help him up.

"I'm sure I deserved that," Kenan said looking eye to eye with the father of the girl he loved.

"And perhaps more," Walker said venomously. "You've got a lot of explaining to do to convince me not to call the police."

43

The chili Stella had prepared proved to be exactly what the family needed to pull them together around the breakfast booth and listen as Kenan spilled the beans and his guts. Walker was kind enough to give Kenan an hour or so to catch his breath before starting his explanations, during which time the tension thickening inside the house could have set off the smoke alarm. Ely arrived on the scene, minus his friend who had a better lunch offer from a female brunette acquaintance, per Ely, and helped to combat the quiet hell that was brewing on Marlin Drive. The sudden noise of a voice caused everyone to jump.

"So, Snoop, you made it back alive," Ely blurted out with glee.

None of the group already inside the house made any effort to respond. Walker looked at the tall Ely before him and thought how totally uninhibited his son was. It wasn't such a bad trait. Honesty, in fact, is the best policy. The drama continued.

"Golly, what happened to you?" Ely looked at Kenan who sat on the sofa holding ice to his jaw. "You look awful. Whose name is on that fat lip?"

"Mine is," Walker spoke for the first time in a while.

"All right, Dad," Ely cheered, dancing around the room in a boxing footwork style and punching playfully into the air. "Ready for round two?"

"Thank you, Ely. That's enough for now, but I am grateful that you resurrected speech in the house once again," Stella admitted standing in the kitchen doorway. "Lunch is ready."

They all filed past Stella one by one, as she stood and held the door open. There were five places set at the breakfast booth that, praise heavens, was roomy. Stella instructed no one on seating arrangements. She had decided to let the cards fall where they may.

Ely was the first to reach the table and he slid all the way around to the middle. Kate and Stella were next on either side of him and Walker and Kenan guarded each end. Walker returned thanks and Stella dipped the chili. Kate looked at Kenan and displayed her nonverbal communicative head nod that they were all accustomed to, and Kenan began the tale of the saga.

"It all started about this time last week, I guess. I'm not sure; the days are all running together. My father called the condo in Pompano."

After a few minutes, Kenan finished the story and looked at Walker.

"Let me get this straight," Walker said pacing back and forth in front of the breakfast booth, or was it the witness stand, with his hands propped on his belt. "You broke into our house even though your father had instructed you to take a vacation?"

The witness answered, "That's correct. I don't know why. Finding the key, or actually having it dropped into my hands, may have been what instigated it all."

"Or maybe, it was fate, so that we would meet," Kate said as if it were fact.

Ely stuck his finger near his open mouth and made a hard gagging noise. He was eyed by all for making light of the situation, so he readjusted himself from a slouched position in the booth and sat up straight and tall.

Stella couldn't blame him, since she was sure this was not exactly how he had hoped to be spending his birthday.

The cross-examining continued.

"How long has your Father had a shrimp boat in this area?"

Stella knew where Walker was going with his line of questioning. He was trying to comprehend the "ring of crime" and determine if Kenan did actually fit into the scheme of things, or if in fact, he was legitimately an innocent by-stander.

"Probably a couple of years. Several months after my mother's death."

"Oh, Kenan, I'm so sorry to know that," Stella interrupted. Walker said that he was as well.

"You bear a striking resemblance to her, Mrs. Stevenson. I nearly fainted when you walked past me at The Ritz." Kenan stood and reached for his cell phone and found a picture of Priscilla. He handed his phone across the table to Stella.

She looked at it closely as Kate and Ely leaned over to look too, and then handed it to Walker still standing by the booth.

"Maybe that was another reason I wanted to look around your house. Subconsciously, I mean. Mom and I were extremely close, especially since my father was never around. We have been trying to build a relationship since Mother's death. I can feel that there is so much about him that I don't know. He says he wants to tell me, but there's never a right time," Kenan said a bit disgusted.

"Kenan, I think there is something you should know. Last night Stella found the capsule that you were searching for and there was a flash drive enclosed and the files on it included many names. Your father's name was one of them." Walker handed Kenan the pages he had printed out. "The police came out today and picked up the flash drive and indicated to us in no uncertain terms, that these names were involved in a crime ring."

Kate and Kenan both looked extremely surprised. Through his widened and concerned eyes, and the endless questions that suddenly poured from his mouth, Walker knew that the young man was innocent. He knew the reactions of a guilty perpetrator. Kenan displayed none of them.

Walker tried to answer as many of Kenan's questions as he could, which wasn't many. The only name Kenan recognized on the list was Paulos.

"His name was in our business index in the computer. This explains his rudeness to me when I called him to invite him for a complimentary vacation to Pompano." Kenan went on to briefly explain that arrangement with their customers.

"Kenan?" Stella asked, "Did your Father ever speak of a woman named Marguerite Dubose?"

"No, but is she related to the kid you found dead?" Kenan asked.

"Yes, his mother."

"I saw her in the ladies' room two nights ago, at The Beach Club. She was holding a handkerchief monogrammed exactly like the one I found on Kate's bedside table," Stella pointed to the counter where she had laid the handkerchief. Kenan got up from the booth and walked to the counter.

"Yes, this is mine. Mother gave us each a set for Christmas. I gave it to Kate during one of our talks." He gave an effort at smiling toward Kate.

"The gentleman she was having dinner with was tall and dark, with deep set eyes," Stella said.

"Sort of scary looking and never smiling?" Kenan chuckled faintly.

"Yes," Stella said.

"Just looking at him used to scare me to pieces when I was a kid. I suppose, this," Kenan said thumping the sheet of names Walker had handed him, "is what he wanted to tell me all about."

Kenan wanted to blurt out that Nathan had slithered into his condominium last night under the cover of darkness and warned him to leave the Island, but he didn't. He was hurt and ashamed of Nathan's involvement with criminals, but there was a dangling string that still existed between them dotted with the hope of a relationship that could have been. The possibility also entered his mind that Walker might call the police if he were made aware that Nathan may still be on the island.

Kenan stood with his back to the Stevensons with both arms outstretched, resting on the counter top. Kate wanted to go and hug him, but she sensed the compassion mounting for this possible fifth member of their family, so she waited to see how her family would react.

Ely nudged her arm and Kate slide around and out of the booth. Ely shuffled over to where Kenan stood. He patted him on the shoulder and said, "This is all really a bummer, isn't it?"

Kate grew a little nervous wondering what would be next to flee Ely's lips.

"Shooting the hoops always makes me think more clearly. How about it? I'll spot you five points and play with one hand."

"Or we could play two against one," a voice from across the room suggested. "Kenan and I against the Clemson star forward," Walker said.

Kenan turned around as Walker walked toward him. "Thanks," he said holding out his hand to the man who had pounded him earlier.

Walker popped him on the shoulder, "Sure."

Stella and Kate watched from the breakfast booth without adding a word as the three males of the family exited through the back door.

Ely's voice lingered through the screen, "Now, you can forget the one hand behind the back deal if it's two against one. Not that you two will be any problem, but I only made that offer because the burglar here stinks at basketball. Maybe if you stick around a while we could teach you a few things. There's hope for him yet, Dad."

44

"What do you know about fishing, Geno?"

"Not a damn thing. What if we really catch something?"

"Well, you'll have to throw it back, cause you can't take it on board the sea plane with you," Mark said definitely.

"What time are they going to be out there?"

"Around 5:45 p.m., straight out there over the horizon," Mark answered.

"Did you tell them to bring some of that good whiskey like our buddy Duncan had stashed on his boat?" Geno chuckled.

Mark was not pleased with this disrespect of the dead, but answered "yes" and showed no outward offense.

"Let's see," Geno said looking at his watch. "We'll need to get started here in a few minutes. Three down, two to go."

"So Nathan was no problem, I take it? Wait a minute, three down?" Mark said.

"Piece of cake. I was in the door with a credit card before I could have even rung the bell. It was about 2:00 a.m. and he was sacked out on the sofa. One bullet through the head. What a way to end a dream."

Mark laughed along with him, counting the minutes until he could put a bullet through Geno's head and dump him from the plane into the sea, as ordered by Paulos. Paulos had lost too much money already and he wasn't about to pay a little crumb like Geno.

"When I was almost out the door of the villa where Gray was hiding, I heard a bumping noise. It kept up, so I followed the noise back to the bedroom. Gray had a broad tied and gagged and stuffed in a closet. I gave her a dose of the same stuff as Gray and came on home."

45

"Andy, I forgot to mention that we would need a table for the gifts," Stella said apologetically.

"That's all taken care of, my dear. Amy is decorating a table on the corner of the gazebo, as we speak, to accommodate the packages."

"You are so thorough, Andy."

"We do aim to please," he said proudly and walked back in the direction of the kitchen.

"Mom, this looks great. You've done it again," Ely shouted down from the disc jockey's stand. No doubt he was approving the music selection for the next few hours.

The guest began to arrive as scheduled and Stella and Walker were able to greet them with a genuine unclouded smile. The talk with Kenan had dismissed most of their concerns about their daughter's safety. Now, their only worry was that of any normal parent when their child falls head over heels in love. Those concerns seemed less significant after what they had been through earlier in the day.

Kenan and Kate had resumed the courtship and were mingling amidst the guests and snapping photos at Stella's request. By five thirty, the birthday party was in full swing and the gazebo was packed with dancers, most adorned in sweaters and turtlenecks to break the chill of the persistent wind.

By now, Walker and Stella had left the arched entrance way to the outdoor entertainment room of The Beach Club and were enjoying the fire on the beach near the roasting oysters along with Kate, Kenan, the birthday boy, and several other guests.

"Now, there's a faithful fisherman," Walker said to the group, acknowledging the presence of the only boat in sight.

"Faithful or stupid, I'm afraid," one guest remarked.

"I suppose you're right. The weather isn't very conducive to fishing, is it?" Walker laughed.

Mark sat in the front fisherman's seat feeling ridiculous holding the unbaited rod and reel. The current was moving so quickly that it felt like there was a fish biting on the line at all times. No doubt it was not fishing weather. Even though the setting sun provided a tremendous picture in the sky, Father Wind was bruising the moment.

"Do you have them in your sight?" Mark shouted down to Geno, leaning against the large cooler across the back of the boat. He had a blue tarp over his head and the only thing Mark could see was the barrel and scope of a gun. He had to be somewhat impressed with this man's expertise. He was a sharp shooter. He had not mentioned the possibility of the choppy waters posing a problem for him. His only concern was the daylight hours fading away and causing a loss of visibility.

"Yeah. The lady and Gray, Jr. are standing side by side, but her husband keeps getting in the way. Isn't that always the problem with a good-looking broad? The husband gets in the way," Geno laughed at his own wit and Mark watched as the tarp moved up and down with his snickering.

"Ely, are you ready to open some of your gifts?" Stella asked.

"You know I am. I was just waiting for the go ahead. Hey, Kenan. You did remember to get me a gift didn't you?" Ely quizzed his new friend.

"Sure I did. It's the big package with a ticking sound inside." Kenan said as he followed the rest of the procession up the stairs to the gazebo.

"Oh, this is great," Geno reported to Mark. "Go ahead and pull your line in, then crank up the motor. They're walking up the steps and I can get them both right in the back."

Stella was first in line, then Walker, Ely, Kate and Kenan.

"I think I'll take a little trip out to Vegas with these earnings and see if I can double my money," Geno informed Mark as his finger pressed against the trigger.

Stella's eyes were level with the floor of the gazebo when a sudden swoon of dread filled her thoughts. Walking toward her in his shuffling style was Mr. Flannery, Fripp Island's town grump. He was clearing a path, waving the guests out of his way with both hands as he went.

Stella stopped her upward motion and remained on the same step where her feet rested when Mr. Flannery had come into her view. This abrupt halt in movement blocked the stairway and Walker bumped into her backside.

"Clear the way," Stella said to the procession on the stairs. "Mr. Flannery is taking an afternoon walk today."

Stella leaned her back against the railing to make way for the old man to pass. Walker moved to the same step as Stella and was turning to lean against the opposite railing when his chest exploded and blood splattered Stella's entire body. He began to fall backward and she grabbed his shoulders and pulled him close to her so that he wouldn't fall down the steep stairs. She heard a voice that sounded like her own screaming hysterically to call for help. Walker's eyes were closing as she held his head tightly in her lap now. Ely's eyes displayed enough fear to last a lifetime as he clung to his father's legs and watched the blood leave Walker's body and drop through the stairs down to the sand below. A spray of bullets whizzed by them as they sank deep into the wooden planks petrified by the ocean's high tide waves.

Kenan, who was on the next to the bottom step when the shooting began, pulled Kate downward and took cover beneath the stairs. He shouted to the guests on the beach to lie down and they did as another round of bullets sent splinters flying.

Geno threw the rifle into the floor of the boat and said, "It's blown. Get out of here now."

The sound of the engine being forced into full throttle turned frightful eyes to the water to witness the departure of their unknown enemy.

Two gentlemen rushed down the stairs and lifted Walker from Stella's arms. She heard a distant voice say 911 had been called and that a helicopter was on the way. Ely helped his

Mother hurry up the stairs after his Father and the two men. Kate and Kenan rushed up the stairs as well.

She watched as they laid him on a lounge chair and carried him to the front croquet court in the open garden of The Beach Club, where through hysteria she assumed this was where the helicopter would land. She held his hand and kissed his brow constantly while she watched friends wrap her precious Walker in beach towels that soaked up the blood rapidly.

Stella spoke softly into his ear words like, "You're going to be all right," and "I love you," but the blood kept escaping his body. She stayed in that position until the wind was so strong that the noise kept her from hearing her words. The few leaves remaining on the trees in the garden were blown away with the force of the air from the helicopter blades and some clung tightly to Stella's heels as if to lend support to a cherished friend.

The paramedics lifted Walker into the chopper and held a hand to Stella to assist her inside. The doors closed and Stella knew they were being lifted into the air. The emptiness inside her heart told her that Walker was slipping away. She held his hand as the pulse in his wrist grew slower and slower.

46

The drive to Kate and Kenan's house seemed endless to Stella, although it was only to the other end of the island. Almost a year and a half had passed since the horrifying happening, but even still when she passed The Beach Club her nerves became rigid.

Stella pulled her car into the circular drive of her daughter's new home and turned off the engine. Kenan had insisted on breaking all ties with his birthplace home and after they were married they began construction on the monstrous home that towered over Stella as she got out of the car. It was big and beautiful and Kate had said they were going to fill every room with a child except for Grandmother's Room, of course. Stella's knees had bent deeply at the mention of the word, but it was growing on her now that Kate was into her fourth month.

They were indeed a perfect couple, just as Stella had hoped. Kate had been an amazing support for Kenan as he dealt with all of the feelings of assuming he was responsible for the shooting. How could he ever make it up to the whole family?

Thankfully, the network criminals who had been responsible for half of the drug trade on the east coast for almost thirty years were now in prison. That included a local Sheriff's Deputy. This helped ease the pain a little and Phillip's death did not seem so useless. He had been solely responsible for the uncovering of these criminals.

The added sadness of learning about his father's involvement with crime, together with the knowledge of his mother's actual cause of death had been terribly hard to hear.

A note had been found by the Police in Marguerite Dubose's villa that was addressed to Kenan at the Pompano Beach address. It had enlightened him on the mystery of his father's life, including another son, and the many questions Kenan always had about his mother's death.

The letter, written in Nathan's hand, helped Kenan to look at his relationship with his Father as one that would have flourished in the end, had it the chance.

Stella walked, alone, up the wide steps to the front door of the mammoth stucco house on the oceanfront. Before she reached the landing the door opened and a welcoming voice said, "I was expecting you."

"Hello Vera. How are you this morning?" Stella asked.

"Trying not to complain. Kenan brought home another pair of these white shoes with racing stripes and I'm giving them a go. Now he's got an excuse that my old shoes will scratch up his new hard wood floors. He's something, isn't he? Get on in this house. You know I like it down here a lot. I haven't missed Richmond one bit," Vera said openly as she closed the door behind Stella.

"Well you have more than graced this island with your presence my dear. We are all truly glad you like it here."

Vera smiled and blushed a little at the compliment and hurried past Stella to lead the way. "Come on, they're in the living room. How do you feel about shrimp scampi for lunch? I just love having all this seafood at my fingertips," Vera said.

"That sounds delicious, Vera. My taste buds are anxious."

Stella walked through the library and into the living room where she found Kate and Kenan sitting on the sofa. They stood to greet her and exchanged hugs. Stella picked up the book on the end table beside the sofa and read the title aloud.

"*Original Names for Your Baby*," she looked at the two parents to be who were staring back at her.

"It's never too soon to start planning," Stella said supportively.

"I'm not sure why I even bought that book, Mother. We've known all along what we want to name our first child." Kate clutched her mother's hands as tears began to burn Stella's eyes.

Stella knew what Kate was going to say next. The tears spilled from her eyes as she walked over to the wide French doors that led to the expansive deck.

Stella stood speechless looking out at the beach in the direction of her own home toward the North. She looked at her watch. The tide was coming in and she felt herself tense up. It had been almost high tide when Walker's chest exploded and anxiety heightened for her even still, as she watched the waves crashing. This happened a lot since the shooting.

"But, what if it's a girl?" Stella asked turning to face them, unable to hide her nervousness that was apparent to all.

"Walker would be a beautiful name for a little girl. There's no changing our minds, Stella," Kenan said casting an unconscious sympathetic glance at his worried Mother-in Law.

Stella had sought the help of a therapist in Beaufort a few months after the incident and he had told her that all of the things she was feeling, including depression, over-protectiveness of loved ones, and most of all anxiety, were all very normal for a person who had been through what she had. She looked at her watch again then peered anxiously through the glass window at the beach now enveloped in a cloud of misting rain.

She breathed deeply as the anxiety kept biting at her brain and she repeated to herself in her mind, "Everything is fine. Be calm."

Kate could tell her Mother was experiencing another low moment and she tried to help her through it by interrupting the silence in the room.

"Don't you think Daddy would be proud about our decision?" Kate asked as she watched Stella look at her gold watch for the tenth time in the past minute.

"Oh, Mother, don't do this to yourself. Everything is fine." Kate moved closer to her Mother for added support.

Stella gazed at the mahogany shadow box on the mantel. It held one lone red leaf. The very leaf Walker had given her the day they fell in love. Stella had framed the leaf and passed it on to Kate and Kenan as a symbol of lasting love the day before their wedding. Stella closed her eyes and took a very deep breath, then exhaled slowly and opened her eyes.

"Tell me what you think he would say," Kate insisted.

Stella quietly cleared her throat and was beginning to speak. Kate was right, everything was indeed fine.

She saw a patch of black hair bobbing up and down on the stairway. With each step up the stairs he took, Walker's face came into view more clearly. She breathed a heavy sigh of relief that he had made the two-mile walk down the beach safely.

Happiness permeated Stella's face as she spoke with joy to Kate and Kenan, "I really don't know. Why don't you ask him yourself?"

THE END

www.ingramcontent.com/pod-product-compliance
Lightning Source LLC
Chambersburg PA
CBHW071454110726
47908CB00003B/604